FOR A GLANCE

BOOK ONE OF THE SERPENT'S THRONE

Dan Ackerman

Supposed Crimes LLC • Matthews, North Carolina

www.supposedcrimes.com

This book is typeset in Goudy Old Style.

For David

Huddled together, some wailing, some rocking and others limp and silent, a hundred human souls waited for judgment. They had come floating down from their world to wander the Empty Plains and there they had been gathered up and herded into the city. They had been chained and marched through the wandering streets of the many districts to the Ninth Precinct.

The demons bustled around now, jabbing the souls into place, into neat rows and columns. Their Prince liked things tidy. Certain things, anyways.

They did not like to disappoint him.

When their Prince entered the room, all the demons genuflected, though some fell to their knees and touched their heads to the floor, or did the best that their bodies allowed. Skarn, snake-thing that he was, simply lay down.

"Stand," came their Prince's voice, quiet and sweet.

The souls shuddered collectively, their wailing and weeping going quiet.

Malketh approached her Prince. "From the Empty Plains, Your Highness."

"This many?" His eyes moved over the crowd, one brow raised. "Is there trouble above?"

Normally only a few dozen souls fell to the Plains, leftover things that hadn't been sorted properly into their afterlives. Numbers swelled in times of war or plague. And, as the Plains bordered Hell, it fell to the Devil to manage them. Angels had no interest in coming to help or in finding the ones who should have gone to Heaven; they worried they wouldn't make it back up to Heaven if they dared to come down.

"None that we know of, my Prince," Malketh told him.

He nodded and waved a hand to dismiss her. He found himself running his hands through his long hair, his fingers braiding it of their own volition. His hands liked to be busy, which meant that no matter how carefully he arranged his hair in the morning, it was always undone by midday.

The demons moved away from the souls, waiting for instructions.

Satan circled the souls, walking between their rows and peering at each one. He stopped in the second row and drew out a young man. He walked him out of the mass and said, "Hindu. Not one of ours. Bring him where he needs to be."

A demon moved forward and took the young man by the arm.

Satan eyed that demon, then shook his head. "No, not you, I want him to make it there." He gestured for Skarn to approach.

The snake creature took the soul by the hand and led him away to his correct destination.

By the time the Devil had finished his inspection, more than half the souls had been removed. The rest were left to be sorted into their proper precinct, where their punishments awaited them.

When the room had been emptied, Lucifer stretched up on his toes, reaching his arms far above his head. He let out a yawn, half stifled as he'd turned his head into one of his shoulders.

"Long day, my Prince?" Malketh asked when he'd finished.

"I am tired, Malketh, always tired."

She nodded. Their Prince was busy, always having something to tend to, either here in Hell or above on Earth. "Perhaps you should retire early. Things have been quiet."

He shrugged, a loose-limbed movement that emphasized the length and thinness of his body.

Rumor said that the Devil had not always appeared so, with spidery long limbs and milk-pale skin. His hair had not always been so inky black and his eyes had not always been such a terrible reddish gold. Malketh had been made in Hell, so she had not known him before the Fall; those who had tended to stay quiet about how Satan had been. Of course, he hadn't been Satan then, only Lucifer.

"There is always so much to do."

He glanced around the room one last time as if he expected to see one last soul lingering. He peered more closely at a shadow, sure that he had seen something glinting.

Malketh asked, "What is it?"

He shook his head. "Probably nothing."

Malketh couldn't take her eyes from the shadows. She stepped forward, hand on her knife, but the only thing there was an orange tabby. Hell was lousy with cats, though no one exactly knew why.

Without a word, the Devil wandered off, leaving Malketh behind and heading to the Eighth Precinct. The Eighth was free of souls to be punished and home to the lower-ranking demons and other creatures that made their home in Hell.

Hedged in by a great circular wall, Hell had nine wedge-shaped districts of unequal size, seven for the sinners and two for those who worked there. Once it had been a great sprawling wasteland, but punishing sinners was difficult when roaming on horseback. Sometimes he missed the days when it had been only him, some hell beasts, and a few friends chasing down those who needed recompense for their deeds. But he had been young then.

In the Eighth, he walked with his hands in the pockets of his silk trousers to keep himself from undoing and re-braiding any more of his hair. Many of the creatures he passed genuflected or bowed. He had never meant to make that a habit for the rank and file, but when he'd forced one cheeky demon to do it, they'd all started.

All the Fallen, no matter their order, touched their heads to the floor at the sight of him. Junius had done it before anyone else, sweet and love-struck thing he had been then, on the first night they had been cast out.

The Fall had been a great scattering, and those cast out had landed all over the human world. Some he had not seen again for many years. Somehow Junius had been with him that night; the poor thing had wept, not used to being confined in an earthly body for so long and heartbroken at the idea of never going home.

Seeing Junius weep had sent Lucifer to his knees. He had taken Junius's face in his hands and promised, "I will see us home, love, you will not have to stay in this place."

In the thousands of years that had gone by, he had not yet been able to deliver on his promise.

Some of the Fallen had chosen to stay on Earth, others had accompanied him to Hell, where he was bound. He could not leave the realm for too long without being compelled back. Hell was his punishment as much as he was meant to punish the souls in his custody.

He knocked on the front door of one of the small houses in the Eighth.

No one answered.

He waited, looking up and down the street. Here all the houses crowded close together, touching or with only narrow alleys in between. This small house was not on the outskirts of the Eighth, so generally, people could pass unmolested if they didn't seem like an easy target.

He knocked again and called, "Eodus, I know you're in there."

The door opened a moment later to show a demon, slight-framed and dark-eyed. His hands shook as he stepped back. "My Prince, I didn't..." He remembered his manners and knelt. "I..."

"We know why I've come, Eodus, let's not be coy."

"I-I don't...is..." The demon's eyes darted around; his thin, ash-colored hands twisted together. "Is something the matter?"

Satan entered the house and closed the door behind him. He glanced around the room. Clean, simple, no sign of the carrion that some demons liked to gather or of the excesses in which some of them indulged.

Eodus had done little of note in his lifetime and Lucifer was surprised to find himself needing to deal with him.

A large, white cat leaped up onto the kitchen table and blinked slowly at the Devil.

"Your Highness, what do you want from me?"

"There is a human in the Eighth, Eodus."

The demon flushed. "A human, surely...with so many souls...there must be so many..."

"A live human, in the Eighth Precinct, where no human, dead or living, has any business being."

Eodus wrung his hands so fiercely that he ran the risk of pulling his own fingers off. "I don't know what you mean."

"Jaspar ratted you out. That one seeks forgiveness for other crimes and hopes pointing fingers will garner it." Satan watched the cat jump down from the table and pause in front of a narrow door. The cat flopped down and stuck its paw under the door. "Bring out the boy."

The demon shook his head, tears glinting in his eyes. "Please, my Prince."

"Bring him out."

Eodus went to the narrow door and brought out a human, young and fair. From Jaspar's report, Lucifer had expected a child. "Small and sweet and *young*, tender," Jaspar had crooned, lips wet with hunger.

Instead, the boy was a slim youth, twenty, or maybe a little younger. He set his jaw and squared his shoulders. Lucifer guessed that, since the Devil lacked the popularly depicted horns and red skin, the youth didn't know who he was trying to stare down.

Satan smiled and the boy's brave posture faltered.

"Your Highness, please, he's no trouble to anyone," Eodus said.

"Tell me your name," Satan said to the boy.

"Jack Callahan."

"And where did Eodus find you?"

The youth answered, "Walter and Shanley Circus, outside of Amherst."

Satan reached out to Eodus, his hand palm up and waiting.

Eodus took him by the hand but flinched when he felt his Prince searching inside of him.

He saw Jack as Eodus would have: tumbling and juggling in white stockings and black leather slippers. He saw him with his brown curls shining in the moonlight after the show as Eodus could not take his eyes away. Every night for the whole time the circus had been set up outside of Amherst. Eodus had taken the young man by the hand and pleaded for his affections. He had covered him in greedy kisses and eagerly knelt before him, pulling down the youth's stockings, infatuated and longing to please him.

Lucifer released the demon's hand, having learned what he wanted to know. The boy had not been taken without consent. Nor was he a child.

"Still, it does me no good to let humans run amok here. Soon everyone will want one." He looked at Jack and found himself wanting to touch the youth in a way he hadn't a moment ago. "A pretty one, too. Tell me, Eodus, why could you not be content with going to visit your lover? So many keep their trysts on Earth where they belong. On Earth."

Strictly speaking, such trips to Earth were not permitted, but there was always a demon who had been granted travel privileges and would sneak others up for the right price. Lucifer let them think they were quieter about it than they were.

The boy's face flushed and Eodus turned his eyes to the floor.

"I didn't want to leave him with Mylas."

"Mylas, Second Fallen?" Lucifer asked, unable to keep the surprise from his voice. Mylas had left centuries ago with no love for Hell or its Prince.

"He calls himself Mylas Shanley now. Trains the acrobats. Keeps the ones he likes best for his own use." Eodus could not meet his Prince's eyes.

"Hmm."

The human had taken ahold of Eodus's hand, his body tense. *Don't send me back*, Lucifer could hear him screaming within, his mind filled up with the things Shanley had done to the other boys who had gone behind his back. Beatings and lashings, castrated while their lovers watched, or simply fucked until they were broken and bleeding so that they'd never again want to take another to bed.

Satan reached for the boy's arm and pushed up his sleeve. Branded into his skin was a string of unearthly symbols. So like Mylas to write his name on everything. "He'd find you quick with this. He searches for you even now, can you feel the runes calling to him?"

Jack nodded, swallowing.

"Do you know where you are?" Lucifer asked.

"Hell."

"And what about me, do you know who I am?"

Jack shook his head. "If I had to guess I'd say you're what he is. What Shanley is."

"We are called the Fallen. Demons, yes, but different from ones like Eodus here, who was born in Hell." He released the boy's arm. "Mylas is rogue, an enemy of Hell."

Jack stared at him, his gray-hazel eyes fixed on the Devil's face.

"I cannot let you stay—"

Eodus let out a small sob.

The Devil tried again. "I cannot let you stay unless—"

"I'll do anything," Jack offered.

Lucifer raised an eyebrow. "Would be nice to finish a sentence for once. Bring me the head of Mylas Shanley and you may request permanent residence in my realm. You have...six months or you must return to Earth to stay."

Jack looked at Eodus. "Your realm?"

"My realm. For those six months, I grant you refuge. Enemy of my enemy." He waved a hand dismissively, then took Jack by the chin and pulled him closer. "Do you accept?"

"If I stay in Hell..."

Lucifer felt the question buzzing in Jack's mind, but the youth wasn't sure how to phrase it. "You live for one lifetime, whatever that may mean for you while you're here. Never had a human stay for long and time is deeply different once you leave Earth."

"I accept."

"Good. This might sting." With one fingernail, Lucifer carved a few symbols into the boy's left cheek, declaring him a refugee. The scarring would be minimal, smooth and white, but visible to all who thought to give him trouble.

When he released Jack, the boy was shaking, blood streaming down his face and dripping onto his shirt.

"Six months, as the human calendar goes. You'll want to keep an eye on it. Eodus, do you have a calendar?"

Eodus shook his head. "No, Your Highness, I don't get sent for Earth-bound work."

"Alright." Lucifer glanced over Jack. "I suggest you get the boy to training, he'll need to do more than tumbling to best Mylas. The barracks are open to you."

Eodus kissed his hand, then kissed Jack.

Satan took his leave, heading back out into the Eighth and towards the Ninth. He liked to walk the streets late at night when even the most raucous demons had gone to bed. During times like now, when the great red sky above them was only beginning to dim, the citizens of Hell were out and ready to engage in whatever they found most pleasing. For some, it was as easy as sex or drink or gluttony, others still preferred dancing and bonfires in the district's center. A handful found so much pleasure in their labor that they continued tormenting others long after their workday was done, this time with willing victims.

He had to walk around a few small orgies and one large feast to get into the Ninth, where the streets were quieter. Not because the demons who lived here were any more restrained, but because they had larger homes and could revel indoors.

The library, crooked and black, loomed above the city. It was home to all manner of books and records. Its towers reached higher than any other building. He had done it so that his people would remember that he knew everything that happened in his realm. Maybe he didn't pay much attention to most of what happened, but he could find out if the need ever arose.

Pieter, the night librarian, greeted him when he walked inside.

"My Prince! What can we do for you?"

"A calendar."

"What sort?"

Lucifer considered what Jack had told him. "Human, modern. For the Americas."

"Yes, one moment." Pieter left his desk and disappeared into a backroom.

The library at night was no quieter than it was during the day. Students sat beneath their little orbs of light, heads bent over tomes and notebooks. The rustle of pages, the scratch of pen nibs and, every so often, an exhausted groan.

Librarians trafficked books here and there beneath the vaulted ceiling, past the stained-glass windows and deep into the stacks, up one flight of stairs and down them again.

Pieter returned and cleared his throat to gain his Prince's attention.

Coming back to himself, Satan peered down at the wooden desk calendar. Red-stained ghostwood blocks showed the day, year, and month in silver; it had extra blocks that could be set to show star cycles or other astrological events. The blocks would change on their own, turning over in time with the human world.

"Is that today's date?"

Pieter glanced over. "Yes, Highness, of course."

"Hmm, almost Halloween," he sighed. He took up the calendar and fiddled with it so it also displayed how many days Jack had left to accomplish his task.

He walked as he fiddled and stepped in a puddle because of it. A puddle of what, he couldn't be sure because it hadn't rained that day.

He shook off his shoe and continued to the large, ostentatious palace he called home. It had been built long ago when he'd still had a wife and had imagined the need for many bedrooms, playrooms, and studies for all the children they were bound to have.

He did still have a wife, as a matter of technicality. She had simply left, without divorce or annulment. As for children, he had those scattered throughout the human world, bastards all of them.

Many believed that the Devil had no love for his children in the human world, but more than anything he feared them, though he would not have admitted it to any who asked. He barely admitted it to himself. He feared failing them as he'd failed his first child, a daughter born to his wife. A princess that should have been his heir.

He feared loving those children, too, because when he loved something, he almost always ruined it.

"Hungry?" a voice asked when he entered.

He turned to see Imogen.

"Oris has soup on, hot if you want it," she offered.

"No."

"You should."

He handed over the calendar to her. Imogen had served as his butler for over a century, since before she'd been called Imogen. "This needs to be brought to Jack Callahan, care of Eodus, in the Eighth Precinct."

She took the calendar, peering at the countdown he'd set. "And who is Jack Callahan, care of Eodus?"

"A pretty acrobat who smells of peppermint candy when he weeps, who likes to bugger Eodus with the demon's hands tied. A pretty acrobat who will bring me the head of Mylas Shanley or die trying."

Imogen smiled a shark-smile and he recalled how much less troublesome her smile had been when her name had been Harold and she had slumped about unhappily in men's clothing. Her smile then had been wan and thin; now she grinned like a witch before a cauldron. Dressed as she liked, with the name she wanted and all the confidence that came with it, Imogen was happier but more worrisome.

"How pretty?" she asked, her fangs flashing. Imogen loved the blood of pretty boys. She was not a demon or a dead soul, but a vampire who still had a vampire's needs.

"Very. Have the calendar wrapped before it's sent."

"Will you write the card yourself?"

He nodded and headed upstairs, his hand on the richly stained wooden banister, his feet sinking into the plush carpet. He stepped over a cat stretched out on the last stair.

The palace had many floors and many rooms, but almost all of them were draped with sheets and covered with dust and cat hair. A least two dozen cats wandered the palace, coming and going as they wanted. Maybe more, as all the cats were black and blended together.

The palace employed two staff full-time to deal with the cats, making sure they were fed, that their bodies were discovered when they died and doubly making sure the cats didn't leave any messes around for the Devil to step in. Only one cat keeper had ever been able to keep all the cats straight, giving them names and knowing exactly how many there were. He had died in an attempted coup and had received a king's burial.

The cats certainly were not the Prince's pets; no one in living memory had ever seen him bring a cat home. He never spoke about the cats to anyone, unless it was to mention, his voice cold and smooth, that there was a mess that needed to be dealt with. Some believed that the cats were witches' familiars drawn to his dark power. A few whispered that they were the Devil's feline children, the product of the time he spent in the shape of a beast. Others still reported that they were enemies he hated, or had once loved, too much to kill.

When the Devil entered his bedroom and saw a cat lounging on his settee, he paid it no mind until he took notice of a particular sound. He turned to see that the cat had four mewling kittens pawing at her belly. Judging by the mess on the cushions, they were newborn.

One kitten lay still and quiet, flopped over on its side.

He crouched beside the settee and wondered if the staff would be able to clean the stains out or if it would have to be reupholstered.

The mother cat regarded him with tired orange eyes.

He poked at the still kitten and it did not move. It had the odd feel of a dead thing, as though it were only a lump and had never been anything more. He put his finger on it and wiggled it a little. Nothing. He scooped it up in one hand, not able to remember if cats were the ones who ate their young.

No, he remembered in a flash of clarity, that was rodents.

The little kitten lay in his hand and he brought it close to his face. The thing had not died long ago and he pressed his lips to its face. The thing coughed up a bit of fluid into his mouth for his trouble. After that, it began to shake and mewl. He spat onto the settee, tucked the kitten back in among its littermates, and noted that the kitten had a great white splotch on one side, shaped somewhat like a hand.

Things brought back from death would never be quite right but in a cat, that would be harmless.

He went to his desk and penned a quick note to Jack in a messy scrawl he'd never been able to improve. He poked his head out the door and grabbed a servant by the sleeve as she passed. The demon, a woman named Gila, flinched, which made him smile.

He handed her the note. "Give this to Imogen."

"Yethyour Highneth, rihaway." Her words came out jumbled and he almost couldn't understand them, but he didn't have the heart to ask her to repeat herself. She hurried away, almost running.

With his problem in the Eighth Precinct handled, at least for now, the Devil retreated into his room and closed the door. He shed his clothes, leaving them in a black heap on the floor, and lay on his bed, staring up at the red and gray pattern on the ceiling. Every night he thought he saw something different in the ceiling, flowers or crows, battlefields or forests. He wasn't sure if it was him or the ceiling that changed.

He wondered if allowing Jack to stay would cost him. He had not been particularly kind to the boy but he had given him protection. There were always a certain number of demons, old things made during his wildest days, who wanted him to be cruel and reckless. They were always ready to see weakness and he, from time to time, would have to remind them that he was not weak.

Alone in a bed made for two, the Devil lay awake, thinking of Jack and Eodus, unable to put aside the memories he'd slipped into. The ecstasy of new love and the heat of intimacy tumbled in his brain, filling up his dreams so that he woke several times, flushed and erect, but also overwhelmingly lost.

He thought of all the creatures who would willingly take him into bed, dozens who wanted it and many more who would allow him to do so because they saw it as an honor to serve their Prince.

He thought of Junius, who had loved him since the start. Right now, far away, Junius lived in New York City, a bustling new metropolis that someday would swell with humans and unnatural things alike. He lived there at the Devil's request, as a watcher. If Lucifer went there, to the apartment the demon had surely filled with potted plants, Junius would take him into his bed and into his heart without a moment's hesitation.

And he would be broken to pieces when he knew that it was only a tryst. In all the years they had known each other, Lucifer had never been able to stand to the idea of taking Junius as a lover. He had a sense deep in his stomach that they wouldn't be good for each other, or, more specifically that he wouldn't be good for Junius.

He loved Junius too much to risk hurting him.

He rolled over onto his stomach, the pressure of his bed against his cock sending a thrill through him. He snorted into his pillow. Here he was, fallen angel and Prince of Darkness, one more lustful dream away from humping his mattress.

He pushed himself out of bed and pulled on a robe, tying it tight around his waist and heading out into the palace. He almost stepped on several cats on his way to the kitchen.

He stoked the coals in the stove and added more wood, then set a kettle to boil. While he waited, he took a mug from the cupboard and puttered through the jars of dried herbs, looking for something that would soothe his longing and let him sleep for more than a few winks at a time.

A whisper-quiet noise from the doorway that led to the servant's quarters made him glance up to find Imogen watching him.

"Apologies, Sire, I thought it was Lolli sneaking things from the kitchen again."

"Lolli?"

Imogen approached, a thick plait of chestnut hair draped over one shoulder. "Oris is bedding her. Or, I suspect, she is bedding Oris just to get in here. She likes those mushrooms you hoard."

"I wouldn't call it hoarding."

She peered into his mug and, with a practiced hand, wafted the smell towards herself. "Valerian and chasteberries?"

He cared less that Imogen knew the herbs by scent and more that someone had been sneaking into his pantry. "Which mushrooms is she taking?"

"I don't know, I can't tell them apart. It's all mold to me. What's got you putting chasteberries in your tea?"

"Mold is a type of fungus, not the other way around."

Imogen sat at the table and looked up at him. "You can tell me."

"About mushrooms? I think they're fascinating."

"You would!" she scoffed. "Who's got your mind all tangled up?"

He stared into his mug, waiting for the kettle scream. "We had a lot of souls in the Plains today. More than usual. Malketh reports no conflict above."

"Sometimes people die."

He regarded her for a moment. Vampires were not unwelcome in Hell, but they were unusual. Sometimes they came down as lovers or out of boredom after an unnaturally long life and more than a handful had been banished here, unable to control themselves on

Earth. Imogen lacked the feral tendencies of the banished ones, was not exceptionally old, nor did she have a lover.

"Maybe there was an accident. Shipwreck or something," she said.

"That could do it."

The kettle wailed and he filled his mug. He took a seat across from Imogen and waited for the dregs to settle.

"That human in the Eighth, I brought him his calendar."

"*You* brought it?" he asked.

She smiled. "Not so many humans down here, I had to go and see."

"If you wanted to see humans, you should have stayed on Earth."

She played with the end of her braid. "I'm not stupid enough to try to bite someone to whom you've given refuge. Everyone remembers what happened when Tore messed around with that fairy."

"Glad to know you're smarter than Tore, at least."

Imogen abandoned her braid. "If Eodus gets a pet—"

"The boy isn't a pet, he's a tool. He'll kill Mylas—"

"Nimble Mylas?"

Lucifer sat up a little straighter. "He was before your time, what could you know about him?"

"People talk."

"So tell me what you know of Mylas."

"You were friends."

He scoffed. "Barely."

She tilted her chin up, not happy at being corrected. "He spent a lot of time coming and going from your bedroom."

"That's true enough," Lucifer admitted.

"And then he left."

"Fled," he reminded.

"Fled bleeding and bruised, cursing your name."

He sipped his tea. "That's the problem with torture, it takes too long."

"What did he do to earn your wrath?"

"Who says he needed to have done anything at all? I have many whims, a great deal of them unkind."

"He was your lover," Imogen reminded.

"So?"

She appeared doubtful, her lips drawn tight.

He thought about telling her what Mylas had done but knew it might reveal too much about himself. "Why did you come to Hell?"

"That doesn't have anything to do with this."

"If you can't tell me, I can't tell you."

She crossed her arms and he really considered telling her about Mylas. He enjoyed the vampire's company well enough, she did her job right and didn't cause him any problems.

"Trust goes two ways and as the great and powerful dark prince that I am, mine ought to be much harder to earn," Lucifer said, unable to keep himself from smirking. He didn't feel like a powerful dark prince, he felt sleepy and no darker than a cloudy day.

The sleepiness was the tea's effect, he hoped.

"If you ask enough people, you'll find all sorts of rumors to pick from, if you're so interested in Mylas." He took one last sip of tea and left the mug to be washed.

The white-splotched kitten mewled continuously. Lucifer attempted to pay the sound no mind, but the letter he wrote already had his nerves wrought. His letters to Elisa were necessary and his heart always quickened when he saw that she had written back.

She hadn't written back in well over a year, though he knew from her keeper that she was alive and well. He also knew that she read each letter, so he continued to write them.

But he could not write with such noise.

He stood and strode over to the settee and glared down at the kittens, all of them sleeping except for the one that had been dead. Things that died never came back right and he felt sure he had been mistaken in bringing this one back. He slid his fingers under the thing's belly and picked it up. It quieted.

The mother cat watched him. She must have known that this kitten wasn't normal.

"No more," he warned and put the kitten back, but as soon as he took his hand away, it began to cry again.

He sighed, lifted the kitten, and tucked it into the inner pocket of his robe, where it remained quiet. Bringing something back from the dead did impart a certain degree of responsibility. He should have learned his lesson by now.

He picked up his pen again and resumed his writing, inane ramblings that he hoped would garner a response. When he could think of nothing else to add, he signed it and set it aside. The ink needed to dry and he needed to eat.

He returned the now-sleeping kitten to its mother's side and went to the kitchen, where he found Oris picking through a basket of raspberries.

"Who sent those?" he asked.

Oris turned, hand to his chest and his eyes wide. "Oh, I didn't hear you come in."

Lucifer reached over to take the basket and check the tag. From Ambrose Weller, a human with whom he dealt rather regularly. A few decades ago, Ambrose had been a man of dreams and ambition with a great deal of debt. Over the course of a few negotiations, Ambrose had managed to erase his debt and begin an ambitious construction project. He carried on sending gifts to the Devil, maybe in the hopes that Satan would go easy on him when it came time for his part of the bargain to be paid.

He worried for his soul, the Devil knew; they all did, but souls came to him anyway and he had no great need for more of them.

He popped a raspberry into his mouth and wandered away, wondering where Ambrose had gotten fresh raspberries with Halloween growing so close in the human world. Of course, Ambrose dabbled in a variety of magics. The berries tasted fine, in any case.

He brought the basket upstairs and picked at them as he sorted through the drawers in his desk, searching for a piece of wax so he could seal the letter. He knew he had one but wasn't sure which drawer he had left it in. He couldn't find it in any of the drawers, but he did find a long, slim dagger that he didn't think he'd seen before.

There was the possibility that he hadn't remembered to put the wax away and a cat had made off with it. Eventually, he grew weary of searching and resigned himself to buying more. He shed his robe and dressed, taking a handful of raspberries with him as he headed toward the door. He doubled back, though, and took the whole basket.

Before he left, he stopped in Imogen's office and asked, "We haven't got any more sealing wax?"

She looked up from her ledger. "Oh, good, you got the raspberries."

"If you're so aware of what Oris is doing, why do you do nothing to stop him?"

"He makes good soup," she said. "And I take everything out of his pay. He hasn't made a serpent of what he's owed this month. Not that he's dared to say anything." She picked up a stick of sky blue wax from her desk. "Do you want to use mine?"

"No, thank you." He offered the basket to her before he turned to leave and she selected a single berry.

As he walked out, he heard her say, "Ugh, still don't like them."

He headed out into the Ninth, stopping at Demic's stationery shop. While Demic and his shop girl fluttered about in an attempt to be helpful, he selected several new sticks of wax as well as a sheaf of crisp linen paper.

"Have them sent up to the palace," he said, "Along with the bill. Imogen will take care of it."

"Of course, Your Highness," Demic said, bobbing his head.

After making his purchases, he wandered a little further into the Ninth and passed by a comely demon updating the sign outside a brothel.

It surprised him to see that this brothel kept up the old tradition of barter instead of pay. Long ago, all pleasure houses had traded for items instead of coin, distrusting the monetary system that had been introduced after things had settled down. They had been the last holdouts for a while, though it had taken a long time to convince the rest of the demons that having a standard system of coin wasn't too organized, too *human*.

In truth, he had done it because he had gotten tired of dealing with endless squabbles about who had gotten the raw end of the deal for something. With coin setting a standard value for most things, the complaints had been reduced by more than half.

"You going to come in or just gawk?" the demon painting the sign asked.

"Hmm?"

"Day shift's just as nice as the night shift, come and see for yourself." With that, she disappeared inside.

He stood outside for a moment longer and considered the things he needed to do when he got back to the palace. Overcrowding in the Fourth, discontent from the workers of the First, a string of unpleasant murders in the outskirts of the Eighth, four deals on Earth that would come to fruition and require his attention soon. Whispers from the barracks about Jack and the trouble one grizzled, old demon was giving the youth.

He stepped inside the brothel, propelled more by curiosity than lust. No one had kept the barter system; it turned out that the demons liked the feel and weight of coins in their hands, liked the way money didn't rot during hoarding periods, either.

Half a dozen demons were scattered throughout the room on silk and velvet pillows and cushions, as well as overstuffed couches. The upholstery appeared fresh and clean but bordered on threadbare in some places.

His eye was caught for a moment by the exposed thigh of a woman. Full-bodied, with lavender skin, she had one leg hanging off the side of the couch, the delicate lines of stretchmarks exposed on her inner thigh.

She didn't notice him, her attention already focused on a winged demon who couldn't take his eyes from her lips. Lucifer looked away, not wanting to catch her eye by accident and have her think she should turn her efforts on him.

The next thing he saw gave the Devil such a surprise that his stomach went cold. A thin-limbed and ash-gray demon lounged against pillows on the floor, his hair the color of black cherries. At first glance, he believed it to be Eodus, but closer inspection revealed a thinner nose and fuller lips, as well as curls instead of Eodus's straight but messy locks.

The demon met his eyes and raised an eyebrow.

Lucifer took a few steps forward and when the demon gestured for him to come closer, he did. The demon wore a thin shirt open at the neck and tight breeches, but no shoes or stockings.

He looked up at Lucifer from the floor, expectant and coy, and suddenly the Devil felt silly holding a basket of raspberries.

"Why don't you have a seat?" the creature suggested.

Lucifer knelt beside his pile of cushions and saw that he held a book in one hand. He now rested it against his stomach, as if Lucifer had interrupted him.

"We don't take credit or coin." A straightforward statement, as though he and the Devil had already decided that there would be an exchange.

"Why not?" Lucifer asked.

"Mistress doesn't trust them."

"But why work here?"

"No choice." The gray demon stretched as though it didn't bother him. "Mistress tells me where I work and this is better than her other enterprises."

Lucifer had come in with no intentions but now felt convinced that he needed to have this creature in his bed. He could leave and come back with something to trade, but he wanted to stay and press his lips to the back of the demon's neck.

One ash-gray hand reached out and hooked a finger around the handle of the basket. "Are these from Earth?"

"Yes."

"Do you get there often?"

Lucifer shrugged and said, "Whenever the mood takes me," which was sort of a lie.

"Mistress will trade for these, I'm sure."

Food grew better on Earth and had a sweeter taste. For those who were sent to the human world for missions, sneaking back bits of food was standard. That which grew in Hell was palatable but limited in variety.

It was not like the Devil to make a deal without careful consideration, but he said, "Take them," without a second thought.

The demon waved over someone from the desk in a corner;

judging by their plain clothes and inky fingers, this creature was not a pleasure worker but a bookkeeper of some sort. They evaluated the half-empty basket and pronounced, "It is sufficient for an hour's time with this one."

"Thank you, Nial," the demon said to the other creature.

Nial gave a small bow, took the raspberries, and returned to their desk.

Taking the Devil by the hand, the demon pulled him behind a curtain that masked the entrance to a hallway full of doors. The demon paused, his hand still gripping the curtain, and looked up at Lucifer. "Unless you'd prefer to be in view of the others?"

Lucifer shook his head and allowed himself to be brought into a room. Clean and tidy, it held no personal touches, which led him to wonder out loud, "Is this your room?"

The demon let out a little laugh but then covered his mouth as if he'd said something rude. "No. Mistress keeps these rooms for customers only."

The demon released his hand and went over to the bedside table, taking an hourglass out of the drawer and setting it so the sand began to run. With that done, he approached the Devil and asked, "How do you want me?"

"What's your name?"

"Ira."

Lucifer took him by the chin and tilted up his face, leaning in close to kiss him. Ira was shorter than him by more than a foot and slender where the Devil was lanky. His limbs didn't seem to have any secret, wiry strength as a dancer might; instead, he was pliant and tender.

When the Devil had him undressed, he pressed his mouth to Ira's belly, his ribs, his chest. He kissed his throat and nibbled at his ear, then pulled back to say, "Would you roll over?"

Ira turned onto his belly and, gripping the sheets, lifted his hips into the air. It didn't seem to be an invitation so much as a surrender to the inevitable. He had his face turned in to a pillow.

Lucifer ran a hand along Ira's back and pressed a kiss to the nape of his neck, then to his shoulder.

"There's oil in the drawer," Ira informed him, then softened his voice and added, "If you don't mind."

"No need yet. You can lie down," Lucifer urged. "And you can relax, love, I'm not in such a hurry."

"Oh." Ira lay flat against the sheets and folded his arms

beneath his head, resting his cheek on his forearm. "What are you going to do to me?"

Lucifer wondered if it was supposed to sound like dirty talk instead of worry. He put his lips to the demon's spine, to the small of his back. "Nothing you don't want."

Ira twisted a little to peer at him. "It's not about what I want."

He couldn't help but smile. "I'm aware how the exchange works and it's more fun when we both like things."

Lucifer almost continued with his kisses, his skin warming at the idea of the things he could do to make the smaller man moan, but Ira didn't relax. The tension in his muscles didn't disappear, nor did the slight quiver in his limbs. Lucifer pulled away, taking his mouth and hands from the demon's skin and kneeling off to one side.

"Would you like things better on your back?"

Ira shrugged. "Anything you like."

"Sit up."

Ira pushed himself up and sat facing Lucifer.

"Do you want me to go?"

"No!" The demon flushed, his cheeks darkening. "I...I don't normally get nervous like this."

"What are you nervous about?"

"I feel like I've seen you before, even heard your voice, and I can't place it, it...I don't know, it's bothering me. Distracting."

Lucifer gave a bit of a shrug. "Just one of those faces, I bet."

"Maybe." Ira didn't sound convinced. "It doesn't matter. I'm wasting your time, you know!" He said it with a smile, as though he wanted to forget about trying to recall where he had seen the Devil before. "Go back to kissing me, I wasn't thinking about anything else then."

Lucifer leaned forward to kiss him, running his hand along the demon's back. Ira twined his arms around the Devil's neck so that Lucifer moved in closer, laying the demon on the bed and straddling him.

The pressure of Ira's body against his cock was a dozen times preferable to that of his mattress and when Ira touched him Lucifer let out a moan that felt like a plea. He couldn't be bothered to fetch the oil from the drawer, instead conjuring up lubricant with an impatiently whispered spell.

He applied it to his length and with the same hand, touched Ira, who took in a sharp breath. With his eyes closed and his head thrown back, he appeared much more at ease.

Lucifer kissed him again, deeply, and then asked, "Are you ready?"

"Yes."

He slid inside the demon, slow and careful, but was not prepared for the heat of the other man's body. It could not have been so long since his last tryst that he'd forgotten. Ira's back arched and Lucifer knew it would be a long time before he forgot the curve of his chest, the parting of his spit-slicked lips, or the sound of his moan.

Ira moved now as he hadn't before, wrapping his legs around Lucifer's waist and pushing himself closer so that the Devil's cock slid further inside of him. He moved his hips up and down, bringing Lucifer in deeper each time.

"Touch me," Ira said, bringing Lucifer out of his fixation with the demon's body.

He wrapped his hand around Ira's cock and made a better effort to move in time with Ira, instead of remaining motionless like a virgin too surprised to do anything. They found an easy rhythm together, both of them coming within moments of each other, giving similar cries of pleasure.

His cheeks pink and thin chest heaving, Ira watched with half-closed eyes as Lucifer took his hand from Ira's length and brought it to his mouth, licking up the spilled seed. He shivered when the Devil pulled out of him and bent his head to lap up what had spilled on his belly and dribbled down his shaft.

He giggled, too, when the Devil kissed him. "Never had anyone clean up like that before."

Lucifer smiled. "I didn't want to leave without a taste of you." He lay down on his side beside Ira.

"I swear I know your face from somewhere. What's your name, anyway?"

He debated between giving a false name or spewing all his titles. Finally, he only said, "Lucifer."

Ira snorted at first, dismissive, but when the Devil didn't smile, Ira warned, "I'm sure he'll get awfully mad at you if he finds out you're giving his name to whores."

"If you see him, make sure you mention it."

Ira shook his head. "Wouldn't dare. I've heard he's...tempestuous."

"Tempestuous!" He couldn't help but laugh a little. Maybe in his younger days, but now it really took something to get him riled. He glanced at the hourglass on the table; only a little while remained.

He put his head against Ira's chest. The demon's heart still beat a little faster than it should have. Ira wiggled so that they were nestled together more comfortably.

When their hour was up, the hourglass let out a chime and, oddly enough, the color of the room's door changed.

"Nial will come kick you out if you don't hurry. Seen plenty get rushed out with nothing on," Ira warned.

Lucifer gave him another kiss and reached for his clothes, pulling on his shirt and smoothing his hair. As he pulled on his trousers and searched for his shoes, he asked, "What's this placed called again?"

"The Trade House."

"Creative."

Ira got out of the bed and began to pull on his own clothes, in more of a rush than Lucifer. He stepped toward the door but the Devil caught him by the arm.

"What?" Ira asked.

"Your hair..."

"Oh." He combed his fingers carefully through his curls and felt around the back.

Lucifer set a few locks straight. "Presentable again."

Ira gave him a smile and opened the door for him. "Don't go telling people the Devil buggered me, I don't want him showing up to prove them wrong. Or right."

Lucifer grinned, amused at Ira's disbelief. "Our secret."

As he walked out, he felt that he should have still been in bed with Ira, the demon nestled close, until both their hearts had calmed.

His walk home turned out to be long and meandering and when he arrived, he stopped in the kitchen to find that Oris had stew on the stove. He peered inside the stockpot and turned to the bespectacled chef. "Is it ready?"

"Yes, Your Highness."

Without being asked, Oris took down a bowl from the cupboard and rooted around for a spoon in the silverware drawer. He hesitated before ladling anything into the bowl, giving the Devil a nervous glance. Oris had not worked in the palace for long, but he had been here long enough that he shouldn't have been so jittery.

Perhaps, Satan mused, Oris was just an uncommonly nervous man. Or maybe he worried about his theft being discovered.

Oris set the bowl on the table once it was filled and asked, "Anything else, my Prince?"

"Bread and wine."

It was times like these when Lucifer missed his previous cook, Tally, a round and sour-faced woman whose mangled and crooked teeth had made speaking difficult for her, but she had listened well and doled counsel in grunts and hums. She had passed away in her sleep, which happened sometimes with demons.

Aging and death were inconsistent in Hell, but they did occur and no one had yet puzzled out how.

Oris returned with bread and wine, then hovered while the Devil ate until Lucifer set down his spoon, took a large gulp of wine, then asked, "Will you fetch Imogen for me?"

Oris bobbed and scuttled away.

When Imogen came, she came unaccompanied. She sat across from him. "Did you need something, Your Highness?"

"No."

She took in his wrinkled clothing, his mussed braids. "What happened at the stationery shop that's got you so rumpled?"

"Nothing."

She frowned a little.

"Am I tempestuous?" he asked.

"No. Perhaps...sensitive on certain subjects."

"Like what?"

She began to list, "Your wife, your daughter, the cats, mushrooms—"

"Mushrooms!"

"Maybe about mushrooms we can say you are passionate," Imogen amended.

He dipped his bread into the stew. "There are plenty of other foods I enjoy, I don't know why everyone fixates on the mushrooms. It is wonderful soup, but I still want to fire him. He...I don't know, he leaves a bad taste. Have you ever had a mushroom that's grown on a grave?"

"Can't say that I have. Have you decided what to do about the Fourth?"

He nodded. "They're all up for reevaluation soon anyways. We'll push it forward and I'm sure some of them will be ready to move to Purgatory."

"The workers won't be happy," his butler pointed out.

"They'll grumble but they'll be content enough when it's done. No more double shifts and missing out on bacchanals. Where did you send Oris, anyway?"

"I told him to go check the cellar for a bottle of mead."

The Devil nodded, knowing that the cook wouldn't find a drop but glad to have him out of the kitchen for a while. "Did you have any of this yet?"

"I am a vampire."

He rolled his eyes. "I know plenty of vampires who like to eat just as well as the rest of us."

"Surprisingly enough, we aren't all the same. I hear that Arak is giving your human refugee a hard time."

"I'll deal with it eventually," he said.

In the past few weeks, Arak had harassed Jack, but so far Eodus and Jack's mark of refuge had kept him mostly at bay. If the Devil intervened too early, he would be seen as overprotective, which would make people think he cared too much for Jack. If he waited too long, it would be open season on the youth.

"What is that smell?" Imogen leaned forward a little.

He sniffed his shirt. "Lavender and hyssop."

"And rosemary. Where did you go?"

Herbs for keeping things clean, all of them; Ira's mistress ran a clean house, at least. He declined to answer Imogen's question, instead finishing his stew and leaving the bowl to be washed. He drank the rest of his wine in one swallow and regretted it when it hurt going down.

In his room, he found his order from Demic sitting on his desk. He sealed his letter to his daughter and penned another to the captain of the Fourth, a woman by the name of Rema, asking her to come to the palace.

He had both letters sent out and then settled into bed with the contracts he needed to review, studying them long into the night and falling asleep with one on his chest.

On Halloween Eve, the Devil took the dagger he had found in his desk and went to the barracks, knowing that Jack would be found there. Every day the youth practiced and every day Arak gave him trouble.

He found Eodus and Jack in the practice yard with Pythea, one of the Fallen who had once counted Mylas as a brother. She had taken his defection from Hell rather hard. It surprised Lucifer not at all that she had taken Jack as her pupil.

When he approached, Pythea and Jack stopped their sparring.

The Fallen touched her head to the ground and Eodus knelt. Jack gave an awkward bow, panting, his damp hair stuck to his face.

"Rise," he said to Pythea, for she would have remained prone until his departure otherwise.

"What brings you here, Your Highness?" Eodus wrung his hands as he asked.

"Am I not allowed curiosity?"

"No, my Prince, I didn't mean—"

Lucifer chuckled. "How are things going?"

"Mylas will slaughter him," Pythea declared.

"So dour." Lucifer produced the dagger and handed it over to Jack. "This is no training blade, it will cut deep." He put his hand under the boy's chin and turned his head to one side, examining a scrape on his cheekbone.

His hands gripping the sheath, Jack set his jaw. "I'll get rid of Shanley."

The Devil took his hand from Jack's face. "See, that's the spirit he needs. You have many more weeks ahead, no one becomes an assassin in a mere month. And with Eodus's tender care at home..." He trailed off with a glance at the demon. "Do you have a brother?"

Eodus hesitated, his tongue darting out to wet his lips. "I...no, not anymore."

"Anymore?"

"He died when we were young. When the Wasting Plague swept through."

"Hmm," Satan hummed.

"May I ask why?"

Lucifer shook his head, not as a negation, but to show that it didn't matter. "I hear Arak bothers you when you come to train."

"Bluster," Eodus said but didn't sound confident.

"You'll tell me if it becomes more."

"Of course, my Prince."

Lucifer turned to Jack and asked, "Do you mind if I watch a few rounds?"

Jack blushed. "Oh, I don't...it's not much to watch yet. Not that you can't!"

Pythea rolled her eyes at the boy and gave him a push back toward the hard-packed dirt of the ring. He set aside the dagger and took up a blunted practice weapon, dropping into a fighting stance. He settled into it easily.

"It's nerve more than skill that he needs," Eodus confided softly.

Lucifer looked over, nearly taken aback that Eodus had said anything to him at all. "Save your worry. Mylas was never one to favor the weak and if he can learn to fight as well as he can tumble, he'll survive."

Eodus nodded, his worries seeming to be assuaged somewhat by the Devil's confidence.

Lucifer did not feel overly worried about Jack; if he had the nerve to do handstands on a tightrope, he would find the nerve to sink a blade into a cruel thing like Mylas.

Probably.

After several rounds of sparring, the Devil took his leave, telling Jack he would check in again sometime soon. He passed Arak on the way out and said nothing to him; from the grizzled demon's countenance, he didn't need to. Arak slunk like a scolded dog beneath the Devil's gaze.

It didn't feel like enough.

He stepped towards Arak and put an arm around the demon's broad shoulders. Arak had the strength to overpower the Devil as he was now without much real effort, but he wouldn't dare. Arak could die, but Lucifer could not and wasn't known for being merciful.

"You aren't doing well, Arak, I've heard."

Arak brawled nightly, couldn't follow his work schedule and when he did show up, he went after the souls indiscriminately and with brutish fervor.

The big demon grunted, "Doing fine."

"Mmm."

He pulled Arak along as they walked. The other demon stood almost as tall as Satan. Of course, when Lucifer had made him, he'd been taller himself. He'd settled into a smaller form over the years.

"Been bothering Jack, you have," Lucifer pointed out.

"Humans got no place here 'cept for torment."

"Jack's been granted refuge."

With a shake of his shaggy head, Arak protested, "Humans got to be punished."

Lucifer sighed. Maybe he should have taken more time when he'd made Arak, but there hadn't been any need for finesse before the walls had been built. "We've got to make some changes, Arak."

The demon pulled away, a harsh snort puffing out through his nose.

"It won't hurt if you relax." The words felt strange on Lucifer's tongue; the way he'd said them reminded him of the things someone, he couldn't remember who, had once whispered in his ear.

He placed one hand on either side of Arak's head and, bug-eyed, the demon took half a step back. Lucifer didn't let go.

Arak didn't relax, grunting and twitching as Lucifer rooted around in his mind, rearranging things. If Arak had been Hell-born instead of made, it would have been much more difficult and the results would have been messier.

Lucifer released him after a few minutes. "What's your name?"

"Arak."

"What's your purpose?" Satan asked.

"To punish."

"And who do you punish?"

Arak intoned, "The wicked dead."

Lucifer nodded. It hadn't been Arak's fault that he'd gotten his wires crossed about Jack. He'd probably never seen a live human before. He gave the big demon's shoulder a squeeze and walked away.

With his business in the barracks concluded, he headed to the Fourth, where Rema had requested his presence. He passed by the Trade House as he walked, though the brothel was out of his way. He had found himself passing by it several times when his route did not call for it, though he had not yet gone back inside.

A glance up at the sky told him that he would be early for his meeting with Rema. She would still be elbow deep in souls to sort and displeased with being interrupted. Or so he told himself, knowing that he shouldn't be wasting time.

He pushed open the door to the brothel, though he had nothing to trade. His gaze went instantly to Ira, lying again on the cushions with a book in his hand. After a moment, he looked up and his eyes widened.

He pushed himself up and the Devil came to kneel beside him.

"I...I haven't got anything to trade, you know," Lucifer informed him.

Ira tilted his head, his brows drawn together.

"Do you only work during the day?"

"No, daytime is my freelance shift. I can be bought for whatever time would please you best." Ira bit his lip. "If you want to buy me, that is."

"I...my days can be busy."

"And your nights?"

Lucifer admitted, "Often sleepless."

His mouth quirking, Ira told him, "I can think of a few ways to tire you out."

Satan reached out to take ahold of the demon's hand. "You don't mind?"

"Getting work?" He tipped back his hand and let out a little laugh. "No, I don't mind at all."

"I'll come back tonight."

"Good, because today has been slow and I want to eat." The words were cheerful but Ira must have noted the concern on the Devil's face because he squeezed Lucifer's hand. "A joke is all. If she starved me I'd be too skinny for anyone to bed. You can ask Nial for me when you get here."

"I will." He leaned forward a few inches then paused. "If I kissed you, would I have to trade something for it?"

"Only if Nial sees."

He leaned in and kissed him quick, then took his leave. He walked directly to the Fourth and found Rema waiting for him at the entrance of the gatehouse between the Fourth and the Fifth. He felt somewhat surprised to see her there, having expected to meet her in her quarters.

"Is something amiss?" he asked.

Rema shook her head, a few wisps of blue hair floating about her head, having escaped from her bun. "I didn't want you to walk all the way to mine just for us to have to turn around and go down to D ward."

"Thoughtful."

She started walking and gestured for him to follow.

"What's happening in D ward?" the Devil probed.

"It's where we've moved all the ones we aren't sure about. The ones that *you* need to look at, not to be too forward, Highness."

"Rema, you are always exactly forward enough."

She glanced back at him.

They took a few steps in silence before Lucifer asked, "How is Ella?"

"Well. I'll tell her you asked. She still fancies you."

The Devil chuckled. "Rest assured, my interest in bedding my own granddaughter is limited."

"Great-granddaughter, she always reminds me."

He laughed that time. Ella's actual interest in him was limited to no more than flirting and innuendo; he doubted that even if she were ever given the chance, she would really take him to bed. It was odd, but Ella was an odd girl from a long line of odd women. Her great-grandmother had been a witch with premonitions that had been hard to distinguish from her normal hallucinations.

"Are there a lot waiting for me?" he asked.

"Have you got somewhere better to be?"

"You know that of all the places in Hell I like the Fourth the least."

Rema tilted her head. "I always thought it would be the Seventh."

In the Seventh resided those who would never leave, those who had done so much wrong that their souls could never be clean. The Fourth, however, was home to the souls so wracked by guilt that they had condemned themselves. After the Seventh, they stayed the longest, all of them craving punishment and unable to move beyond it. Some of them had done no wrong at all but could not be admitted to Heaven with their souls so unwell. The Fourth served as a waiting ground while they tortured themselves.

In the Fourth, the job of the demons was not to torture but to push these souls into forgiving themselves. It was not a job to which demons were well suited, which led to a high staff-to-soul ratio. It caused overcrowding and burnout.

He tried to recollect the current population of the precinct. He asked, "How many have you sent to Purgatory so far?"

"Just shy of ten percent."

He winced. That number was lower than he had hoped. "Rema...how many are there for me to evaluate?"

"We have sixty-eight percent unready to move on, plus the nine-and-a-half that were sent up. Two even went to Heaven once they'd come to peace."

"Two *percent?*" Satan asked.

"No, two souls."

"That's over twenty percent in D ward?" He tried to keep his tone neutral but knew he'd failed when Rema cast a glance his way.

"And spilling into E a little."

"And what's stopping you from mediating them?"

"They're beyond my ken," she admitted.

He didn't like the sound of that. Rema had been the captain of the Fourth since the days of Charlemagne. She excelled at what she did, so to think that there were souls beyond her ken worried him.

"I have an engagement later tonight."

She stopped before the gate into D ward and took a key from her belt. "Highness, if you think you'll get through them all in one day, you haven't been paying attention to how many souls are in the Fourth."

She pushed open the gate and brought him into the chancery for D ward, where he saw several haggard demons sitting before stacks and stacks of portfolios.

"They're still matching up files to cells in the back." Rema gestured for one broad-chested demon to come forward. He had the build of a soldier, not a paper-pusher. "This is Inri. He's…he's sort of forgetful when it comes to anything but paperwork, so I mean, if you ask him to bring you lunch, make sure you write it down for him. He'll be able to get you what you need, he knows these files better than I do."

He gave Inri a nod, though Inri kept his eyes fixed on the wall behind Lucifer.

Rema prompted, "Inri, say hello."

"Hello," Inri said, his voice having the cadence of imitation, not engagement.

Rema gave him a pat on the shoulder. "Inri, this is your Prince, he's here to get all this sorted. You've got to help him. Bring him what he needs."

"Staying?" Inri asked.

"Who's staying?"

"You. Rema."

She promised, "I'll come check in. He'll be here for a while, though."

Inri glanced at Lucifer.

Soothing and calm, Rema assured Inri, "He'll do alright. Write things for him if he's too dense to understand you."

Inri nodded, turned to Lucifer and said, "Don't touch."

"Don't touch what?"

"The papers. Ask me when-when-when-when you need papers."

The Devil nodded. "Of course. I'm not here to go poking around."

"Alright, Inri, that's all, back to what you were doing." Rema gave Inri another pat on the shoulder and he returned to the stacks of folders. "He understands, so don't talk down to him. It just makes him upset."

"I won't." Lucifer watched Inri among the papers for a moment, then returned his attention to Rema. "You're sure *all* of these need my attention."

"You are the Devil, aren't you?"

He made a face. "That's what they tell me. Should I bother to visit the cells or get right into the paperwork?"

She peered at her pocket watch, a complex thing that showed time in Hell and on Earth. "There's one more thing I need you to see."

As they headed out of the chancery, he contemplated the grimness of her tone, wondering what could be so bad that it had her worried. She paused before a cell and unlocked it. He stepped into the doorway but no further.

Within he found a child in a nightdress, a little boy of perhaps nine. He stood beside a bed in a room lit by a single candle. The earthy smell and dampness made Lucifer think this room was a basement. A door on the other side of the room, a door that led to nowhere but his imagination, began to open. A man in medieval dress entered, carrying a plateful of food.

From outside the cell, Rema informed him, "Hundreds of years have passed above since this boy came here."

Lucifer could not help but watch as the man sat on the bed and pulled the boy onto his lap. He fed the child by hand, stroking his hair and gripping his thigh.

"He doesn't belong here, Highness, but none of us can coax him out. He needs more help than a demon can give."

The Fourth saw many who could not move past what was done with them. Many men who had taken their own lives rather than submit to their need for another man's flesh, or women who had died, chaste and miserable, in abbeys thinking of their sisters' thighs. Of course, many more such souls moved on without guilt, able to embrace their love of their own gender, or able to lay blame on those who assaulted them rather than themselves.

The Devil watched, stomach cold and face hot, as the man moved the boy from his lap to the bed, pulling up his nightdress and pushing the boy onto his stomach.

Rema pulled on his sleeve, but he didn't leave the cell, didn't take his eyes away until the act was done. A thousand times, this boy had lived his nightmare. What right did the Devil have to look away? If he looked away, he wouldn't remember, he wouldn't go home feeling sick, but if he looked away, the need to fix this wouldn't be as pressing.

When the man left, the boy lay and cried for a while, bleeding and raw, until he fell asleep.

"Every day, this is it. Exactly one human day," Rema said, giving his sleeve another tug. "We've tried everything we can think of for him. Staying with him, stopping the man, blocking the door, talking to him. It is beyond my ken to fix."

"And mine, too."

He left the cell and Rema closed it behind him.

The captain cleared her throat a few times before she managed to say, "If it isn't too much, maybe you could appeal to Heaven for him. At least for them to send...I don't know, someone good! He needs *help*."

"An angel, you mean."

"Maybe. There has to be something He can do."

Lucifer thought of a hundred bitter things he could say about God, but none of them were useful. "I've appealed to Him before about all of the Fourth. Souls cannot go to Heaven until they are ready and that means by their own standards, too. But I will write, don't look at me that way. I'll write to Him, I'm not too proud for that."

In silence, he walked back to the chancery and started to go through the files. Inri brought him some that he hadn't asked for as soon as he sat at a desk.

"Good to start," Inri told him.

While reading the files, Lucifer noticed that this first batch was all annotated in neat handwriting with suggestions on how to deal with the soul's ailment, complete with reference to similar cases in the past.

"Inri," he called.

The demon came, his arms full of portfolios.

"Did you write this?"

"Yes."

Satan glanced at the notations again. "Have you done this for all the files?"

With a stiff shake of his head, Inri replied, "No. Just easy ones."

"Alright, that's all. Thank you. Actually, tell me when it's getting dark."

Inri nodded and left.

By the time the larger demon returned, the Devil had written up a score of reports, his work expedited by Inri's help. He sealed them and set them aside, ready to be distributed in the morning. Each report contained a treatment method to set each soul on their path to Purgatory or the suggestion, based on the soul's wrongdoings, to simply move them to another district.

Sometimes a change of scenery and some active punishment was enough to move a soul out of their self-inflicted pain. It never failed to amaze him that humanity would punish themselves readily enough, but when faced with accusation for the same crime, take the defense.

"Dark outside," Inri informed him.

"Lovely, thank you. Those reports are ready."

Inri nodded and gathered the reports.

"I'll see you tomorrow."

Inri nodded again and gave a small wave as the Devil walked out.

By the time Lucifer made it to the Trade House, the sky had gone nearly black. He'd needed to stop at a store to buy something to trade, which seemed pointless. With a small velvet bag in hand, he entered the brothel and found it rowdier and more crowded than during the day.

He approached Nial's desk.

"How can I help you?" they inquired.

"Ira."

The bookkeeper asked, "For how long would you like him?"

The Devil had no want to bed the demon, not after what he had watched in the boy's cell, but he had promised to come.

Nial repeated, "For how long, sir?"

"I don't know. Can I...can I pay when I leave?"

Nial stared up at him then looked down at their ledger. "You may pay for an entire night and collect the remainder when you depart. What have you bought to barter?"

Lucifer handed over the little velvet bag, full of assorted

gemstones. Word on the street said that Ira's mistress did not trust minted coin, but liked the flash of gems and precious metals.

Nial sorted through the bag, picked out half a dozen of the largest gems and returned the bag. "These will buy his trade for the night."

"And when does the night end?"

"When the sky begins to glow."

Lucifer nodded.

Nial rang a bell and when another plain-dressed servant appeared, they gave instructions for Lucifer to be brought to a room and for Ira to be brought from his quarters.

The servant brought him to wait in a room that was different from but almost identical to the one he had been in last time. Ira entered a few minutes later, bright-eyed until he set eyes on Satan.

"You don't seem pleased to see me," Ira demurred.

"No, I...will you sit?" Satan gestured to the bed. Standing in the middle of the room staring at each other felt wrong.

Ira sat, tucking one leg under himself and letting the other dangle off the side of the bed. The Devil sat with his legs crossed Indian-style and his hands in his lap.

"I came because I said I would, but..."

The demon guessed, "But you changed your mind." His voice came across flat but not surprised.

"Not..." Ira's disappointment was clear and Lucifer wanted to soothe that, but he had spent too much time hunched over pen and paper today. "I told you my days were busy and I find myself more tired than I anticipated."

"Oh."

"I didn't want you to think I'd forgotten," Lucifer assured.

"Then why did you get me for the whole night?"

"Because I don't want to go home, either. I'll leave if you want me to, I have no intention of taking back what I traded if you're worried about that."

With a shrug and a glance around the room, Ira said, "I wouldn't mind if you stayed."

"No other clients you'd rather see?"

"I haven't got any regulars."

"How could that be?" Lucifer wondered.

Ira shrugged. "All sorts wander in on the day shift, especially university students, but I don't think any of them care enough to notice who they're fucking. There's one girl who's traded for me at least three times and each time she asks my name like we've never met."

Lucifer watched his hands as he spoke. He was always moving them, fiddling with the stitching on his shirt or picking at his nails, plucking fuzz from his breeches or simply gesturing around. He didn't move them with any particular vigor, but a languidness that suggested he was bored with everyone else in the room. "And you know her name."

"Amila. She's studying agriculture."

Lucifer snorted.

"You really want to just sit here all night?" Ira asked when too long had gone by in silence.

"It wouldn't be terrible if one of us was talking."

Somewhere between petulant and guilty, Ira told him, "You know, I didn't eat. I didn't think you'd want me for so long."

"Should I go?"

Ira gave another shrug like he didn't care if Lucifer stayed or went. "No, but you should order something from the kitchen. It isn't wonderful, but it's food."

"How?"

He gestured to a little bell pull beside the door. "It's all standard fare, nothing so fancy as raspberries."

The Devil pulled the cord and ordered when a servant came, exchanging a tiny gem for an order of bread and cheese and a bottle of wine. The kitchen had no fruit, he was told when he requested apples. While they waited, Ira told him of the last time he'd had fruit. A patron had asked Ira to handfeed her grapes while another had serviced her; her eyes had been closed so often that he'd been able to sneak half of them into his own mouth instead.

Roots grew well enough in Hell, turnips and rutabagas, potatoes and carrots. There was no lack of hearty things, but fruit trees and vines were hard to tend and therefore cost more than the average demon could pay.

"Mistress had me whipped when she found out, but it was worth it. She never does it hard enough to leave scars anyway."

Lucifer didn't want to dwell on that for too long so he inquired, "Have you ever tasted something from Earth?"

He shook his head. "It can't be that good, can it? What difference would a great big star make to things anyways? I like the sky red."

"Because you've never seen it blue."

Ira shrugged.

When a knock came at the door, Ira answered it and placed the tray on the bedside table. He poured Lucifer a glass of wine but didn't take one for himself. He didn't touch the food but eyed it eagerly.

Lucifer had his glass halfway to his mouth when he realized that Ira was waiting. He pulled the glass back, gestured to the food, and said, "Go ahead, you're the one who wanted to eat."

It would have been a lie to say he wasn't hungry, but it was a distant feeling, suppressed by the memory of the child's torment.

He sipped at his wine and watched Ira eat. At first, the demon took small bites, trying to be polite, maybe trying to maintain an air of sensuality, but that faded when Lucifer let out a small, accidental burp.

Ira laughed. "That's what you get for drinking on an empty stomach!" He reached over and took the wine glass from Lucifer's hand and replaced it with bread and cheese. "Before you make yourself sick."

He took a bite of the bread, finding it dense but pleasantly chewy. The cheese was semi-soft and rather bland. "Is this what you eat all the time?"

"It's nicer than what I eat all the time," the demon told him.

Lucifer shook his head, took another mouthful of food, and said, "I'll have to bring you something to eat next time."

Ira shrugged.

"You don't think I'll come back," Satan guessed.

"I don't know. Haven't even told me your name."

"I did, it isn't my fault if you won't believe me." He ate the last of his bread and took his wine back. "Drink something, I didn't get a bottle for myself."

"You're sure?"

He nodded.

Ira poured a glass for himself. "Besides, there's no way the *real* Lucifer would come here."

"Why not?"

"Because the Trade House is...acceptable, certainly, clean as anything," Ira explained, "But it's not nice enough for the Prince of Darkness himself. Good for students and those from the Eighth who don't want to worry about getting crabs or lice."

"You wouldn't say that if you saw how much cat hair there is in the palace."

Ira sipped his wine. "Instead of lying, why don't you tell me what's got you too tired to bed me?"

"I was in the Fourth today. We moved up the reevaluation and I've got...more files than I can count to go through."

"Bad at counting?"

Lucifer couldn't take the bait. He wanted to tease back but instead, he stared into his wine glass, thinking of the blood on the boy's thighs.

Ira reached out and gave his hand a squeeze. "You'd be surprised how many people come to whores to talk. I mean, most of them wait until after they've come to do it, but it hardly ever takes a whole hour."

"There's a little boy, he's trapped. Raped every day by some man...I told Rema I'd write to Heaven, but I know they won't even write back. I doubt they'd read it. What could happen in Hell to interest Him? After all, there's a reason He left it the hands of..." Lucifer sighed. He'd started to ramble. "And the angels all have their heads up their asses, anyway. Stiff new bunch of rule followers. But I guess that's what you make after a rebellion."

"Children don't come to Hell," Ira protested.

"They do if they think they deserve it. Oversight, I hope, but rules are rules and once He writes a rule, you don't change it." He twined his fingers with Ira's, running his thumb over the demon's skin. "Nothing changes."

"Tell me about something else," Ira said, the words tumbling out of his mouth.

"There's nothing else I can think of, I'm sorry."

They sat together quietly for a long moment until Ira downed the rest of his wine with a flourish and refilled both their glasses. "Do you read?"

"Daily," Lucifer replied.

"Business or pleasure?"

"Business, mostly."

Ira inquired, "Did you like the last book of poems Phaedrus Queen published?"

"Oh, sappy love poems, all of them!" he pronounced.

"I like them."

With a scoff, Lucifer told him, "If you saw their husband, you wouldn't be so impressed."

"A human, isn't he?"

Lucifer nodded. "Tall, skinny thing. A mage and a Reinhart,

too, and those are *always* trouble. But they're happy enough together, really. I never thought Phaedrus would settle down again. I should be happy for them."

"You sound jealous."

"No, not hardly. Phaedrus and I never had any sort of spark and I'm definitely done fooling around with Reinharts altogether!"

"Still, I liked the poems." Ira thought for a moment then added, "Especially the third one."

"You ask me if I'm Scheherazade..." The Devil sipped his wine. "When it comes to poetry, I've come to like Dickinson."

"Who?"

"'Because I could not stop for Death, he kindly stopped for me,'" Lucifer quoted.

"I don't know it."

"That's alright. What about cats?"

"The...the animal?" Ira ventured.

"Of course."

"Well, they're everywhere."

"Do you like them?"

Ira smiled. "Do you?"

With a smile creeping over his face, Lucifer admitted, "I don't know, I can't decide. There's a litter of kittens in my bedroom, sweetest little things you can imagine, wobbly on their legs, prancing around but as soon as I lie down to sleep, I'm Everest and they have to climb me."

"Everest?"

"It's a mountain on Earth. Humans are going to start trying to climb it soon, I mean the European ones, and I'm going to create a special place here for them when they die. Idiots."

Ira chuckled and refilled his glass again. They finished the bottle together not too much later but did not order another from the kitchen.

When the last drop was gone, Lucifer stretched out on the bed and then rolled on his side, gazing at Ira. "Would you mind if I called regularly?" He didn't want to look away.

"No," the demon answered as though it were a ridiculous question.

"You could come to call on me."

"If I ever happen to wander by the palace," Ira teased, shaking his head at the Devil's insistence. "He doesn't like it when people use his name. Everyone knows that."

"So I live on the edge. Come lay next to me so I won't be so afraid of the Devil swooping in to take his vengeance."

Ira lay down beside him. "You'll have to tell me your real name if you're going to be a regular. Everyone will laugh at me if I say our Prince has come to fancy me."

Butterflies grew in his stomach. "You think I fancy you?"

The demon slid his fingers along the Devil's jawline. "Don't you?"

"I'm not sure." Lucifer changed the topic. "Have you got a brother?"

"Somewhere."

"Dead?" he guessed.

"No." Ira's mouth twisted. "He must be in the Eighth somewhere, that's where our parents lived. Probably live there still."

"And what are you doing in a brothel in the Ninth? Runaway?"

"They sold me. Traded me to Mistress during the Wasting Plague."

Lucifer felt like an ass for asking at all and could only summon, "Oh," in response to Ira's frank answer.

"Twins are bad luck all around. I'm lucky they didn't kill me outright since it was plague times."

"Lucky indeed," Lucifer scoffed under his breath.

"Besides, what's bad about having people come and barter for the right to make me spill? Better than the other things she runs. Good thing I was sort of pretty."

Prettier than your brother, the Devil thought as he buried his face in Ira's shirt, wrapping one arm around the demon's waist. Not, of course, that he bore Eodus any ill will or found him unpleasant to look upon.

"Are you going to fall asleep?"

"You should, too."

Ira protested, "I'm going to get a bad reputation if anyone finds out that I've charged to let you cuddle me all night."

"Or maybe the lonely but impotent will come out of the woodwork."

"This silly after half a bottle of wine? I don't think the Devil would be glad to hear that he's got a lightweight stealing his name."

Lucifer insisted, "I'm not drunk, I'm tired. Fucking kittens keeping me awake all night and a mountain of paperwork to deal with in the morning."

"Sounds like Satan to me."

Lucifer had a retort in his mind, but it was meaner than he wanted to be, so he tightened his grip on Ira and fell asleep without another word.

Lucifer arrived at D ward in the Fourth smelling strongly of lavender, hyssop, and rosemary. Nial had roused them at dawn and urged Lucifer out. Ira, still mostly asleep, had shuffled away with just a wave.

He arrived before the other workers and settled into the same desk as yesterday, pulling a sheet of paper from the drawer and staring at it. He could think of nothing to write that would move Heaven to action and by the time the others started to arrive, he had only penned two words.

Dear Father.

God was not his father in the sense that he had been born, but He had created Lucifer and all the other angels and had always referred to Himself as such. References to paternity were scattered throughout the religions He had organized around Himself. *Our Father, who art in Heaven* went the prayer and He'd even called Christ His son. Maybe all the old fool had ever wanted was to be a parent in the genetic sense.

He would call the bastard 'Daddy' if it would get this boy out of Hell.

If this letter reaches your eyes, then your angels are not the pompous idiots I remember from our last meeting.

He knew he was being too unkind, but it had taken a lot even to write those words.

I would bring this message myself, such is the importance, but barred from Heaven as I am, I rely on paper instead. There is a boy, or to be more accurate, a boy's soul here that does not belong but cannot move past the things done to him. He is guilty of nothing and deserves to ascend to his place in Purgatory.

My demons in the Fourth have worked to help him, but they are Hell-born and not suited to such tasks. If you cannot bend a rule to take him out of his self-imposed torture, will you at least send an angel to guide his healing?

As much as I can, I beg.

Ever your creation—as much as it chafes me,

Lucifer

P.S. Best you hear it from me than someone else: There is a human living in Hell, he's taken up with one of the demons. Quite happily, I might add. No need to send any soldiers to stomp around and bring him back to Earth.

He set down his pen and reread the letter. It was the best he could do. He didn't think detailing the boy's circumstances would do anything to sway the Almighty because there was nothing that was unknown to Him. It was merely a matter of making something interesting enough to provoke His interest.

He tapped his nails, black and shiny, against the wood of the desk for a moment, then sighed and reached past the skin of reality into the cosmic webbing that connected all things and felt around for a string that would reach to Heaven. He found one, tied it around his letter, all the while hating the resonating tingle that worked its way from his fingers to his head, and then gave the string a strong enough tug so that it would bounce up to Heaven.

From the doorway, Rema said, "Thought it was horseshit when they said you could reach into the underneath."

"I wouldn't be a particularly good Devil if I couldn't," he said. "No way to get to Earth or to move in time? I'd be as useless as the last fellow."

He clenched and unclenched his hands in an effort to banish the feeling of the underneath on his skin. He checked the urged to pull at his hair and hit himself in the head to distract from what had seeped into his skull. *It will pass*, he told himself over and over again.

"Uncanny." Rema shook her head. "Are you wearing perfume?"

"Hm? No, that's just the smell of whorehouse."

"Ah." She nodded.

He reached for the files that Inri had put on his desk. "Anything else you needed?"

"Wanted to make sure you settled in alright."

He assured, "I'm settled in fine. About Inri—"

Defensive, she answered with terse enunciation, "He does fine."

"Yes, but what about his name?"

"Hm?"

"Iesus Nazarenus, Rex Iudaeorum," he elaborated. "That's what it means."

"Oh, well, I think it's short for something. Inri!"

The demon approached.

"What's your whole name?" she asked.

"Inrepentious and Hortent Flagellation the Sixth."

Lucifer made a face, forgetting how appallingly bizarre demons could be at times. It was his fault, really, but it always served as a shock.

"Ugly name," Inri agreed with a nod. "Don't like it."

"Well, I wouldn't either. I'm sorry."

Inri nodded, accepting the apology and setting a half dozen more portfolios on his desk. "More notes."

Lucifer shuffled through them half-heartedly. "Thanks."

Inri glanced at his face for a moment then walked away.

"You ought to promote him," Lucifer suggested to the captain.

Rema sighed. "He always fails part of the exam."

"What exam?"

"The exam *you* put into place after that fiasco in the First," she reminded.

He thought back. "Oh, right. The exam's easy enough."

"It has a panel interview."

With a wave of his hand, he told her, "Oh, give it to him written! He's got lovely handwriting, I don't know if you've noticed but it's something else."

"Better than your chicken scratch."

"Give him the interview written, that's an official decree." He picked up a portfolio and waved Rema away, sure she had better things to do.

He wrote another dozen reports that day and Inri informed him when darkness began to fall.

Before he left the Fourth, he checked in on the boy and found him lying in bed, face down and aching. He stepped into the cell to pull his covers up, but when he did the boy tensed. He sat up and pulled away.

"Oh, don't worry, little thing, I've no interest in buggering you. You get enough of that, don't you?"

The boy stared at him, his eyes huge and blue. "Who are you?"

"The Devil."

The boy nodded, accepting the answer easily enough. "Papa said I would go to Hell."

"Is that your papa that comes to you every day?" he asked with a glance toward the door.

"Yes."

"You know you don't have to stay here."

He shook his head. "Papa doesn't like it when I leave my room."

Lucifer sighed. Rema had reported that they'd tried to take the child's soul from the cell, hoping that a change of scenery would break the cycle, but the man had come anyway, dragging the boy back to the cell and beating him bloody. "Your papa doesn't seem very nice."

"He loves me."

The Devil put a hand on the child's face, cupping his cheek. "When he comes next time, tell him to go."

The boy bit his lip and looked down at his lap, his small hands clenched together.

"Get some sleep."

He nodded and nestled into bed.

The Devil pulled up his covers and left him, feeling that there should have been more he could do. If the boy had been alive, he could have gotten rid of the father, but the soul's torment wouldn't end until he thought it should.

When he arrived at home, Imogen greeted him with a frown.

"What?" he asked.

"Where've you been?"

"In the Fourth," he answered, more than a little nonplussed at her concern.

"For two days!"

"I didn't know you cared for me so much, Imogen, love." He put an arm around her shoulder and pulled her close. "If I had, I certainly wouldn't have gone sulking around whorehouses."

She pulled away, wrinkling her nose. "You've gone this long without making a pass at me, let's keep it that way."

"I could be a girl if you'd like me better that way." He grinned wickedly and she visibly shuddered, crossing her arms tighter.

"God, I hate that smile."

He smiled wider. "Touched as I am, you don't need to worry. The Fourth will keep me busy for days to come. Could you have Oris send up something to eat? I'm starving."

She nodded and turned away from him.

As soon as he sat at his desk, the white-splotched kitten dug its claws into his legs and climbed onto his lap. He gave the thing a gentle pat on the head and had to continuously put it back on the floor once his food arrived since it kept trying to eat from his bowl.

When he settled into the bed, the kitten shoved its way underneath his chin and lay across his throat.

"Should have left you dead."

The kitten began to purr.

He turned onto his side and the kitten made itself at home between his chin and his shoulder, curled up and kneading his throat with razor-sharp claws every so often. He managed to fall asleep eventually.

No more than an hour or so later, something clattered to the floor and woke him. He sat up so quickly that three fully-grown cats fell off him, none of them pleased. One leaped off him, digging its claws into his gut to get away.

He rubbed his eyes and recalled that it was Halloween night, the night when idiots on Earth gathered in drunken groups to make ill-advised sacrifices to the Dark Lord. It was invariably cats. Black ones.

"Fuck," he swore and reached for the oil lamp on his bedside table. He hesitated to light it, not wanting to see how many more cats he'd been sent.

Before his hand reached the lamp, something large and probably not a cat leaped into his bed and plunged a something sharp into his shoulder. His first thought was that someone had sacrificed a tiger, but immediately dismissed the idea. It was a blade, not a claw, sunk into his flesh.

He grabbed his attacker and pushed them off the bed. He scrambled off the other side, hoping to put space between them. His eyes took too long to adjust to the darkness and he didn't like that he could hear something scrambling. He conjured a light that filled the room with a cozy, golden glow. This revealed a woman, bloodied knife in hand, coming around to his side of the bed.

With her pale hair pulled back tight into a bun, she looked like a soldier, something offset by the plain, homely dress she wore. Together they reminded him of something and as she took a lunge at him, he realized that she looked like a Puritan without a coif.

He grabbed her by the arm and wrenched the blade from her grip, but didn't expect her to turn into his hold, hitting him in the gut and then twisting away.

No less than six black cats dashed around the room, scrambling for a place to hide during the tussle.

The woman lunged again and this time he grabbed her more firmly, pulling her close and wrapping his arms around her. Once in his grip, she would have a slim chance of worming free. She bit into his arm and he said, "Oh, a little nibble like that barely gets my attention these days."

She let out a scream and slammed her boots into his bare feet. He lifted her up so that her feet dangled above the ground, though it only led her to bash her heels into his shins. The hard leather of her boots scraped away at the skin of his legs, unshod as they were.

He tried to think of the right spell to immobilize her, but she kicked so ferociously that his thoughts scattered. He pushed facedown her onto the bed and straddled her back to hold her down.

"Be still!" he demanded.

She wormed beneath him, her mind alight with the things he would do to her.

On his pillow, the white-splotched kitten sat looking concerned by all the commotion and the Devil thought he would have to name the kitten.

The little cat mewed and he soothed, "Oh, don't worry, darling, just a madwoman come to kill me."

The woman let out a cry of anger and continued to lash out with her limbs, though her blows landed infrequently.

He grew bored with her thrashing and increasingly irritated with the pain in his shoulder. "I don't imagine that if I let go of you, you'll be able to calm yourself."

"Devil!" she screamed at him, "Get off!"

He could hear her fears within her mind, fearing that when he raped her that she would like it. She alternately imagined him eating her alive as he assaulted her, blood dribbling down his chin as she shrieked her throat raw.

"I'll get off when you stop trying to *hurt me*," he said.

She went still and he waited a few moments before he stepped back, leaving her on the bed with the skirt of her dress pushed up. A glimpse of her calves showed them to the thickly muscled.

She immediately rolled over onto her back and pushed herself away from him. Her hair had come out from her bun and bright red blotches covered her pale cheeks. She watched him like a cornered animal, her breaths coming fast and hard.

He glanced around the room until he found his robe. He snatched it and was glad for the slither of silk against his skin when he pulled it on. Naked had never been his favorite way to fight.

Her eyes darted around the room and he saw them settle on the blade he'd taken from her. "Don't," he warned, but she moved for it anyway.

He grabbed her by the arm and maneuvered her back onto the bed.

They stared at each other for a while; if he moved to call for assistance she would strike and he had no wish to be stabbed again.

Not when the blood from the first wound soaked into the fabric of his robe, making the garment stick to his skin unpleasantly. He thought he even felt a dribble of blood leak all the way past his hips and down his leg.

"What brings you to Hell?" he asked casually, waffling between annoyed and curious.

She didn't answer.

"What about a name? Or you can tell me how you got here! You aren't dead at all." He resisted the urge to poke her. "Did one of my demons bring you in?"

He couldn't think of another way for the woman to have made her way to Hell. Even the most powerful and foolhardy mages conjured demons from the underworld instead of braving it themselves. Only demons and angels could move between the worlds with any sort of ease and even then, they only moved with the permission of their monarchs.

She spat at him; the glob of spittle landed on the bedspread and he sighed.

He could grab her, walk her to the dungeon himself. He could also kill her but she wasn't a real threat to him; he was more curious than anything. Holding her in the dungeon would give him time to sort himself out and get all the extra cats out of his bedroom. Maybe Imogen would be able to get some answers from her. She was female and human looking, the woman might trust her better.

The dungeon and then Imogen, he decided.

Definitely Imogen. He needed someone to sew shut this wound and didn't relish the idea of doing it himself. The vampire had never balked at his requests for medical attention, either.

He approached his bed and informed the intruder, "We're going for a walk. I'd prefer not to have to drag you the whole way."

She shook her head and he took her by the arm.

When their skin met, he felt a confusing rush of emotions from her. There was, of course, the hatred and anger he expected, but also something he identified as lust, though not without a bit of revulsion. Perhaps only a residual effect of the fight or maybe she was more interested in gangly monsters than she had anticipated.

He pulled her along to the dungeon and she constantly tried to twist out of his grip until he grabbed her by both arms and pulled her close. "Just because I haven't hurt you yet doesn't mean I won't."

She went still, staring up at him with dark green eyes.

"Every little worry about what I'll do running through your head I can hear, and I can do them all if you give me the slightest reason."

"Beast," she accused.

He shook his head and resumed his trek to the dungeon, though this time without her resistance.

He placed her in a cell and shut the door, then peered at her through the bars. "How did you get down here?"

She ignored him, testing the bars.

He watched her for a stretch of time and finally had to ask, "Are you stupid or what? This is Hell, no one *escapes*."

She spat at him again and he left before his temper got the better of him. He had little interest in raping her as she so worried, but it had been many years since he'd taken a good bite out of a human.

He headed toward the servants' quarters but found all his staff gathered in the kitchen, huddled and whispering. They went silent and pulled apart when he entered.

Imogen was the first to speak. "You're bleeding."

"I'm aware."

"We all heard screaming," she prompted.

"Surely not for the first time."

She crossed her arms. "The rest of you go!"

The other staff grumbled but went. When they had gone, she asked, "So what was it, some overenthusiastic lover?"

"Not hardly, I think she was trying to kill me. Come on, I put her in the dungeon."

"*Who?*" Imogen demanded.

"Some woman."

"You'll really need to be more clear."

"She showed up in the middle of the night trying to kill me, that's as clear as I can get," he said. "I'm hoping you can talk to her. Also, would you mind?" He pointed to the bloodstain on his robe.

She nodded and took a small sewing kit from one of the cabinets. He leaned against the counter as she worked.

"Why do you want me to talk to her?" she asked as she tied the last stitch.

He walked away before she could mop up the rest of the blood and she wrinkled her nose but followed after him as he headed back toward the dungeon.

"Well, I'm the Devil and she seems to have an issue with it," he explained. "Maybe you can, you know, have a heart-to-heart with her or something."

"Why *me?*" the woman clarified.

"Well, Oris is bright goddamn red and Gila has *far* too many teeth for even me and as for the cat keepers, one of them is covered in scales and the other has that problem with her eyes."

"Holly is a good worker—"

With a sigh, Lucifer asked, "Is she or is she not constantly bleeding from her eyes?"

"She is."

He stopped before the door to the dungeon and opened it. "And that aside, you're my butler which means I trust you the most."

"You don't trust me at all."

"Imogen, I'm wounded you think that!" He pretended to pout. "Go ahead, she's right in the first cell. Anything you can find out."

She rolled her eyes but entered the dungeon.

"Keep me posted."

Imogen had no luck getting any sort of answer from the woman; she had recognized Imogen immediately as a vampire and now treated her with the same contempt she treated the Devil.

She lurked in the back of his mind as he read through the dozens of files in the Fourth. The only time he forgot about her was when he visited the boy's soul, which now he did each night before he went home.

This night, as he stepped out of the cell with the same mild feeling of sickness, the skies parted and a beam of light appeared before him. He watched, unimpressed, as an angel descended.

Once his feet had touched the ground, Lucifer asked, "Did you give Him my letter at all?"

The angel announced, "Our Father has read your letter and wishes me to give you a message."

Lucifer's shock showed plainly on his face. An absurd amount of hope bloomed in his chest and made his hands unsteady.

"He says that you have taken your share of angels from Heaven already."

"He would! Useless, all of you." He wanted to weep but pushed it away.

Unaffected by Lucifer's reaction, the angel continued, "He will not send you help. This is your job."

"It isn't about me!" Lucifer protested.

The angel's face remained passive.

"I can't believe—but you know, I can!" Lucifer cried. "You've come all the way down here just to be unhelpful. If you saw..."

He glanced towards the cell door and a thought grew in his mind. The angel must have noticed the smile growing on his face because he reached for Heaven, but the Devil grabbed him by the arm.

Lucifer pulled him close, redoubling his grip on the angel. "If you saw then you would know, so you will see and you will go back to Heaven and you can tell them what our Father will allow!"

"Release me, Lucifer, or—"

"Or what! I am barred from Heaven already."

He pulled the angel toward the cell and pushed him inside. The boy slept but stirred when the door slammed shut.

"Lucifer!" the angel screamed but Satan walked away. He didn't want to keep the angel, only make him sick to his stomach. He wanted someone else to see what he had seen, to know that the boy needed help the Devil could not give.

His feet brought him by the Trade House and he handed over the fountain pen he had in his pocket, not sure what it would get him.

Nial inspected it for a long time. "I have to say, no one has ever brought me a pen for trade before."

"It's made of silver."

Nial nodded and explained, "Still...I must decide to take its value in silver or as a pen."

"This is why you should just take coin like everyone else."

"Mistress doesn't trust coin," the creature intoned.

Lucifer searched his pockets again; he found a hard candy that Inri had given him and a few bobby pins. He ran his fingers through his hair and found another pin holding his hair out of his eyes, things one set with a small jewel. He slipped it out and handed them over. "Silver, too, and that's a diamond."

Nial nodded. "I will consult with Mistress about the pen, but the pins are enough for an hour. The candy I do not need."

Lucifer took the candy back, rolling it around between his fingers, enjoying the crinkle of the wrapper. He sat on the bed and played with it the whole time he waited for Ira in another one of the mostly identical rooms.

"Didn't make me wait weeks this time," Ira said when he entered. "Here to cuddle again?"

"I did have something a little more intimate in mind."

Ira nodded toward his hand. "What are you playing with?"

"I think it's a butterscotch." He held it out to Ira, who slipped it from his fingers.

"What's a butterscotch?" The demon peered at it.

"Candy. You can have it."

Ira looked up, his dark eyes wide. "You don't mind?"

"Of course not."

Ira pocketed the candy and came over to the bed, where Lucifer waited. "You look tired."

"I am several millennia old, I am always tired."

Ira ran his fingers along the buttons on Lucifer's shirt, undoing them one by one. "You didn't seem tired the first time you bought me."

He took Ira's hand and kissed the inside of his wrist. "You don't always have to think of something to say."

"Are you telling me to shut up?"

"No, but I can tell when words are empty."

Ira slipped his hands inside Lucifer's shirt and pushed it off his shoulders, pausing to glance at the wound on his shoulder.

"I'll tell you about it later," Lucifer said, pulling Ira closer to kiss him. The demon climbed onto his lap, straddling him and running his fingers through the Devil's hair.

Lucifer pulled off Ira's shirt and worked at the laces on his breeches, pushing them down over the meat of his backside but not able to get them off with the demon on top of him. He scratched down Ira's back and then gripped his bottom, kissing him all the while.

He put both hands on the demon's ass and squeezed, thinking of how he wanted to have him, of where he wanted to put his tongue.

Ira winced, sucking in a sharp breath, and Lucifer paused.

"No, it's nothing, keep going," Ira urged.

"You're sure?"

Ira nodded and returned to kissing him, his tongue sliding inside Lucifer's mouth and banishing thoughts of anything else from Lucifer's mind. He pushed the Devil onto his back and undid his trousers, pulling out his cock and toying with it for a moment before tugging off the rest of Lucifer's clothes.

"And what about you?" Lucifer asked when the demon climbed back on top of him with his breeches still on.

"Right." Ira stood again and tossed aside his remaining clothes.

Lucifer took him by the hand, pulling him close, letting his length press against the demon's behind between his cheeks. He gave a bit of a thrust, hungry for the demon's touch.

Ira bit his lip, this time able to check his recoil better.

"There you go again. Ira, what's the matter?"

He shook his head, his curls bouncing. "I'm fine."

"Empty words."

With an irritated sigh, Ira said, "Some like it rougher than others and some bastards are too stupid to use enough oil, that's all. It's fine."

"You should have told me."

"Why? So I could lose work for the night or so you could do it anyway?" Harshness crept into Ira's voice.

"Love, there are other things we can do together and none of them have to be unpleasant." He kissed Ira and wrapped an arm around his waist, lifting the smaller man and moving him from his lap to the bed. "Better if we're both enjoying things."

He pushed Ira onto his back and kissed his belly, his hips and thighs. He wet his lips and then ran his tongue along the demon's shaft. Ira did not seem to know exactly what to do with himself while the Devil pleasured him. He writhed, gripping the sheets, and every so often he began to say something but never finished his sentence.

He let out a moan, melting into the bed when Lucifer took the length of his cock into his mouth, and then shivered when the Devil pulled back.

Lucifer savored the sight of him like that for a moment, his skin flush and damp, his cock slicked with spit and twitching.

"Do you want me to finish you like this? Or would you like to fuck me?"

Ira's eyes opened. "Like this, please, like this."

Lucifer kissed him and then returned his mouth to his length, glad for the taste and feel of him against his tongue. It had been too long since he'd had someone spill in his mouth and when Ira came, hot and thick, he swallowed it down, taking all he could get.

The demon's tongue ran over his lips and the Devil wrapped his arms around him, burying his face in his shoulder for a minute. Ira kissed his throat but when he reached between Lucifer's legs, the Devil pushed his hand back.

"You don't need to."

"I'd be a miserable whore if I didn't." He kissed the Devil's throat again and ran a finger along his jaw. "I'm not some delicate thing you need to save, I know my work."

One finger circled the tip of Lucifer's cock, an offer the Devil had no wish to refuse.

"Use your hand, kiss me while you do it." He wanted Ira close, his whole body pressed against him.

"Anything you like."

He pressed his mouth to Lucifer's and, with skilled fingers, brought him release. Afterward, with a silly smile, he asked, "Do you think I should clean up the way you do?"

Lucifer shook his head and handed him one of the neatly folded towels from the bedside table's drawer.

As Ira wiped his hand, Lucifer watched and asked, "Does she let you rest?"

"Hmm?"

"Your mistress, if you're unwell, does she let you recover?"

With a shrug, Ira assured, "If I'm too sick to work no one

would want me anyways."

"I don't just mean being sick."

Ira scowled at him and he almost managed to look cross. "I told you, I'm not delicate, I don't need saving."

"I'm not trying to save you, it's poor practice on her part is all."

Ira shrugged again and tossed the towel on the floor. He played with the fine hairs that grew on his legs, swirling them so a circle appeared.

Lucifer prompted, "You should try the butterscotch." He wanted to do anything but think of whether or not someone was taking care of Ira.

"I was saving it for later."

"I'll bring you more next time."

"Promise?"

Lucifer nodded. "Of course."

The demon fetched his breeches and took the candy from his pocket, peeling off the wrapper and placing it on his tongue.

Seeing the face he made, Lucifer reminded, "Tell me if you don't like it or you'll end up with a whole bag of things you don't want."

"No, but it's so sweet!"

"It's mostly sugar."

He contentedly watched Ira roll the candy around in his mouth for a minute and soon enough the whole room smelled of butterscotch.

"They'll be able to taste it on me all night," Ira told him.

"I thought you worked freelance during the day."

"I've got others booked tonight."

"Who?"

"Don't go getting jealous," Ira teased, but it had a real note of worry.

"Just curiosity, don't worry," Lucifer assured.

Ira ran his hand through his curls, messing them so badly that Lucifer reached over to put them back into place.

"They're just a couple of girls from the university...or maybe the library? Either way, they like each other more than they like me, watching and telling me what to do to the other. It's sort of fun."

"Sounds sort of fun," Lucifer agreed.

"They like Uri better but he's booked full up tonight."

The hourglass chimed.

As they dressed, Ira asked, "Should I expect to wait days or weeks to see you again?" His voice was a purr, his question asked with practiced flirtation. It was funny how that sultriness came and went.

"I don't know."

"You...no, never mind."

"What?" Lucifer insisted.

"It makes me sound desperate and that never looks good on a whore."

"Ask anyways," Lucifer urged.

"I will see you again, won't I? It's nice to have sort of regular work and I don't want you to think..." Ira rubbed his arm. "Well, you know, I'm usually up for anything, I could have done it tonight if you'd wanted."

There was no hint of flirting anymore.

"I don't know when, but I'll be back." Lucifer fastened the last button on his shirt, touched Ira's arm for a moment, and walked out just as Nial was coming to knock on the door.

"Mistress doesn't want your pen," the creature said and held it out to him.

"She's missing out, it's a wonderful pen." He pocketed it.

He passed a sweet shop on the way home and doubled back. He peered inside to see a single confectioner at work. He tapped the window and she looked up, her brow furrowed.

She came over to the door.

"Open?"

She grinned. "Let me guess: honey? Always someone out on their way to an orgy and needing honey."

He chuckled. "No, not honey."

"Come in anyway, look around."

He browsed the glass jars on display and the confectioner offered him a bag to fill. He plucked candies from this jar and the other, making sure he put in at least a couple of butterscotches. When he finished, he set it on the counter.

"All set?" she asked.

"Do you deliver?"

She pulled over a notepad and took a pencil from her apron. "Sure. Where to?"

"To Ira, care of The Trade House, Ninth District."

She scribbled it down. "Anything else?"

He purchased a handful of caramels and had the bill sent to the palace. When he did that, the confectioner seemed to realize that she hadn't recognized her own Prince and grew overly deferential.

At home, Imogen reported that the woman in the dungeon still had not shared anything about herself. As he walked away from the vampire toward the dungeon, he heard her mutter, "Reeking of rosemary and hyssop again."

She would figure out soon enough that he saw the same whore each time; what she would do with that information, he didn't know.

Satan gave the bars of the cell door a gentle kick, just enough to get the woman's attention. She glared briefly and spat in his direction, though she barely worked up enough spittle to do so. The food and water she'd been offered were untouched, as was the change of clothes someone had brought her. It had probably been Imogen who'd brought them; she cleaned herself with almost ritualistic regularity and seemed to think others wanted to do the same.

He sat on the floor, his legs crossed Indian-style, and watched her for a minute. She didn't move, her eyes fixed on the cell wall.

He unwrapped a caramel and she looked over.

Lucifer gestured to the food. "If I were going to kill you, it wouldn't be poison."

"I'm not afraid to die."

"No, obviously not, coming to Hell with nothing but a knife," he scoffed. "Don't they use swords anymore? At least that would have had some reach on it."

She didn't respond.

"So then why won't you eat, if you aren't afraid of poison?"

She stared him down like he was stupid. "It's *tainted*."

"The food?" He leaned a little closer toward the cell to peer at the food. No hint of mold or rot. "I don't think so."

"Tainted by Hell."

"Oh. The food here does have a certain...tang to it, a little bit like...ash, right on the back of the tongue," he admitted. "But it won't do you any harm, moral or physical."

He placed the caramel in his mouth and she watched. He once again got the odd sense of longing and revulsion coming from her.

"Imogen says you called her a false woman."

She growled, "A dress doesn't make you a woman."

"No, of course not, lots of people wear dresses, but she's gone and got herself tits. It was an awful mess to find someone who could work that spell, so you know she's committed." He thought for a bit and added, "About having tits anyway. I'm not an arbiter of whether having them makes you a woman."

At the word 'tits' the woman's face had turned pink. Or, at least, he thought it was because he'd said tits.

"I don't know if she's done anything about the other bits, but really, cock or no cock, if she says she's a lady, it's enough for me."

The woman blushed again, this time at the word cock. He wondered what she'd do if he told her of his time with Ira.

"Want a caramel?" he offered.

"You're a foul beast."

"And that's a dowdy dress!" He took a caramel from the bag and tossed it into the cell. It skittered across the floor and landed right beside her. "If you tell me how you got in, I can send you back. Humans aren't supposed to move worlds unless they're dead. Which you aren't."

She shook her head.

"Then you'll stay here."

She didn't answer.

"Look, you can't want to be here any more than I want you here! Be *reasonable*," he demanded, though it felt more like whining.

"If I go without you dead, I'll have no welcome at home."

He rubbed his eyes. "What makes you think I can be killed? I'm *the* Devil, not some Hell-born demon or one of my poor bastards up on Earth. I am eternal."

"Only God is—"

"You don't think He's the one that made me this way? That my life isn't part of His stupid clockwork plan?"

"Clockwork?"

He felt the real need to ask, "You do know what a clock is, don't you?" He almost dreaded the answer.

"What does clockwork have to do with anything?"

"You don't seriously think He's up there tinkering with every little bit of time and fate, do you? Humans, vain as ever," he scoffed.

He pelted her with another candy. This time it hit her in the head. He grinned and stood, stretching on his toes. His shirt, only half-tucked after his time with Ira, pulled out of his trousers to show a bit of belly. He felt her eyes on his skin as surely as he'd felt the gaze of men on a breast or thigh when he'd spent time as a woman.

She had to be at least thirty and was too old for the confused yearning of adolescence. What a frustrating place her mind had to be.

"You should eat, though," he reminded her.

He left her after that, to sulk or pray or whatever it was she did during her confinement. He wondered what would happen if he opened the door to her cell. Would she be brave enough to set foot outside? Would she make another attempt on his life or run out into Hell? That would be an ill fate, considering that she didn't share Jack's status as a refugee.

In his room, he set the bag of caramels on the bed. Marlow, the once-dead cat, pawed at it and he shooed her away. When he settled into bed, she burrowed into the blankets beside him. He had resigned himself to it at this point. Maybe when she was weaned, she would drift away from him the way she would drift away from her mother.

He fell asleep thinking of the woman's hideous dress and was awakened at what must have been a disgustingly early hour because his eyes remained sticky with sleep.

"...an angel!" Imogen shouted at him, pulling his covers back.

"Hm?" He hadn't caught the start of her tirade.

"You *trapped an angel* in Hell!"

"Oh, only for the night, I'll let him out when I go to the Fourth. What time is it? Is it morning?" he asked, rubbing his eyes.

"It is dawn and there are three score angels *here* looking for their missing comrade."

He had never seen her like this before. "How many?"

She repeated, "Three score," as though that should mean something to him.

He frowned, trying to do the math.

"Sixty!"

"And they're, what, here specifically or just here in general?" he asked.

"Here, they are in the palace, they are *here* specifically."

"Oh, Imogen, I didn't know angels got you in such a tizzy."

She pulled his covers back the rest of the way, leaving him exposed and unpleasantly chilled. "Get dressed! Or don't, but get these angels gone."

"What's the worry?"

She hissed, "Because everyone in the Ninth saw them walk inside. Everyone's either going to work or slinking home."

"Ah." That was something to be concerned about.

"They are one pissy loudmouth away from rioting," she warned.

"Oh, I hate riots," he whispered.

The idea of an uprising was enough to take him from his bed. He grabbed his robe and headed downstairs.

The sight of sixty identical golden men in his foyer took him by surprise. They had the same blond curls and tanned skin, the same orange eyes and glittering armor. All of them bore a spear or a sword and none of them appeared pleased.

He glanced over the crowd and broadly asked, "Is there one of you, in particular, I should speak to or...just a general sort of address?"

One angel stepped forward, distinguishable only by a badge on his armor's chest piece. "Our Father demands the return of his messenger."

"He isn't hurt."

The angel declared, "If you do not surrender him, we will take the search into our own hands."

"I was going to let him go in a few hours anyway," Lucifer sulked.

"The messenger."

"I'll go. Wait here."

The angel began, "We will—"

"You can't all go parading through Hell! One of you come, if you're going to insist." Lucifer tied his robe tighter about his body, feeling that maybe he should have dressed better for the occasion. Sleep-rumpled hair and a robe embroidered with pretty designs didn't strike the authoritative image he needed right now.

"We will—"

"One!" he shouted, feeling himself grow a little larger in size, feeling the corners of his mouth stretch so that his mouth would be more a maw. His fingernails were one terse word away from turning to claws and he hoped things didn't get out of hand. He had a hard time putting himself back together when he lost his temper.

The angel acquiesced with a nod.

"I'll be back in a moment."

"Where are you going?" the angel demanded.

"To get some pants. Jesus!"

He dressed in a hurry, forcing himself back down to his normal size so that he could fit into his clothes.

While he and the angel walked through Hell, he felt the eyes of every demon on him. He needed to do something to take control of this back or his citizens would revolt. They were wild things and distrustful of Heaven. If they thought he had gone belly-up for God, things could take a rotten turn.

The last coup had been short-lived, but bloody and destructive. Thousands of souls had gotten loose and it had taken decades before everything had been sorted again.

Lucifer looked at the glittering soldier again. "What's your name?"

The angel responded, "I have no name, we are all soldiers."

"That's got to get confusing."

"No."

"What if He needs just one of you?" Lucifer asked.

"Have you forgotten Heaven so much that you don't remember how He speaks to us?"

Satan grimaced. "Haven't forgotten why I took my leave of it all."

"You were expelled."

"And you weren't even made then so don't talk like you know how things were," Lucifer snapped.

The angel went silent for a long while so when he pronounced, "You stink," it took Lucifer by surprise.

"Pardon?"

"The stink of this place is in your skin."

Lucifer wasn't sure when the angel had smelled his skin. "Well, I didn't get the chance to wash yet, but it's just a bit of herb and—"

"No, it's not sulfur but there's a stench to this place," the solider elaborated.

"Oh, you mean the misery, yes, you'll get used to it. You know, I've had more people say it smells like high tide than brimstone. I think it smells like cigarettes and baby powder. I sort of like it..."

"It stinks."

Lucifer shrugged. "You can tell all your friends about it when you get back home. Make sure you tell them how handsome I am in person."

The angel frowned, his grip on his spear shifting.

Neither of them said anymore until they arrived in D ward in the Fourth. Lucifer went to the boy's cell and heard the other angel's cries before he had the door open.

The boy sat on the bed and looked up when Lucifer came in. On the floor, the angel knelt, weeping raggedly. He sounded like he'd been at it for a while, too.

"He won't stop crying," the boy said.

"Nor should he." Lucifer took the angel by the elbow and dragged him out to his comrade. He pushed him into the other angel's arms and declared, loudly, "When you get back there, make sure you tell them what happens in Hell! Tell it to the bastard's face, make sure all His loyal angels know what it is that He condones!"

A crowd of demons had gathered and he had raised his voice for their benefit. Hopefully, a bit of disdain and bravado would keep things in check.

He spat at the feet of the angels. "Now go, before I decide that my hospitality has been too generous."

The angel soldier reached into the underneath with the messenger held close to his side. Within moments they were gone, no fancy beams of golden light this time.

The demons who had gathered watched for a moment more, but Lucifer didn't know what else to do to impress them, so he strode into the chancery for D ward and began his reports for the day.

Imogen came down herself later to inform him that the other fifty-nine angels had left without incident and that, aside from the normal malcontents, the threat of riot had died down.

"Some are talking of another rebellion."

He grimaced. "Oh, quell that as best you can, I've got too many other things in the works right now."

She leaned against the wall. "I can't believe you were stupid enough—"

"It wasn't stupid, it was rash. It was angry." So many centuries and he still hadn't learned to check his temper when it came to his father.

"You don't think you're trying too hard for His attention?"

"I don't *want* His attention, I want that boy out of here," he corrected.

"And what will making that angel watch get you?"

He set down his pen and found his fingers braiding his hair not a moment later. "Hopefully, angels will be just as gossipy as they were in my day. Maybe something will happen to force His hand."

"I'm just a dead lady, but I don't know if you want to be forcing the Almighty to do things," Imogen suggested.

"I've got an heir if things don't play out."

She snorted. She picked up a handful of the portfolios, glanced through them and inquired, "How many more of these are there?"

"Should be done at some point."

"Six percent," Inri said from another room.

Lucifer called, "Six percent done or left or what?"

"Twenty-two and a half minus six is sixteen and a half."

"Thanks, Inri."

"At least someone knows what he's doing." Imogen set the stack back on his desk. "Make sure you eat."

"It's not like I can die. Make sure that woman eats."

Imogen flipped her hair over her shoulder. "I don't care if she starves to death, nasty thing that she is."

"If you get her to eat, I'll let you go to Earth for a night."

"And what would I want on Earth?" Imogen asked flippantly.

"The blood of pretty boys."

Her stance changed and he knew that he had tempted her. "Maybe I'll try, but I won't be trying very hard."

"Thank you."

Imogen left without saying anything else.

When he returned home that night, he checked in the dungeon and saw that the woman had an empty plate in her cell. He also spied caramel wrappers on the floor and he wondered if she'd given in to the candy's temptation before or after Imogen had gotten to her.

"What about a name?" he asked.

She ignored him.

"I'll give you another candy."

Her mouth contorted as though she were trying not to smile.

"What?"

"I'm not a child."

Lucifer made a face that he hoped expressed his exasperation with her. "Are you sure? Because here you are pouting about being in jail after you tried to kill me."

"If you can't be killed, why worry?"

He laughed at that. It was a poor attempt at word-twisting on her part. "How did you get in?"

She turned her head away, returning to what must have been an interesting contemplation of the masonry.

He rubbed his nose and tilted his head. There was a smell here he hadn't noticed before, one that hadn't been there the night before.

"Did Imogen bite you?" he asked.

"What?"

It wouldn't be like Imogen at all to do so, but he pressed, "The vampire, did she take your blood?"

"No."

He stepped closer to the cell. "Someone's bleeding and I don't think it's me."

She couldn't meet his eyes and kept her hands carefully folded in her lap. She hadn't moved an inch since he'd come in. The hem of her skirt was torn in a way it hadn't been before.

"Do you need some rags or something?" he asked, not sure if

his guess was correct.

She didn't answer but her cheeks colored.

"Oh, were you not going to say anything? You're impossible. Making this worse for yourself."

He turned and left. He found Gila and had her go out into to town to see what she could find for the woman's cycle.

"And get her some water to wash with...with which to wash? Tell her we can get her the ugliest dress in Hell if she wants to change."

"Yethmy Printh."

Before he made it to his bedroom, Imogen caught up with him halfway up the stairs. "And what about my end of things?"

He turned, almost stepping on a cat and gripping the banister to maintain his balance. "Which end?"

"To Earth."

"You want to go right now?"

"If it wouldn't be too much trouble."

He translated that as a firm *send me now*. "Fine, come here. Six hours on Earth you'll have."

She pursed her lips.

"Unless you'd rather stay up there altogether?"

"No."

"Good, I'd miss you so," he said and gave her a winning smile. She kept her distance and he beckoned her over. "You really have to come here, I can't do it without touching you."

She approached.

"Can you do me a favor?" he asked.

"What?"

"Bring back apples."

"I'll give it a shot."

He placed one hand on either side of her face, pulling the threads he needed from the underneath and then gave her a push. Instead of falling down the stairs, she tumbled into nothingness and was gone from his sight. The threads would pull her to Earth in no time at all and they would pull her back to Hell when her stint was up.

He rubbed his hands on the legs of his trousers and then squeezed them together.

Maybe the woman in his dungeon had found a way into the threads of nothingness that connected all things; he didn't think any human had managed that yet. When mages pulled demons out of Hell or sent them back, they did it by breaking them down in one place and rebuilding the demon's body in another rather than sending them whole through the in-between spaces.

Both methods had their own unique messy ends if done wrong, but he hadn't botched such a thing in some time.

While he lay in bed with Marlow on his chest and his fingers running down her spine over and over again, he wondered what he could do with the woman. She hadn't trusted Imogen and she was the closest thing to human that he had in his service.

Except, he recalled, for Jack.

Jack was entirely human and handsome to boot. Maybe she would ogle him the way she eyed the Devil and maybe she would open up to him.

Marlow sunk her claws into the skin of his chest and he winced. He picked her up and set her aside, but as soon as he had rolled over onto his stomach, she climbed on top of him again.

When the sky was at its reddest and brightest, the Devil took leave of the Fourth and headed to the Eighth. Pressing as his work there was, he wanted to catch Jack during his training. From across the barrack's courtyard, he saw that the acrobat still struck at his opponent with hesitation, but not as much as he had before.

Eodus spied him first and knelt as he approached. Pythea and Jack didn't notice.

"He seems somewhat improved," Lucifer noted.

"Yes, Your Highness, we have hope for him," Eodus confirmed.

"I need to borrow him."

Eodus gaped at him. "Oh."

Pythea took notice of her Prince and ended the spar, touching her head to the ground and approaching when asked to do so.

"I need your pupil."

Jack looked to Eodus, who didn't meet his eyes. He turned to the Devil and asked, "Now?"

"If you don't mind."

The boy's hand went up to touch the pink scar on his cheek. "No, I...whatever you need, of course." He bowed at the waist.

Lucifer gestured for Jack to follow and said to Eodus, "Don't worry, I'll bring him back just as I took him." He glanced over the youth's sweat-stained clothes and dampened curls. "Well, maybe a little cleaner."

"As you wish, my Prince."

Lucifer walked away and Jack followed a few steps behind. Lucifer took him by the wrist and pulled him so that they walked evenly. "How have you found Hell so far?"

"It's...not like I thought it would be."

"Oh?"

"And I never thought I'd be here so soon!" Jack had a crooked little smile on his face, amused but a little rueful.

Lucifer put an arm around his shoulder. "And how would a sweet thing like you end up in Hell?"

Jack raised his eyebrows. "You don't let someone bugger you and think you'll make it to Heaven, and certainly not if you let them as many times as I have."

"Mylas, you mean."

The youth shrugged. "And whoever else he let have me. He liked to watch a pair of us go at it while he had someone's ass for himself."

"Not so bad if that's what you enjoy."

Jack nodded. "No, it wasn't bad. Shanley's only bad to you if you're bad to him first."

"How long were you with him?"

"He picks us out when we're just boys, starts us with tumbling right away. The buggering comes later if that's what you mean. Waits until we've got some hair on us," Jack noted appreciatively, as though it should be counted as something noble that Mylas hadn't taken to fucking small children.

"I see."

"I was...six, I think. My sister..." Jack shook his head. "It doesn't matter."

"No, go on."

Jack explained, "My sister knew what I was, always pinched me when she caught me trying to kiss the other boys. It was just playing around, you know how kids are. The little boys were always chasing the girls around, pulling their hair. She would hit me for it sometimes and she said, 'If you don't stop that they're going to send you to Shanley's tent and he'll shove his pecker right up your ass.'"

"Sounds like a nice girl." Lucifer hadn't meant to comment but the words slipped out on their own.

"She was trying to scare me, trying to get me to stop, but it didn't work. I didn't know what she meant by it, I was six, I didn't understand what fucking was really...but I snuck out the night she said that and peeked into Shanley's tent."

"Oh?"

"They were such pretty boys, laughing together and with their arms around each other. I saw them kiss each other and I felt so...I don't know." Jack licked his lips and glanced towards Lucifer, his cheeks a little flushed, though more with emotion than lust, Lucifer guessed. "Breathless. Butterflies. You know the feeling."

"I do." He did. The very mention of it brought images of a particular gray-skinned demon to mind.

"I didn't see more than that, my pa dragged me back home, but a few days later, Shanley came to visit." Jack paused and looked up at the palace. "This is where you live?"

"Sure is." He took his arm from around Jack's shoulder to open the door. Once inside, he took the acrobat by the hand and led him upstairs. He pointed him toward the bathroom. "Wash up if you want."

Jack fixed his eyes on the floor. "It wasn't bad with Shanley, it was all in fun but...you know, with Eodus...it's something else altogether with him."

Lucifer watched and waited, knowing the lad had more to say.

"I love him, I really do. I don't mean any disrespect, I know you don't have to let me stay but..." A few tears slid down Jack's cheeks and he still hadn't looked up.

"Oh, you've misunderstood, I'm sorry." The Devil took Jack by the chin and tilted his head up. "I didn't bring you here to fuck you, there's just...this woman, I need you to talk to her."

"A woman?"

"A human one," Satan explained. "You're the only other one I've got down here."

Jack wiped his face on his sleeve and sniffled. "Oh."

"Poor thing, you should have said something sooner." Lucifer should have paid more attention.

Jack shook his head. "No, you're...*you*."

"That I am." He gave Jack a push toward the bathroom. "Wash up, we'll get you a change of clothes. You do smell...I hate to say it, but just terrible. When you're all done, my room is right next door."

Jack laughed nervously and gave the Devil a small smile. He closed the door and Satan went to his bedroom, combing through his closet to find something for Jack to wear. He turned up a few items that wouldn't be absurdly long on him, though they would still require cuffing.

He spied a bag on his desk that hadn't been there when he'd left and peeked inside to find it full of oranges. A note from Imogen informed him that he'd sent her to Florida and oranges had been easier to find.

He shrugged. They would do well enough. He penned a quick note to Ira, saying that he hoped he liked the fruit, and slipped it inside the bag.

Jack knocked, then entered the room and Lucifer waved a hand toward the clothes on the bed.

"Just leave the other stuff, I'll have it washed."

"Eodus will never believe you didn't bed me if I come back in your clothes," Jack noted, setting aside his towel and dressing with all the modesty of a performer used to a shared dressing room.

"Do you think he'll like you less for it?"

"No, but...it's not that he'll be jealous, he isn't like that, but..."

"But he loves you." The Devil smiled. "Don't worry. I'll reassure him."

Lucifer took the bag from his desk, opened the door, and led Jack down into the dungeon.

The human glanced around. "What've you got a jail down here for?"

"Where better to keep an eye on my enemies?"

Jack shrugged. "So what about the woman?"

"She won't tell me anything, not why she came or who she is or how she got here. Anything you can find out would be helpful."

"Oh."

The Devil reassured, "And your help won't go unrewarded."

"Oh, I don't need anything."

"Don't put such an offer aside so readily, think on what you could want first," he warned. He gestured for Jack to go into the dungeon. "She's in the first cell."

"Should I tell her you sent me...?"

"Tell her whatever you want, Jack."

The acrobat nodded and entered the dungeon. He looked like a child in his father's clothes, if his father's wardrobe had included silk and linen.

Lucifer returned upstairs to Imogen's office and placed the bag on her desk. "There's laundry that needs doing in my room. And I need these delivered."

She didn't look at him. "To?"

"Ira, care of the Trade House, the Ninth."

"That's a brothel."

He nodded. "And an odd one at that. They still use the barter system. How was your time on Earth?"

"Satisfactory."

"I borrowed Eodus's human since the woman didn't take to you very much."

Imogen set down her pen. "You can't have really thought she would."

"Why not?"

"Why do you think I left Earth?"

He shrugged. "I haven't puzzled it out yet."

She scowled. "I don't know why you pretend to be so dense. It isn't charming."

"I'm not much interested in charming you, Imogen, you're my butler. Why did you leave Earth?"

"Because they're rotten, all of them."

"If they were all rotten, I'd have more souls," he pointed out.

"You know what I mean! They look at me and they..." Imogen trailed off.

"They what?"

"They know, as soon as they look at me, that I'm not a woman. Just some pervert in a dress," she spat.

"Oh." He had not expected that answer and hearing her say it sent a twinge through his gut. She had never seemed to care much at all what anyone else thought of her and he hadn't considered that she'd been hiding it.

"In Hell, no one cares. If I say call me Imogen, they call me Imogen, if I a wear a dress or grow my hair or trade with some toothless witch to get breasts, no one bats an eye."

"Farrah was a mage and she had at least one tooth left," he corrected.

She glared at him, then pushed herself back from her desk and stood, going over to the door to her office and pointing out. "I've work to do if you don't need anything else."

He clucked his tongue. "Imogen."

"Don't."

"Her tooth was right in the front, all snaggled and yellow, I don't know how you missed it. I couldn't stop staring. I think she noticed."

Imogen scrunched up her face, tried not to laugh, but she couldn't manage. It came out as a weepy sort of chuckle. "Go. Haven't you got things to do?"

"Lunch, right now, I think."

He left her alone after that, going to the kitchen. He had Oris ladle him a bowl of the soup that simmered on the stove.

"Why always soup, Oris?"

Nervously, Oris asked, "Does it displease you, my Prince?"

"No, not really, but I mean...is soup a pathology for you or just easy to cook?"

"It's what I'm best at, Your Highness and...to be honest, with your hours as irregular as they are, soup keeps well."

"Hm," Lucifer mused.

"And I do make bread every morning," the cook assured.

"Is this old soup?"

"No, no, of course not, my Prince, it was made this morning." Oris had begun to sweat a little, drops beading on his brow.

"Are you still seeing Lolli?"

"Who?" the demon asked, his yellow eyes going wide as

saucers.

"Imogen mentioned something about it. Said she liked mushrooms..."

Oris fumbled for an answer. "No, I..."

"I wish to eat in peace, Oris, if you don't mind."

"Of course, my Prince, of course." The demon bobbed and bowed his way out of the kitchen.

Lucifer dipped his spoon into the soup now that it had cooled somewhat and found himself closing his eyes as he tasted it. It was plain onion soup, but it was good and he had been hungry. He reached over toward the counter and almost tipped out of his chair to reach the loaf of bread, but managed to grab the bread and right himself without incident.

After he'd eaten, he didn't know what to do with himself. He didn't want to leave Jack alone nor did he have any real desire to return to the Fourth that day.

He poked around in the cupboard and found two mugs; he filled them with soup and, with half a loaf of bread tucked under his arm, went to the dungeon. He pushed open the door with one foot and caught the murmur of their voices, so he paused, listening.

The woman seemed to think that she could get Jack and herself out of here if she could find the amulet she'd lost in the Devil's bedroom.

"If I could get back there—"

"If you want to get into my chambers, you just need to ask nice," he said, coming through the door.

The woman glared and Jack looked up. He'd taken a seat right in front of the cell and the woman had come to kneel next to the bars.

"Hungry?" Lucifer asked.

Jack reached out his hand to take the mug the Devil offered, and then the loaf of bread when he was handed it.

Lucifer set the other mug just inside the cell. "Has she talked to you much?"

"When I said that you'd asked me to talk to her...uh, well." Jack rubbed the back of his neck. "She said my soul could still be saved."

Lucifer nodded and sat beside Jack. "And do you want your soul to be saved?"

"Not if it means I'll have to apologize for loving men and settle down with some woman." Jack looked at the woman briefly. "Not that there's anything wrong with women, you know. I haven't got anything bad to say."

"Do you think she'll tell you anything else?"

Jack made a face. "I don't think so. I'm not good at this sort of thing. That's why I was so quick to run from Shanley, I'm no good at deception."

"I can hear you," the woman said.

Lucifer turned his eyes towards her, surprised. Apparently, she disliked being ignored. He turned back to Jack. "What about a name? A mission?"

"Just that she's got to kill you. Something about her honor, I didn't really follow but she was being awfully vague," Jack apologized.

"Nothing says honor like stabbing a man in his sleep," Lucifer agreed.

"You are *not* a man," came the growl from the cell.

He paid her no mind; he tore off a small piece of bread and fed it to Jack. The act drew the gaze of the woman and he confided to Jack, "I think she likes me."

The entirety of her face went blotchy red.

Jack took a sip of soup. "You are handsome."

"And it moves you not at all."

"No, just..." The youth gave a bit of a shrug and bit his lip.

"Eodus moves you more." He couldn't help but smile at being considered second-rate when compared to an Eighth Precinct demon. "What if you could have the two of us together? No need to choose, really. I don't imagine Eodus has taken you to one of the orgies around town, has he?"

Jack shook his head. "No."

"It would be too rough, I bet, for a tender thing like you. What if I only watched? The two of you make a comely pair and I can pleasure myself well enough," he purred.

Even Jack's cheeks had gone pink now. "I..."

Lucifer let out a laugh. "I'm teasing, love, forgive me. I can't help it when it's so easy to get a reaction." He finally gave his attention to the woman. "What about a name, though?"

"Mercy," she breathed and then seemed to realize she'd broken her silence.

He grinned and she recoiled, maybe because of his black teeth or maybe because she was ashamed she'd given in. Dirty talk was not the interrogation method he'd thought he'd need but if it worked, it did. Who was he to question the absurdities of the human mind?

"Soups going cold, Mercy, dear," he reminded.

He would be kind to her, polite and charming. She would give in eventually or he would change to more unpleasant tactics.

When Jack had finished his soup and bread, Satan brought him back to Eodus in the Eighth and declared, "See, I hardly laid a finger on him."

"What's mine is yours, my Prince," Eodus said from his kneel.

"And if I wanted him, I'd have him, but I borrowed Jack for something else today. He'll tell you about it, I'm sure."

He gave Jack a pat on the shoulder and left, not worried about anything more than finding the amulet she'd lost in his room. It must have come off in their tussle.

Back home, he enlisted Imogen to help him search. After about an hour, she pulled something from underneath his settee and said, "I think I've got it."

He took his hand from beneath the side table and examined it. "No, I lost that ages ago."

"Maybe if you let Gila clean your room."

"My room is the way I like it," he told her.

"It smells like cat."

"Doesn't."

She pressed her lips together but didn't argue.

Beneath his bed, he found three wax sticks and an earring that had been his daughter's. Tucked beneath the mattress he found the last thing his wife had ever written him. Seeing it sent a wave of nausea over him and he had to sit down on the floor.

Imogen took notice and asked, "Found it?"

"No. Just..." He shook his head.

She peered at the note. "Oh."

Luci, I need some space. Only one line. How much space she had needed and when she would be done taking it, he'd never found out.

"Your wife, right?" Imogen asked.

"Yes."

"She called you Luci?" the vampire asked.

He nodded and said, "Satan doesn't really leave much in the way of room for pet names."

Imogen sat on the edge of his bed. "Do you think she's forgiven you yet?"

He looked up. "Forgiven me? For what?"

"Everyone says she left because you weren't faithful."

"I wasn't...!"

Imogen shrugged. "It's just what everyone says."

"If she'd cared about fidelity she wouldn't have taken so many lovers of her own...not that it mattered, not that any of it mattered. I never cared who she slept with," he said.

"No?" Imogen didn't sound convinced.

"If you think Hell is wild now, you should have seen it in those first days. Hunting down souls to torment and sleeping in hide tents on beds of furs. Firelight and so many bodies...not an orgy but all her spent lovers." He tucked the note back where he found it, hoping he'd forget about it again. "She liked to fuck, had more of an appetite for it than I did."

Her ravenous appetite, her wild laugh, the way she loved things to exhaustion, that had been what he'd loved about her. What he would have still loved, if only she were around.

He cleared his throat and announced, "She'll come back if she wants. I'm not her keeper."

Marlow batted the earring they had found back onto the floor.

"In a palace full of cats, we might never find that amulet." Imogen picked the earring back up.

"I know," he admitted. "Ask Gila to look for it, too, just...any stray thing they find, have them bring it to your office."

"It might not be in the palace anymore. Sometimes things go missing."

"I'll eat them alive if they've made off with it. Make sure they know that and it'll turn up if it can be found."

Imogen nodded.

"You can go, I think we've searched the whole room." He didn't think that but finding his wife's note had put him in a melancholy. Coupled with the thought of more paperwork tomorrow, he didn't want company or conversation.

She touched his shoulder briefly, then left, closing the door behind her.

He spent a while petting Marlow until his eyes grew heavy, though he didn't fall asleep until it was almost time to wake.

Lucifer entered the dungeon and was surprised to find Mercy wearing something other than her dowdy dress. It was still plain and loose-fitting, but it wasn't made of the same heavy material.

He had ignored her for the past week, not in the mood for much. He hadn't stopped by the Trade House or anywhere else. Now he found her standing near the bars; if he wasn't mistaken, she was inspecting the lock.

He asked, "Got tired of looking like a frump?"

"You should let that boy go home."

He couldn't help rolling his eyes. "He doesn't want to go home. I didn't even bring him here."

"You should let *me* go home."

"Once you tell me how you got here," he bargained readily.

"You know how I got there, you heard me tell him about the amulet," she said.

"Which, interestingly enough, no one has found. Were you lying to Jack?" he asked. He might have been impressed if she'd said yes.

She shook her head and stepped away from the door.

"Do you like it here?"

"No!"

He sat in front of the bars, close enough that his knees touched. His usual spot for their one-sided conversations. "Do you like me?"

"You're a beast," she growled.

"I can feel the way you look at me," he shared. "It sounds like nonsense but...there's something about the way you're feeling that's not quite Christian."

Quickly, Mercy told him, "No, it's *not* you."

"Then what?"

"You look like him," she admitted.

It felt like bragging but he said it anyway. "I don't look like anyone."

She shook her head.

"Go on, tell me who I look like or I'll keep thinking you go to bed with your thighs wet at the idea of me," he warned, though he made sure his voice had more purr than threat.

The idea seemed to disgust her enough to compel her to answer, "You look like Reg."

"And who's Reg?"

"One of yours. A great-grandson or less. But I swear, his

face...you could have been twins. Except for his eyes. They were more brown than red. Like rust." Her voice had gone soft and she twisted her hands in her skirt.

"Ah."

"But he was a demon nonetheless," she said, her tone growing brusque.

"How did you know him?"

He did not expect the question to provoke much of a reaction, but she seemed to lose some strength and sat, pulling her knees close to her chest.

When she started to weep, he said, "Come on, Mercy, I've not done a thing to you. I just want to send you home."

"I can't *go home*."

That surprised him. A moment ago, she'd been scolding him for keeping her here. "Why not?"

She sniffed and wiped her face. "Because of what I did."

Feeling like he was talking in circles, he asked, "What did you do?" He vowed that if she didn't give a straight answer, he would kill her and be done with it. His concern about how she had gotten in dwindled with each day.

Mercy wiped her face on her sleeve. "Reg was a captive, bound for the pyre."

He grimaced.

She continued, "It was my job to police the cells, make sure there wasn't any devilry or witchcraft going on, no escape attempts."

"The cells?"

"A dozen, no more. When they're filled, we burn what we've caught."

"Ah." The idea sent up a flare of anger but he pushed it down.

"Reg was in there for months, it had been a slow year and..." Mercy trailed off.

"And you liked him, I see." A common enough story, not impressive at all. He found himself somewhat disappointed.

"I let him go free, I thought the rest would be out on a hunt all night, but they came home early and found us gone."

"And found you in some inn the next town over with your skirts about your waist," he guessed. "Slit his throat or bashed his head in, I'm sure."

"My husband..."

"Your husband! That's a twist I like. Cheating wife, handsome devil, you could publish that if you put pen to paper."

"My shame is not for your amusement!"

"You wouldn't be so ashamed if you hadn't got caught," Lucifer pointed out. She didn't argue and he asked, "So what, they brought you home?"

She nodded. "Flogged and cast out."

"And that brings you to Hell...?"

"Because if I bring your head, they'll take me back," she admitted, more desperate and forlorn than determined.

The corners of his mouth turned down. "I don't know that redemption works that way. Why do you want to go back? They killed the fellow you were bedding."

"I was *weak* to let him touch me."

"And you're weak still if you fancy me because I've got his face."

She lunged for the bars and grabbed his sleeve. "If you think I'll leave this place without you dead—"

He took her hand from his sleeve and she tried to pull back. At the contact, he felt her revulsion, but also a need to touch something. She was lonely in her cell. She missed her family, she missed her lover, too. "I can't die, Mercy, I've told you before."

He released her hand and she fell back, landing hard on her rear.

"Your husband must have been a lousy lay, huh? Bad enough for you to have slept with the enemy." He recalled his plan to be charming and polite. Too late now. Maybe he would try again another day. "Or maybe you loved him, that Reg. Love can do things to you, it'll have you doing things you never thought you'd do."

With red-rimmed eyes, she glowered at him. "What could you know?"

As much as he didn't like the accusation, he seemed to have broken down some of her barriers. One step closer to whatever way she'd gotten in so he could keep an eye on it. He didn't want more competent assassins to find their way into his bedroom. "Just because I'm the Devil doesn't mean I don't feel. As I recall, and I do get muddled sometimes, feeling things too much is the whole of my problem."

"Your pride—"

"And who are you to lecture me on pride? Rather starve and sit in your own blood than accept the hospitality of the Devil just because of, what, exactly? What have I done that's so horrible?" he demanded, more for show than anything.

"You are the root of evil—"

"Isn't that money?" he quipped, feeling clever for a moment.

"The progenitor of a thousand vile bastards, husband to a million foul witches, father of lies and stealer of souls," Mercy listed.

He wrinkled his nose. He certainly hadn't fathered a thousand children on Earth and he didn't think he'd bedded anywhere close to a million different people, let alone witches. "Is this the turn Christianity has taken lately or should I assume that you are part of some insular group?"

"My family is one of the few that continues to crusade against wickedness."

"By rounding up demons and witches and whatnot to burn?" he asked with careful inflection, hoping that she'd pick up that lighting people on fire would surely be counted as wicked when her soul was to be judged.

"To cleanse the Earth and take it back from the unnatural scourge," she recited.

That phrase rang a bell and he thought for a while until he remembered where he'd heard it before. In Triviai there had been a civil war over the ascension of Ashley I; those who had opposed him had used the same words. "Moralists, right?"

She nodded.

"Tried to kill my heir, you did. If that's the lot you run with, I'd be better off slitting your throat than trying reason."

"Then do it." She had her jaw set and her eyes locked on him, green like pine needles.

The dungeon had blades and bludgeons galore, anything he could want to use for such a cold-blooded murder. She didn't tremble when he selected a knife from the wall. When he pulled open the cell door, she adjusted the way she stood, taking a lower stance and turning her body so that she presented a narrower target.

He had no wish to kill her and couldn't be sure what had actually compelled him to enter the cell, let alone with a blade in his hand. He knew, with a cold but distant certainty, that Mercy would most likely be dead on the other end of this encounter.

"You could still be sensible," he offered.

She put up her hands to defend herself.

"Or I could be very unkind and leave you to my demons. Let you loose in the worst parts of the Eighth," he mused.

"All talk."

It was goading, he knew, but he moved forward anyway, making a lazy grab at her. She ducked out of his way. It wasn't until he'd backed her into a corner with his slow approach that she truly pushed back, lashing out and knocking the blade from his hand.

It was the dress, he knew, ugly and plain, that threw him off. He didn't expect such a competent fighter to wear such a thing. It made him underestimate her. His heart wasn't in the fight, either, he wasn't sure why he'd started it.

He watched her dive for the knife, scooping it up and backing away from him to reevaluate. Her eyes darted around, taking in the surroundings before she lunged in toward him. She drew first blood, as she had last time, slicing his arm when he put it up to defend his more vital organs.

At the same time, they both realized that her back was to the open cell door. She turned to run and he leaped after her, knowing that having her loose in Hell was not an option. She would be broken to bits and his reputation would take a hit for letting her slip through his fingers.

His hand closed around her arm and she spun, attempting to slash his face, but he caught her wrist and knocked the blade from her hand. With a maneuver that impressed him, she hooked his leg with her own, throwing off his balance. She used the momentum to spin them around and push him against the wall. He could taste her breath, they were that close, and he could feel her pulse hammering in her wrist.

She stared at him and didn't seem afraid at all.

Knowing he ran the risk of being bitten, he closed the space between them and kissed her, curious more than anything. He wondered if she missed Reg or hated him more. She did bite him and pulled away with blood on her mouth, but she didn't let go of him.

"You're the one holding me now," he said with a smile. He liked the taste of blood in his mouth, especially his own. It made him think of his wife.

She pushed harder against him, her arm against his throat and he closed his eyes, letting out a pleasured sigh.

"How bad do you think you can hurt me?" He pulled her arm away and slid down the wall so that he knelt before her. She didn't look or sound like his wife, she didn't smell or act like her, but she had hurt him and he liked it. He missed it because he missed her.

Mercy didn't pull away when he wrapped his arm around her

waist and pressed his face to her belly. "What trick is this?"

Blood from the cut on his arm soaked into her dress, darkening the fabric. "It isn't."

"I don't want to hurt you," she said.

"A minute ago, you wanted me dead." He began to pull up her skirt, inch by inch, and she started to tremble when his skin touched hers, his hand just above her knee. "Tell me to stop."

"No."

He gazed up at her. He had expected her to back away, to insist he take his hands off her, but she didn't. She just stared down at him until he stood and pulled her back to him, his arm around her waist. He put his lips to her throat, feeling her blood rushing through the thick vein in her neck. If he bit, she would gush blood, coughing and dying in his arms.

She seemed to know this because, though her body molded against his and her fingers wound into his hair, she urged, "Kill me."

"I don't want to." He moved to kiss her, tasting his blood on her lips, running his tongue down her chin and throat to trace where it had trickled down.

She gripped his hair harder, tilting his head back. His wife had pulled his hair like that, pulled it even harder. She had choked him until he couldn't breathe, until his vision grew black. She had hurt him terribly, leaving scratches and bruises all over, and all he wanted was for her to come back.

Mercy sucked hard on the tender skin of his throat and he let out a groan. He lifted her skirts all the way and pulled one of her legs onto his hip, his hand on her bare thigh. He could feel the heat and wetness of her on his cock, even through the silk of his trousers.

"Should we fuck?" he asked, asking for advice as much as he was asking for permission.

"If you won't kill me."

He wouldn't, so he undid his trousers and picked her up so that he could slip inside her. She bit his lip hard when he entered her, drawing blood again, then kissed him deeply. She came before him with a wild moan and he could feel it, waves rippling through her, starting between her legs and squeezing his length. She came again when he did, this time more quietly. He thrust deep into her as he spilled, closing his eyes and burying his face in her neck, panting his wife's name.

He held on to her for a minute more, breathing hard and trying to gather his thoughts and remember what he had been doing in the first place.

There was information he wanted from her, he recalled that much. The whole thing had been a bit strange, even for him. He set her down and rubbed his face, pulling his hand back when he felt blood on his chin.

"Who's Tabby?" she asked.

"How did you get into Hell?"

"I don't know."

"What do you mean you don't know?" He tried to put himself back together, fumbling with the fastenings on his trousers as he tucked himself away. It hadn't been this hard to undo them.

"I didn't ask how. I just had a witch send me."

He finally managed to put all his clothes back on the right way. Her answer seemed too straightforward, but maybe that had been the problem all along. He had been too caught up thinking that mages *didn't* send humans to Hell to consider that they could. Of course, that sort of traveling, being taken apart and put together again, was probably worse for humans than demons. Mercy must have been desperate or ignorant of the dangers.

"A witch or a mage?" he asked.

"What's the difference?"

He thought to take the time to point out the difference between low and high magics but just shook his head. "And the amulet?"

"It's how I was getting back. A signal to the witch. I'm sure she thinks me dead by now."

He informed her, "I'm sure she never thought you would last more than a few minutes in the first place. The amulet is probably bunk altogether."

Mercy frowned. "I paid for a trip two ways."

He reached out to wipe a bit of dried blood off her face. She allowed it, to his surprise. "Yes, but it's like paying for a two-way ticket into a volcano."

He looked at her for a moment then rubbed his face again. His thoughts were still muddled. He stepped away from her, toward the door of the dungeon. He wanted to be somewhere else.

He stopped and glanced back. "Home. That's where you want to go."

She shrugged. "I don't have a home while you live."

"Listen...did, you know, did your family *say* you had to kill me to get back into your little cult or did you just assume this would do it?"

Her mouth opened, then shut. Finally, she said, "It's the ultimate goal of the Moralists..."

"You assumed, then. Listen, either way, I'll send you back to Earth."

She shook her head.

"What do you mean no?"

"I need to think."

He eyed her for a minute, frowning and taking in the odd, faraway aspect in her eyes. "Are you going to kill yourself?"

"I don't think so."

He didn't quite trust her answer and he didn't think she trusted it either. He needed to say something to pull her back so he offered, "Tabby is my wife."

"Your wife?"

"Don't worry, she left me. You reminded me of her."

"Oh."

He gave a crooked smile. "Just the way you bite."

"She left you?"

He nodded. "Don't ask why because I don't know." He looked at his hands, then the floor. Blood oozed down his arm to drip off his fingers onto the floor. "I just know I want her to come back. I don't think she will."

He realized it was the first time he'd said it aloud. He'd always said that she would come back when she'd wanted, when she was ready, when she'd gotten her fill of whatever she'd needed elsewhere.

His voice cracked when he said, "I really don't think she will."

Mercy shifted uncomfortably.

He rubbed his eyes. "So. Uh. Why don't you come upstairs?"

She glanced around the dungeon and followed him when he walked away, lingering a few steps behind him the entire time. He brought her to Imogen's office and knocked on the doorframe to get the vampire's attention.

He needn't have done it, though, because her nose was twitching as soon as he entered. When she looked up and saw the blood on his face, her mouth popped open.

"What...?"

He gestured to the human woman at his side. "We, uh..."

"You fucked her."

He corrected, "It was mutual. Anyways, she's got this look about her, sort of dazed."

"You've got it, too," Imogen said.

"I'm sure I do. Keep an eye on her for me."

"Keep an eye out for what?" Imogen asked. "You're getting blood on my carpet."

From his side, Mercy answered for him, "He thinks I'm going to kill myself."

Unimpressed, Imogen asked, "Are you?" She had her eyes fixed on the blood drops on the floor.

"I don't know."

"So you can see the issue," Lucifer said to Imogen.

The vampire shrugged. "Not really. She tried to kill you. But I'll certainly keep an eye on her if you want me to."

"Thanks. I've...I don't know, I need to go for a walk."

"Eat something."

He waved a hand as he walked out. "I ate in the Fourth."

"You should wash first!" Her voice carried down the hall after him and he let out a half-hearted chuckle.

He didn't clean up but went out into the Ninth with blood on his face and a variety of fluids on his trousers. The cut on his arm would scab over eventually, he hoped.

Not many others were out on the streets; the sky had long since gone black and his citizens were surely all inside at their revels. The tamer ones might even be in bed. Eodus would be in bed, he knew it in his bones. Him and Jack. Asleep, Eodus might even be still for once.

The Devil didn't know where he wanted to go but found himself in the Fourth as the sky started to redden. He let himself into the boy's cell and closed the door.

The boy stood beside the bed in his nightdress as always. "You have blood on your face."

Satan wiped his chin on his sleeve. "Did I get it?"

"Yes."

"What's your name?"

"I don't remember."

Lucifer sat on the floor and gestured for the boy to come over. The boy hesitated.

"Don't worry, I won't hurt you," Lucifer vowed.

"No interest in buggering me, that's what you said."

"Do you remember all of it?"

"Every day." The boy approached finally and sat beside him.

"Why do you stay?"

The child answered, "I belong here."

The Devil let out a sigh. "*I* belong here. You're just a kid. Not even a bit of peach fuzz. When the angel was here—"

"What angel?"

"The one who wept."

The boy said, "He didn't have wings."

"Most of us don't. What did he say to you?" Lucifer asked.

"Nothing, he just cried." The boy thought briefly, his blue eyes clouded, then added, "He cried more after Papa came."

"Did he try to help?"

The boy shrugged. "Sort of. For a bit. It was like...like he couldn't touch anything. Like he was a ghost."

"Hmm." Lucifer hadn't expected that. It probably had something to do with the way the angel had perceived things; so much of Hell was about one's perceptions. He put an arm around the boy. "Do you mind?"

"No." The child leaned against him. "But Papa will be here soon."

"Not today."

"He always comes," the boy pronounced.

"Not today."

It was not permitted for him to prevent the torment of an uncleaned soul. It was his job to prepare the souls for Purgatory and if they would never be fit for Purgatory, he was to punish them. But Hell was his realm and the Almighty had shown no interest in helping correct this oversight.

Lucifer had never cared for rules in the first place. He pulled the boy a little closer. "Do you want to go to Heaven?"

"I belong here."

"You can't like it, this endless buggering."

The boy shook his head. "No. But it's where I belong. Mama said so, Papa did, too. I went to Hell, I was good."

"Unfinished business, I understand that. You're like a ghost." Lucifer reconsidered. "Sort of."

The door handle began to turn but Lucifer waved one blood-encrusted hand toward it. The door slammed shut and a lock appeared. The door handle jiggled.

"You try to follow the rules, you know? You think you're lucky

He didn't do something worse to you..." He sighed. "So you try to play at being the Devil all the while skulking around under someone else's rules."

The boy shrank closer to him, his eyes trained on the doorway. He had some of Lucifer's shirt bunched up in his hand.

"Do you hate him?"

"Who?" the boy asked.

"Your father."

"I don't hate anyone."

It was the answer he wanted. Souls filled with hatred were unmanageable, he'd learned that the hard way. He stood and then bent back down to pick up the boy. He carried him out of the cell and began to walk.

"Where are we going?" the child asked.

"To the library."

The boy put his arms around the Devil's neck and rested his head on his shoulder. "Why?"

"I'm going to make you one of mine. If He wants to go leaving perfectly good souls down here, I'm going to make the most of it. You don't mind, do you?"

"No. I belong here."

Lucifer wondered how many times his parents had told him that. Bad parents were a plague, begetting and twisting children who grew up to be worse parents. Maybe it was good this boy had died before his soul had gotten too mangled. At least now he could have a purpose, find something else to do with his eternity.

Once inside the library, every head swiveled to watch him, though he thought it had more to do with the soul in his arms. He approached the day librarian and informed her, "In the stacks on the third floor of the west wing, there is a book I need."

"The third floor?"

He nodded. "If you don't mind, Shiraz."

She ripped a piece of paper from a notepad. "What book?"

"It's the only book on the third floor."

She looked at him and set aside the pencil she'd taken up. "Oh."

"Don't open it," he advised.

She nodded and left.

Lucifer set the boy on the counter, his bare feet dangling down. "You'll be different afterward, but not too different."

The soul asked, "It won't hurt, will it?"

"I'll never do a thing to hurt you."

The boy looked down at his feet. "Papa gets angry when I leave my room."

"He won't be able to hurt you anymore."

The child reached out and took Lucifer's hand, waiting quietly.

"Never again," Lucifer promised.

Shiraz returned with the book, still wrapped in the cloud gray shroud it had been stored in. She handed it to him like it was a baby she was afraid of dropping.

He remoced the shroud and helped the boy hop down from the counter. He pressed the book into his hand and instructed, "Open it and look right in. You'll know when to close it."

A crowd had gathered around them and when the boy opened the book, the assembled demons let out a collective gasp.

With his hands gripping the book like a lifeline, the boy's soul began to shake violently, his neck snapping around at disturbing angles. He threw back his head and at one point his body turned inside out starting at the mouth.

When he closed the book, he was taller by half a foot, as well as broader through the shoulders. His skin had darkened to a pleasant orangey brown that reminded Lucifer of dying leaves in autumn.

Seeing his quickened breathing, the flush in his face, Lucifer felt compelled to ask, "Did it hurt?"

"Uncomfortable but not painful." His voice had a different cadence now and had deepened in pitch.

He handed the book back to Lucifer, who wrapped it in the shroud and returned it to Shiraz.

"Do you still feel like you belong here?" the Devil asked.

The new-made demon nodded. He ran his hand along his arm, pushing up the sleeve of his too-small night dress to see his skin. "This was my favorite color, you know."

"What's your name now?"

Eyes wide, he asked, "Was I supposed to get one?"

Lucifer shook his head. "I thought you might want to pick one out."

The demon gave a quick shake of his head, seeming like a child again for a second. "I can't think of anything good." He bit his lip. "Pick one for me?"

"Elisha." The name came to his mind easily.

The demon nodded. He reached out to take Lucifer by the hand but then drew back. "I...What do I do now?"

"First you'll sleep. After that, I think there's work for you in the First if you're ready."

"What's there?" Elisha asked.

"I don't know, I never make it to that Precinct."

Elisha frowned and Lucifer laughed.

"No, that's a joke, sorry. It wasn't funny. First Precinct is all soft sentences. Everyone cuts their teeth in the First. You'll be good at it," the Devil assured.

"Are you sure?"

He nodded. "Yes."

He took Elisha by the hand and brought him to the palace. After a good night's sleep, he'd be better settled into his new body and not so nervous. It had been more than a millennium since Lucifer had corrupted a soul. With the way demons reproduced, he hadn't needed to; when the Devil saw Elisha smile for the first time as he nestled into bed, he felt justified in what he had done.

No one in Heaven would even notice his trespass.

Mercy didn't try to kill herself, but she did spend a lot of time playing with the cats and after a week or so, Lucifer considered it worrisome. He voiced this concern to Imogen, but she brushed it aside.

They stood together in the door of her office watching Mercy dangle bits of string for half a dozen cats.

"Shouldn't you be in the Fourth?" Imogen asked.

"I promoted Inri," he explained.

"Who?"

He shook his head. "Anyway, he's been writing reports for me, I just need to stop by and initial them."

"You don't think this is a dereliction of duty?"

"Ask me if I care."

She sighed. "Do you care?"

"Not at all. Now ask me where I'm going today."

Not at all sounding like she wanted to know, she asked, "Where are you going?"

"To see a whore—"

"Ugh." She turned away from him and returned to her office. "Enjoy yourself, I have a job to do."

As he walked to the Trade House, he felt unusually jaunty. Elisha had transitioned well to the First and Lucifer had put him into housing near Eodus, who had readily agreed to keep an eye on the new-made demon. Jack had bubbled with all kinds of questions about how demons were made, and though Elisha hadn't known exactly how to answer, he had tried his best.

When Lucifer entered the brothel, he didn't see Ira right away and found himself panicking until he spied him sitting in one of the overstuffed armchairs. As he approached, the demon glanced up and said, "Oh."

"Oh?" The flatness of Ira's voice took him aback. "I thought you'd be a little happier to see me."

"I'm happy to work, you know that. Whatever you want." He closed his book and set it down on the small, round table beside his chair.

He traded with Nial for Ira's time, but couldn't figure out why the demon's reception had been so cool.

Once they were alone in one of the rooms, he touched Ira on the arm. "I know it's been awhile, I told you I didn't know when I'd be back."

"I know."

"I've been busy."

Ira shrugged. "I'm not asking to know your business."

Lucifer sighed. "Tell me, what's got you in a mood?"

"I'm not in a mood."

"Ira!" Lucifer whined.

The demon shook his head, silent for a moment. He gave Satan an irritated glance, then admitted, "Mistress told me what you said. I told you I would have done it. You could have taken me any way you wanted."

Lucifer hadn't exchanged a single word with Ira's mistress. He did not like that someone had lied and lied about the Devil's own opinion, but he felt more concerned with Ira's unhappiness. "If I wasn't pleased with what we did, I wouldn't have sent those things over for you."

"What things?"

"The candies and things."

Ira shook his head. "Not that I ever heard of."

"Not a single thing came to you?" Lucifer asked.

"No."

"Not even the notes?"

"No," the demon answered.

The pieces came together easily. If Ira had not gotten the things Lucifer had sent, there was only one place they could have ended up. And if his mistress knew about his reticence to bed a wounded whore, then she had read his notes. He had referenced it with the cheeky promise to take Ira from behind if he could avoid anything too rough for a while. If she had read his notes, then she knew the way he'd signed them. *Thinking of you.*

"I wish to file a complaint," he announced.

Ira shrank at his words. "Not about me, I'll do what you want, I told you I would. Let me try again."

He reached out to touch Ira's face, cradling his cheek for a moment. "Not about you, silly. Should I ask Nial?"

Ira nodded, his eyes glittering. Lucifer took his hand and walked back out into the main room of the brothel with him, approaching Nial's desk as every set of eyes in the place followed him.

"I want to talk to the madam."

Nial informed him, "Any request or grievance can be registered with me."

"No, I want to talk to her."

Ira took his hand back, stepping away from Lucifer.

Nial shook their head. "No one speaks with her."

"I will."

"Mistress does not—"

Lucifer interrupted, "If you think for one moment that I care what your mistress does or doesn't do, you've mistaken me for some common groveling thing like the rest of you."

Nial stood and stared at Lucifer. "And who would I tell her is asking?"

"Tell her the Devil is here."

It didn't get the reaction he wanted. No one said anything until one person whispered; a stifled giggle followed that whisper.

"Don't, you'll get us all in trouble," Ira insisted.

Lucifer paid him no mind. If they did not believe him, then they would believe their eyes. He threw back his head and flung out his limbs, swelling in size until his back touched the ceiling and he had to hunch. His teeth grew longer and sharper; his mouth stretched into a maw and his fingers turned to claws. Spindly and grotesque, this was a shape anyone in Hell would recognize.

He crouched down and took Nial in both of his hands, his fingers wrapped around their waist and chest. He drew the creature close to his face. He could smell the fear and sweat on their skin. For effect, he screeched into Nial's face, not quite capable of true speech in this form.

When he returned Nial to the ground, everyone else in the brothel had gone prone. Except for Ira. Ira stared at him with his mouth agape.

Lucifer growled affectionately and ran a single claw along the side of Ira's face. After that, despite how his stomach demanded food and his teeth begged for flesh to tear, he forced himself back into his usual form. Even then, his teeth still felt too large and his limbs felt disjointed and wobbly.

Ira seemed to remember himself and dropped into a kneel, his head bowed.

Without needing to be asked again, Nial scurried away and returned with their ear in the grip of a woman of middling height. She was not thin or fat, nor did she have a terrifying countenance. Lucifer wondered what lurked behind that face to make the others worry so.

She pushed Nial back behind their desk and examined Lucifer.

She inclined her head slightly. "My Prince, I'm told you have a complaint you wish to file with me directly."

"Yes." When he spoke, his jaw cracked and settled into its proper place.

"With this one?" She nodded her head toward Ira.

"With you."

She touched a hand to her chest in false surprise. "Me? My Prince, what could I have done...?"

"I sent three packages to this place, all of them addressed to Ira."

"Perhaps—"

"If you are going to suggest that the packages never arrived, I would rethink that immediately," he snapped. "I know you received them and I know you read the notes I sent with them. Think before you speak this time."

"A misunderstanding, I'm sure," she suggested.

"Unacceptable."

"I can offer you recompense for the missing goods."

"If it happens again, you will offer me your heart and watch me eat it." His stomach growled at the thought and he seriously considered eating her then and there.

But then Ira would probably be too distraught to do anything fun for a while and Lucifer would be spitting up bones for a week.

"Yes, Your Highness." She inclined her head slightly. "Is there anything else you need?"

"Three dozen candies and a bag of oranges. A book of poems by Dickinson."

At that, some color came to her face. "The book I have—"

"And the rest you can procure while I wait. Have them sent to my room." He took Ira by the hand again and led him back through the curtained hallway and into their rented room.

With the door closed, he let out a groan and stretched, all the bones in his back cracking and popping unpleasantly.

Ira watched from a distance.

He held out his hand but Ira didn't approach. He took his hand back, letting it dangle at his side. "What?"

"You aren't angry with me, are you?"

"With you?"

Ira nodded. "Because I didn't believe who you were."

Lucifer touched his cheek with a smile, but Ira shrunk back. "I frightened you, didn't I?" he asked, keeping his voice soft.

"No."

"You don't have to lie. I won't come back if you don't want."

"No, it's...you're him, you're the Devil." Ira buried his face in his hands and started to weep. He dropped to his knees. "I'm sorry, I should have known who you were, I'm a miserable fool. She's going to whip me for this, I know it. I served you so poorly."

Lucifer knelt beside him and gently pulled his hands away from his face. "You served me exactly as I asked. A Prince couldn't want for more." With his sleeve, he wiped Ira's face.

New tears replaced what he wiped away. Lucifer gathered the demon into his arms and cradled him close. It must have been a terrible shock for him. His larger form was unpleasant enough to drive humans to madness, so it couldn't have been an easy sight for a common demon either.

Instead of the mouth he'd kissed, Ira would always imagine that maw, the one that had eaten disobedient and unpleasant monsters. A maw that could have swallowed him easily, gulping like a snake, shaking him till his neck snapped if he was lucky. Otherwise, he would have been crushed and torn, suffocated, or burned by stomach acid.

You'll be eaten by the Devil was what parents whispered to naughty children in Hell and it was something even grown demons feared. A threat driven home by the public devouring of treasonous subjects; the last one had been some years after the Wasting Plague. Ira must have seen it and been a child at the time.

Lucifer tightened his arms around Ira, not knowing what comfort the embrace of monster could bring, but the demon ceased his weeping after a few more moments. Lucifer asked, "Do you want to talk?"

Ira shook his head.

"Tell me if you want me to go."

"No." He gripped Lucifer's shirt and nestled closer to him.

"Will you let me feed you orange slices?"

Ira looked up at him, dark eyes opened wide in disbelief. The Prince of Hell should not handfeed his subjects, let alone one he paid to serve him. Not in the nicest of brothels, and certainly not in this place. "Yes."

"And will you let me cover you with kisses, sticky as they'll probably be?"

"Yes."

"And can I tell you about the rather curious sex I've had since I last saw you?"

Ira snorted, losing that doe-eyed expression. "If you want."

"I'd like to get your professional opinion about it."

Ira laughed at that. "How could I know more than you?"

"I don't get around as much as I used to," Lucifer admitted. "I know I've got a reputation, but I'm not young anymore."

Wiping his face on his own sleeve, Ira stood and sat on the bed, gesturing for the Devil to join him. "The oranges aren't here yet, you might as well tell me about the weird lay you had."

"There's this woman. Human. Tried to kill me," he began.

Ira settled into the bed, lying on his side with one arm tucked under his head. He listened carefully and when Lucifer finished his tale, he said, "You called her by your wife's name."

By that time, the oranges, as well as the book and notes, had arrived and Lucifer had started to peel one of the oranges. "I know."

"Sounded like good sex, though, at least. I didn't think you'd like being hurt. Figured you for the other way around." Ira glanced at the notes again. He had read them without batting an eyelash. Now he tucked them inside the book of poems.

"That's the thing, though, I don't like it! I mean, with anyone but Tabitha, I never cared for it. And I mean, Mercy barely hurt me. A little blood and a hickey, nothing like what my wife used to do to me." It felt like sacrilege to say her name aloud. He peeled off a section of orange and offered it to Ira.

Lucifer watched, waiting to see his expression when he bit into the fruit, taking it from the Devil's fingers with his mouth. His eyes widened right away, his whole face lighting up.

"I knew you'd like them."

Ira ate the entirety of the orange with the same reverence, talking out the odd details of Lucifer's experience with Mercy.

Finally, he consoled, "I don't know what to tell you, really. Sometimes fucking is just...weird."

Lucifer sucked a dribble of orange juice from his finger. Ira took him by the wrist and licked up what had spilled down his arm, sending goosebumps prickling over Lucifer's skin. He kissed the Devil, putting one hand on the back of Lucifer's neck and drawing him close.

He didn't hold him like that for long, though, because the Devil's response was mild. He pulled back. "Do you think about your wife a lot?"

"I try my best not to."

"Will she be mad if she comes back and finds you've been

bedding whores and assassins?"

"I don't think so."

Ira wrinkled his nose. "Why not? Isn't that why she left you?"

"I..." Lucifer leaned back, half-propped on his side. "It's..."

"Tell me."

"She never cared what I did unless it was something she'd told me not to do."

"Oh."

Lucifer explained, "Tabby was...she was always different. When I met her, I didn't think much of it. I just thought she was one more Hell-born thing. This was in the wild days before the walls were built. She was more, of course, and I fell in love. She told me that real love could never be had between people who weren't equals."

Ira took the Devil's hand in his, kissing his fingers.

"So I gave her everything. Magics, immortality...everything I had, I shared. I made her my queen. She could have been the Devil if she'd wanted to be, leaving me to be naught but Lucifer again."

"And?"

Lucifer shook his head. "It was never her that needed to be more." He rolled onto his back. "She loved me, I'm sure she did. I think she found me uncomplicated, easy to be around. I never knew what she meant by *real* love, though."

Ira played with the buttons on Lucifer's shirt, though it seemed to be more out of the need to do something with his hands than an attempt at flirtation. "Can I tell you something?"

"Hm?"

"You should feed me another orange."

Lucifer glanced over at him to see a silly smile on his face.

"If you're not going to fuck me..."

"I could," Lucifer said slowly.

"Unless you want to talk about your wife some more."

"Is that mockery I hear in your tone?"

"Never," Ira said, his tone grave. "I wouldn't dare."

Lucifer poked him in the side and he batted the Devil's hand away. "I think it was, I think you were *mocking* your Prince." He had never been so delighted to be ridiculed.

"Don't!" Ira squirmed away when Lucifer moved towards his ribs. He grabbed Lucifer by the wrist.

"I wasn't."

Ira released him and he ran his hand along the demon's side. He stopped at his waist and started to lift his shirt, inching it up so

Ira's belly was exposed. He traced along the top of his breeches, his fingers pale as snow against the backdrop of the demon's ash-gray skin. He liked gray and white together more than he liked the pallor with the inkiness of his own hair, nails, and teeth. It was too stark then.

He pressed his mouth to Ira's hip and noticed a tattoo he hadn't before; black ink proved hard to see against Ira's dark skin. He ran his tongue over the symbols.

He didn't want to talk about his wife anymore, he didn't even want to think about her. She'd come back when she wanted. If she ever did.

"You're still thinking about her," Ira scolded.

Lucifer raised his eyes to look at him. He had an answer on his tongue, some smart retort that he didn't care to say. He climbed on top of Ira and kissed his throat. "Last time you declined my offer to be the one doing the fucking. Is that because you don't care to?"

Ira's head was tilted back, his eyes were half-closed. "It was because of the way you used your mouth."

"Would you like to now?"

His eyes fluttered open. "It means you'll have to come back."

"What?"

"You promised to take me from behind in that note. If you don't do it today, you'll have to come back."

Lucifer touched his forehead to Ira's shoulder for a moment, then lifted his head, unable to keep a disbelieving smile from his face. Always trying to secure another day's work. "Then I'll have to come back."

Ira grinned. "Good." He ran his fingers through Satan's hair and drew him closer, kissing him sweetly.

Ira's hands moved just as sweetly over the Devil's body as they shed their clothes and caressed each other. Ira's touch was gentle and slow, his kisses deep and long. He rolled Lucifer onto his belly and slipped well-oiled fingers inside of him.

Lucifer let out a long moan at that and Ira asked, "Too much?"

"Not enough."

Ira let out a breath through his nose, amused. He kissed Lucifer's shoulder blade. "I wasn't sure what you were used to." He pulled his fingers back and Lucifer sighed, shivering a little.

The Devil licked his lips in anticipation, waiting for Ira to enter him when he felt the demon's cock against his ass. He did so just as gently as he had done everything else and it took Lucifer a little while to realize that Ira was not just being careful with someone who might be unused to receiving. He was being *tender*; he was not fucking or buggering, he was making love.

The sensation of having a caring lover was unfamiliar to him now, like a distant memory brought back by finding something that had been lost. The Devil had no objections, though, to Ira's tenderness and turned himself over to the experience, moving in time with the demon's unhurried thrusts, closing his eyes and winding his hands in the sheets. Ira brought Lucifer to climax without even needing to stroke his cock.

After Ira came, he didn't pull back right away but instead wrapped his arms around Lucifer for a moment, his cheek warm and soft against the skin of Lucifer's back. When he did move away, it was to dampen a small towel and wipe up what he had spilled, dabbing the Devil's rear and thighs.

Lucifer closed his eyes, burying his face in the pillow.

Ira tapped his arm. "Roll over, let me get your belly."

Lucifer rolled over and took the towel. "You don't need to." He cleaned himself and attempted to do the same for the sheets, but they would have to be washed.

Ira came to sit beside him, trailing his fingers along Lucifer's chest. "See? I'm good at my job if you'll let me do it."

"How is it that you aren't booked every night?"

Ira shrugged. "Men that want me want to be the ones doing the taking and men that want to be taken aren't moved by a thing like me. Too skinny, too short, and a baby-face to boot." He glanced at the hourglass that had chimed long ago. "Not to mention, when people are paying, they like to get things done quick. They want to come more, not better."

Lucifer looked at the hourglass as well.

"I guess Nial isn't too worried about hurrying you out now that they know who you are."

"I'll make up the difference. Have I mentioned how incredibly inconvenient her no coin, no credit policy is?"

"I wouldn't mention it to anyone."

"What about you?" Lucifer asked.

"Hmm?"

"Wouldn't you rather be earning coin?"

Ira shrugged once more. "I earn my keep, it's all I'm worried about."

Lucifer did not allow himself to make a face. He had no right to judge how Ira lived his life. Still, the way things were run at this place chafed him. As someone whose business was deals, it seemed abundantly clear that Ira was getting a raw one.

A tentative knock came from the door. Ira padded over to answer it and had a short conversation with Nial, then turned back to Lucifer to say, "I've got someone else booked soon."

"Oh."

"Should I...do you want me to turn her away?"

"No, no, I don't want to cost you any business." Lucifer wanted to curl up in the bed with Ira's skin against his own, but he reached for his clothes anyway.

Ira nodded.

Once they had both dressed, Lucifer headed for the door and Ira grabbed his arm. "Don't forget to come back."

"I won't. You should put those candies somewhere safe, I bet there are thieving hands already itching for them."

"Oh, well, I'd share with everyone anyway."

Lucifer laughed, appreciating the irony of a demonic whore eager to share with his fellow demonic whores. Humanity would never believe it. He gave Ira a last kiss and made his way home, though it was still early enough in the day that he could have found people hard at work in the Fourth. He should have checked in on things there, or on Elisha in the First.

Instead, he just went home. He found Marlow on his pillow and picked her up, cradling her in his arm and going over to his desk. There he found a letter with an unexpected word printed across the front.

Father.

He flipped it over and recognized the seal of his daughter's ring. He broke the wax and scanned the letter, then read it again more carefully.

That building of Ambrose Weller's is finished, my suite is being furnished. It's larger than where I am now. I wouldn't mind it if you had some of my things from the palace sent up.

xoxo

Elisa

Below her signature was a list of the things from her old bedroom that she wanted to be delivered. As he read the list he saw that some of the things she asked for were not hers to begin with; they were her mother's, things for which she must have known he had no use.

Of course, it was that she needed something. Of course, she wanted him to move furniture between Hell and Earth. And of course, he would do it and do it happily.

With Marlow still cradled in the crook of one arm, he went down to Imogen's office. He rapped on the doorframe.

"How was your whore?" she asked without looking up.

"Pleasant."

"I heard that you terrified an entire brothel."

"Word spreads fast."

She informed him, "Your people are exceedingly pleased with you these days. Emotionally scarred an angel, turned a young boy's soul into a demon, showed your nastier form."

"Oh, not even the whole thing," he scoffed.

"Enough to make them forget about your fondness for that human boy."

"I feel like you're trying to get at something," he said.

"You should capitalize on things is all."

He handed over the list his daughter had sent. "Can you have these things gathered and sent to Earth? The location is noted at the bottom."

She skimmed the list. "I can't send things to Earth."

"Call Shiraz, the day librarian, then. She can do it. Or Yatha, she's a schoolteacher. And someone else. It's written down somewhere, I'm sure." He scratched Marlow behind the ears. "Where's Mercy?"

"Around, I don't know. She isn't going to kill herself and thus my vigil is ended."

"She hasn't left the palace, has she?" he asked.

"Not unless she snuck out a window."

"Imogen."

The vampire rolled her eyes. "No. She hasn't. Last I saw her she was in the kitchen making what appeared to be an incredibly boring meal."

He turned and took his leave of the office, heading to the kitchen. There he found Mercy eating a bowl of plain porridge, something he doubted had ever been prepared in the Devil's palace before.

"Don't like soup?"

Her eyes still on her porridge, she informed him, "I've given into temptation too easily."

"The temptation of a hearty chowder?" He sat across from her and set Marlow on the table. The kitten sprawled out, rolling on her back and exposing the fluffy black expanse of her belly.

"A bland diet will calm my mind. I'll be able to think clearly then."

"And if you masturbate, you'll go blind," he intoned.

They hadn't spoken much since their coupling. A few words. He'd asked if she'd needed anything. She'd said no. He'd insulted her dress. She'd ignored him.

She ignored him now, too.

"I don't normally associate with Moralists and therefore I'm not clear on their personal codes of conduct, so can I ask if you're not supposed to enjoy sex or just sex with inhuman monsters?" he asked.

"I'm not going to lay with you again."

The idea made his skin crawl. "Nor do I particularly want to lay with you. I was wondering about your husband."

"Why?"

"He's your husband, don't you want to go home to him? Don't you feel...some yearning to be with him again? Or was he, as I already guessed, a bad lay?"

"Webster is...he's a good husband," she informed him. "A good man."

"You love him?"

"No." She immediately looked at him, as if she hadn't meant to say it. "I should, though. He's *good*. He's moral and strong."

"So why don't you want to go to him?"

She replied, "He won't take me back."

Lucifer guessed, "He doesn't love you?"

"I was unfaithful."

He reached out and touched Marlow's belly. The kitten stretched, then wrapped her front legs around his wrist. She put out her claws but didn't dig into his skin. "So?"

"What do you mean, 'so'?"

"If you love someone you love them anyway," he told her. "If you love someone, they're worth more to you than the sum of their good parts. If you love someone, you forgive them."

She stirred her porridge. "He hit Reg from behind. Hit him so hard I saw brains when he fell. Kept hitting him till there was no way he could heal." She let go of her spoon with a sigh, resting her forehead against her hand.

That made more sense. He clucked and agreed, "So then I

imagine you're not going back to him."

"I loved Reg. I miss him."

He had to ask, "How'd a demon win your heart anyway?"

"He told jokes. All the time, nonstop."

"Ah, well, laughter does have a certain effect on the soul," Lucifer mused.

"He wasn't funny. Not at all. The worst jokes I'd ever heard and I told him as much. So he dared me to find a funnier joke."

Lucifer nodded.

"Want to hear a dirty joke?" she asked.

"Certainly."

"Seven white horses fell in the mud."

He stared at her for a minute, then covered his mouth, giggling. He couldn't stop giggling and had to put his head down on the table. So, that was the joke that could make a demon love a woman who considered his kind to be a scourge upon the Earth.

When his mirth died, he straightened up and dabbed his eyes with his sleeve.

"Hell is no place for you, Mercy."

"I know."

"Even if your family won't take you back, even if your love is dead, there must be somewhere you want to go," he said.

"I know six ways to kill a vampire, but I don't know enough of the world to know where I want to be."

"There's always the library," he suggested.

"You really should kill me and be done with it."

"Too easy for you. Harder to go back and rebuild a life. That's your sentence for your crime against the serpent's throne."

"I barely drew blood."

"You left a scar. Two of them," he reminded. "You know what? I'll have Imogen send for the atlases. It's better, on second thought, if you don't go to the library on your own."

"What's an atlas?"

He blinked at her, not sure if he should pity her or not. "Were you raised a Moralist or did you convert?"

"Raised."

Pity, then. "An atlas is a book of maps." He scooped up Marlow and stood.

In his room, with the cat on his lap, he penned a note to his daughter to let her know her things would arrive shortly. He told her how glad he was to hear from her. He didn't mention that he had plans to visit Weller.

Marlow walked across the page and left a paw print in the ink he had used to sign his name. He didn't bother to rewrite it.

Lucifer peered at the calendar that sat on Eodus's kitchen table. He had come by that night to check in on the acrobat after he'd finished his reports in the Fourth; he stopped by the little house in the Eighth every so often, though he never felt expected or overly welcomed. The calendar showed that it was, on Earth, coming up to the end of December. Jack still had about three months left.

Without warning, the numbers on the blocks tumbled forward to show that it was New Year's Day.

Jack gave the calendar a dirty look, as though a mere object could understand his displeasure. "I hate it when it does that! Sometimes it doesn't change at all for a whole week."

Lucifer rested his elbow on the table, knowing that it would be rude to tilt back in his chair and put up his feet. "Time is different here."

The youth nodded. "I know. It's just...this business with Shanley makes me nervous, is all."

"Pythea says you're doing well."

Jack shrugged and rubbed the back of his neck. "I know..."

"Worried you won't be able to do it?"

"Sort of. Shanley, he...cruel as he could be, he taught me everything I know. He was the only one who looked out for us."

Eodus, who had a kettle on for tea, huffed loudly and pressed his lips together.

"What?" Jack snapped.

"Nothing," Eodus answered mildly.

A terrible silence sat in the room and Lucifer broke it by saying, "Jack, if you're having doubts, I can send you back to Earth. Your deal with me is...not something I'll hold you to if you don't want to stay in Hell."

Eodus gaped, knowing better than Jack the offer the human had been given. The Devil enforced his deals, to a fault.

Jack shrugged. If Lucifer wasn't mistaken, he was a little broader through the shoulders than he had been when he'd first gotten here. "As soon as I'm back on Earth, Shanley will find me. Better that I go to him and go prepared."

Lucifer wondered what had happened to cool things between the lovers. "You don't sound so happy to be here as you were. Is my realm not to your liking?"

Jack glanced at Eodus but then pulled his eyes back. He shook his head, looking at the floor. "No, it's fine here."

He clucked his tongue. "Sounds like a lie to me. If I moved a little closer, I'd be able to taste it."

Wide-eyed, Jack stared at him for an instant, then forced his eyes back to the floor.

It shouldn't matter to him whether they loved each other or not, or if Jack was happy in his new home. Lucifer tapped his fingers on the table, wondering what to do next. From Jack, he felt discomfort as well as the desire to do something. To speak. He had something he wanted to say but he held it in.

Humans were not emotionally more complex than demons, but given that Lucifer often had access to their feelings, if not entire thoughts, without effort, he found them taxing. Right now, he felt especially taxed and it drove him to say, "Out with it, Jack, if you've got something to say."

"No, I..." Jack trailed off.

Eodus started to say, "My Prince—"

Quiet and calm, but with careful enunciation, the Devil said, "Eodus, if you're speaking it is to tell me what I want to know. I do not want to think I was overgenerous in allowing your lover to stay here."

"I miss the circus is all," Jack hurried to say. "It isn't anything to do with Hell!"

Lucifer found the answer almost disappointing. If the acrobat was keeping secrets, he should have been keeping good ones. "Oh, well, no shame in that. Eodus, why don't you take him to Siobhan's place? What's she call it again? In the Ninth, to the west of the university and up the street a little?"

"Dreams of Eulalia?" Eodus guessed.

"That's the one! Take him there."

Eodus glanced at Jack. "He doesn't like women. Neither of us does."

Lucifer shooed away the concern with a wave of his hand. "It's not a whorehouse, it's a stage. The sex that happens there is incidental."

Jack's interest didn't seem dampened by the fact that women would be the featured act. "A stage?"

"They do a variety of dance and acrobatics or did, last time I went. Sometimes a little theater. Haven't been in a while." He lost himself in the memories of the last time he had gone, then turned his eyes back to Jack. "Do you want to go?"

"Now?"

"Well, no, tea's on and the best shows are always after dark. Not to mention, Jack, love, you stink."

The human flushed. "I didn't expect you to come by...I was with Pythea all day."

"And you're with her every day, aren't you? Naught but training and this place?" He looked around the small house. Neat and tidy, it was a nice home, but it wasn't the pinnacle of excitement. "No wonder you miss the circus. Go, wash."

Jack went with a glance at Eodus, a glance that said *I'm sorry he's paying attention to me again.*

"Don't trust my intentions with your pretty acrobat?" Lucifer asked.

Eodus initially glowered, but then must have realized the mistake, because he rearranged his face back into its usual nervous servility. "No, my Prince, I trust you."

"Trust the Devil? Seems like a mistake."

In a grave, muted voice, the demon answered, "Not as much of a mistake as it would be to anger him."

Lucifer let out a little bark of a laugh. "Which one is more dangerous, do you think?"

Eodus squeezed his eyes shut and bit his lip.

He must have been trying hard to contain himself. Lucifer couldn't recall what he had done to make people fear him so. He kept Hell in check, of course, but demons could really run amok if given the chance. He had his darker passions, but he had never imposed upon his subjects. He had never taken someone to bed without their unbridled consent and he wondered why so many thought he would.

The kettle screamed and he stood, going over to the stove, brushing past Eodus as he did. He poured water and set the mugs on the table to steep. He touched Eodus on the shoulder and gestured to the table.

"Come sit, Eodus, perhaps we should speak."

Eodus sat, his hands wrapped around the mug and his eyes fixed on the water. "Whatever you wish, Your Highness."

"You wish I had less interest in Jack but I..." the Devil sighed and wondered how much would be too much to tell the demon. "You're one of my tamer citizens and you seem to be reliable enough. I hope that I can speak openly without it being common gossip by next week."

Uncomfortable to the extreme, Eodus shifted in his seat. "Yes, my Prince."

"Neither of you should matter to me. I should have sent Jack back to Earth to be done in by Mylas. Humans have no place in Hell...but I saw him through your eyes, Eodus, and it..." Dramatic. His father had always called him dramatic and maybe he was. "It picked open a wound I thought couldn't be made raw again. You love him and I am envious. That's all it is. I'm here because I like to see that the two of you are happy because you have something I might never have again."

"Your Highness..."

"I don't come to visit in any attempt to take him or win his love. I come because I am genuinely hopeful that he will be successful and happier because of it."

"Um." Eodus cleared his throat.

"My feelings exactly."

They sat in silence for a while until Jack came back from washing and looked between the two of them. Lucifer gestured for him to come over and sit, which he did.

"Eodus and I were just discussing the terms of our relationship...hang on, that's not what I meant." He took a sip of his tea and tried to find the right word. "Details? Maybe. Either way, I'm not here because I want to bed you or do anything else untoward. That said, I would still like for us to go out and see a show unless you'd like to tell me to get fucked altogether."

Jack stared and seemed to forget to breathe because after a moment he inhaled sharply. "Um, I..." He looked at Eodus. "No, it's...I want to go, too. I do. Really."

"I'm glad."

Jack reached over to take Eodus's hand.

Lucifer reached over and put his hand on top of both of theirs, just to make them uncomfortable. He smiled his worst smile and told them, "And I can be so much fun if you're not wasting time worrying about what I'm going to do to you."

Jack laughed and didn't seem perturbed at all. Most people, at the sight of the Devil's smile, felt a little uncomfortable, if not deeply disturbed.

"You aren't afraid of me at all, are you?" Lucifer asked, pulling his hand back. The action had produced the appropriate effect in Eodus.

"Not really," Jack said. "I mean...I should be, you're the Devil and all, but...when you smile, it...I had this poster tacked up next to my bed of my father in his clown paint."

"Christ Almighty, I remind you of your father?"

"Something about the mouth," the youth admitted.

Lucifer laughed. Circus people were invariably more comfortable with freaks of nature and apparently, the Devil was included in that.

They sipped their tea together; Eodus seemed no more comfortable than he had before, but Lucifer felt better now that he'd stated his intentions clearly.

Although, he reflected, intentions were one thing; what happened was another. He hadn't stepped into the Trade House with any intention to make it a habit, he hadn't kept Mercy around with the intention to bed her, nor had he brought Marlow back from the dead with the intention to have her constantly glued to his side.

But going to take in a show at Siobhan's promised a fairly predictable night and he didn't think it would have any unintended consequences. The girls there could be somewhat free-wheeling when it came to taking their lovers to bed, but the place was generally calm. It was a place of performance and art, not of raucous carousing.

When they walked into Dreams of Eulalia, Lucifer found himself wishing for the smell of rosemary and hyssop with the ever-present hint of lavender.

Siobhan appeared by his elbow not a moment after he entered.

"My Prince, we're so happy to see you back." She bowed slightly. He didn't expect her to kneel; he'd known her for too long and she'd seen him at his worst too often.

He glanced down at the woman. She had an ethereal thinness, like a wisp of silk, and only reached to his waist when she straightened up. He bent down to kiss her cheek, though once he would have scooped her into his arms in a tight hug. "You know me, I always show up."

"Like a bad penny."

He put a hand on her shoulder and said, "Eodus, Jack, this is my sister-in-law, Siobhan."

Jack took in the tiny woman, emerald-skinned with large black eyes and a crop of spiky dark hair. "I didn't know you were married."

"I hardly notice myself. The missing wife helps."

"Missing!" Jack's eyes went wide.

"Missing from his side, not missing from the rest of us," Siobhan said. She put her hand on Lucifer's elbow. "This way, dear, I've got some seats right next to the stage. You'll like the show tonight, Sabal is opening."

"Sabal's visiting?" He hadn't been aware.

"Just for a little while."

Siobhan settled the three of them into plush velvet seats by the stage and gave Lucifer's hand a squeeze before she disappeared backstage. A serving boy came over with drinks they hadn't ordered and Lucifer chuckled when he saw what she'd sent them.

"What?" Jack asked.

"Last time we drank, we had whiskey sours and I puked up a ring that belonged to someone I'd eaten a hundred years ago."

Jack grimaced and Eodus's hand shook when he took the drink the serving boy handed to him.

The lights dimmed around the stage and the curtain went up to reveal Sabal, a brown-skinned woman in a bright, beautiful saree. With her hair done in an elaborate bun and decked-out in silver jewelry, Sabal caught the attention of everyone in the room. When her dance began, each movement was controlled and fluid, the red paint on her fingers and feet drawing in the gaze, the ringing of the bells on her ankles adding to the music.

"What's she doing?" Jack whispered, his eyes still on the dancer.

"It's a temple dance. She's a mahari from Puri. Or was, before...well, never mind, shhh."

Jack nodded, leaning forward in his seat, his drink forgotten.

Lucifer had not forgotten his drink. He drained it, as he did to all the replacements the serving boy brought him. After four he started to feel warm and he couldn't stop rolling his latest empty glass against his bottom lip. It was cool, smooth and he was warm.

Jack, when Sabal had finished her dance and the lights started to grow brighter, tugged on Lucifer's sleeve. "Where's Puri?"

"India."

"India? In the Orient?"

"That's the only India I've heard of."

Jack took his first sip of his drink all night. People milled around between acts but as soon as the lights dimmed again, everyone hushed.

The serving boy brought Eodus his second drink and refreshed Lucifer's again.

When the curtain came up again, half a dozen girls ran on the stage. Each one dressed in a leotard and stockings of a different color, they began to tumble and leap about the stage when a bright, lively tune began to play. When a few swinging trapeze bars descended from the rafters, Jack let out an audible gasp, covering his hand with his mouth.

He tugged on Eodus's sleeve that time, whispering, "*Look, aren't they beautiful?*" when the girls took to the air.

Eodus took the acrobat's hand and pressed it to his lips.

Lucifer, bizarrely, wished that Eodus would kiss his hand, too.

At the end of the entire show, Siobhan reappeared and Jack went right over to her, saying, "The trapeze..."

"What about it?" she prompted.

"Would you mind, I mean...could I give it a try?"

"Jack!" Eodus scolded.

Siobhan glanced at Lucifer, one corner of her mouth tipped up.

Lucifer waved a hand towards the stage. "Let him try it out."

"Please." Jack stepped towards Siobhan, his eyes wide and beguiling, his hands clasped together in a pleading gesture.

"Stop it, Jack, you're being rude," Eodus hissed.

"Eodus, you don't understand!"

Lucifer stood, wobbled, and then took Jack by the arm, pulling him toward the stage. A few stagehands were heading toward the trapeze and he said, "Hey, leave it," and when they gave him an odd look, he added, "Your Prince demands it."

They backed off and he gave Jack a nudge towards the trapeze. Jack hesitated for a second, but then wrapped his hands around the bar and pulled himself onto the trapeze. He grinned and kicked his legs like a child, but then a moment later he leaned back, hooking his legs around the bar so he could hang upside down. His shirt slipped down and covered his face and he laughed.

He righted himself and asked Lucifer, "Want to see me do a backflip?"

"Sure."

Jack tucked in his shirt, then began to pump his legs so the trapeze began to swing back and forth. When he was satisfied with the momentum, he swung back down so he hung upside down again. At the height of the trapeze's arc, he let go and did a backflip. He landed lightly, then took a bow, beaming all the while.

"Trapeze always goes on last, you know. You should hear the

people scream. They want to see us fall so bad!" he declared brightly.

"Did you?" Lucifer asked.

"Everyone falls." Jack stared back up at the trapeze bar, then took Eodus by the hand and pulled him over. He proceeded to goad the demon into coming up onto the trapeze with him.

While Jack coaxed his lover, Siobhan touched Lucifer's elbow. "I'd heard there was a human down here, didn't think you'd let anyone keep a pet."

"He's not a pet, he's...I don't know. He's going to kill Mylas for me."

"If you wanted him dead, Luci, you could have done it yourself."

Lucifer shook his head. "No. I couldn't. I...God, gutless thing that I am, I couldn't..." He rubbed his face. "Jack will do it and Eodus will keep him and they should be happy together." He trained his eyes on the pair, now perched on the swing together. Jack touched his head to Eodus's, both of them smiling. "Don't they look happy together?"

"Very," Siobhan agreed.

He put an arm around Siobhan's shoulders and pulled her close. "Was it my fault, Siobhan?"

She sighed. "It isn't anyone's fault. You *know* how Tabby is."

"I do. Is she happy...I mean, I know you see her still. I won't ask where she is or anything, but..."

"She's fine, Luci, she's happy and well," she assured.

He nodded. "Bill me for anything you want to bill me for. Tickets, drinks..."

"Maybe."

"I'm going."

She raised an eyebrow. "What about your friends?"

"Hire the acrobat."

She snorted.

He left, nothing else to say, not wanting to interrupt the moment that Jack and Eodus shared. He almost tripped when he stepped down from the doorstep into the street. He unsteadily made his way back to the palace. He was not that drunk, really, but he was somewhere far beyond tipsy.

At home, he did finally fall, tripping up the stairs, though only because he'd had to step around a cat and hadn't been able to reach the railing to balance himself.

Upstairs, someone stirred, either in reaction to his falling or the cat's yowling.

A candle appeared at the top of the stair. He righted himself and made it to the top without further incident to find Mercy standing there.

"Cat scared me half to death," she grumbled.

"Scared me, too, Mercy, dear."

"You smell of drink."

He leaned in close. "*You smell of drink,*" he mocked. "Say it like it is, Mercy, tell me I'm drunk."

She scowled and turned away from him.

He didn't want her to go. He didn't want to go back to an empty bed with only Marlow for company. He didn't necessarily want Mercy for a bedmate, either, but beggars couldn't be choosers.

He reached out and touched her shoulder.

She shrugged him off like a spider. "Less interest in bedding you drunk than when you're sober."

"What interest do you have in bedding me sober?"

"None."

He reached for her again and she stepped out of his reach. "Leave me be, Devil."

"No salt to throw over your shoulder?" He smiled but realized he was leering, so he fixed his face into a somber mask. "I don't want to go to bed."

"What?"

"I'm not trying to fuck you, I just want someone to stay and I...when I tease you, you look at me. When I'm nice, you ignore me. Have you read through the atlases yet?"

"It's the middle of the night."

"You're already awake!" he cried.

She shook her head and walked away, closing the door to her room. He heard the lock click as if that would stop him if he wanted to get in there.

He returned to his own room and Marlow pounced as soon as he lay down, ready to knead into him with her pinprick nails. She began to purr right away and he realized, as he stared into the darkness of his bedroom, how mawkish he'd been that night. Something was not right. He blamed his upcoming visit to Ambrose Weller's building for his mood.

Lucifer went to New York with two things on his agenda: meet with Ambrose Weller to cash in the favor he was owed and check in with Junius. He had a third item, which was to see his daughter, but he didn't admit that hope even to himself.

After he'd had Shiraz and Imogen send everything to the location she'd specified, he'd gotten no further letters from her. Of course, it could be that she hadn't had the time to write back. More likely, she wanted to play with him. He had taught her that much, at least, though he had meant his advice to be used when she took his throne, not against himself.

When Elisa had been born, he'd loved her instantly. He'd loved her, really, from the moment he'd known she was growing in her mother's belly. As a baby, she had screamed at all hours for any reason or sometimes no reason at all. As a toddler, she'd had tantrums of an intensity that reminded him of God when He'd decided to flood the Earth. When she had learned to talk, the tantrums had ceased, to be replaced with demands stated calmly and with an ultimatum.

If I can't have it, I won't eat and then I'll die.

If you won't let me, I'll throw myself out the window.

If I can't go, I'll hit my head against the wall until my brains come out.

He wondered which time had been the time when he'd finally given in too much. He'd hated to hear her cry, he hadn't known what to do to calm her tantrums, and he'd had nothing to prepare him for threats of suicide spoken in the sweet, babyish voice of a five-year-old with ribbons in her hair.

He had given in again and again until he had stopped giving in altogether. One day, something in him had simply broken. He had not cared anymore if she followed through with her threats. He had told her no and she had run out of the room, up to the highest tower in Hell and he hadn't followed her. He hadn't cared if she jumped or if she never came back.

She hadn't jumped, but she had come home hours later and hissed, "I hate you," at him for the first time.

He didn't know if his daughter had ever loved him. He didn't know if she loved anything or if his doting and weakness had robbed her of the ability to feel for others. He must have done something incredibly wrong because when she had been born, tiny and pink, she had been sweet. She had wrapped her hand around his finger and he had wanted to weep.

He let himself into the building, knowing Ambrose would be on the top floor in the penthouse he'd made for himself. He passed a crew in coveralls carrying paint buckets and rollers. No one offered to help him or asked him what he needed. They simply watched him walk by.

Ambrose turned around as soon as Lucifer walked in. After meeting so many times, the man seemed to have a sense of when the Devil was about.

He barely looked at Lucifer, though, and turned back to his newspaper a moment later. "So soon? Half of the tenants haven't even moved in yet."

"You sound bored, Ambrose."

The man corrected, "Hungover is more like it. Any time for last goodbyes?"

"I don't know. I'm not here to kill you." He entered further into the room and sat on the couch. He made himself comfortable, resting against the arm and putting one foot up.

"No?"

"No. I want a favor, not your soul."

"What could you need from me?" Ambrose asked.

"Something I don't want to do myself, that much should be clear. It has to do with my daughter." He hesitated. It felt wrong to think, let alone say aloud. "She has rented a room in your building."

"I'm aware. Elisa?"

He nodded. "Once she enters that room, you must never let her out."

Ambrose's eyebrows shot up. "What?"

"That room must be her prison. I'll work the magic but I need you for it."

"Why me?"

Lucifer explained, "Because you own this building and that's a gateway to an ancient magic, same as making deals or knowing a name. You and whoever owns this after you will be the key, in a literal sense, to that room."

"And why lock her away?"

Lucifer thought about lying, but knowing Ambrose, figured the truth would have a better effect. "Because she is worse than I am."

Ambrose studied his face for a moment, then set down the newspaper. "I don't suppose it matters to me either way, right? It's my part of the deal. She's moving in tomorrow morning."

"I know." He stood and held out his hand to Ambrose, who

frowned before he stood on his own. "Don't want to hold hands?"

Ambrose didn't answer.

They walked down to the suite on the third floor where his daughter would live. White sheets covered all the furniture, but he recognized the shapes of the ones he had sent.

Ambrose watched uncomfortably as Satan prowled the room, rolling up his sleeves as he examined the space. The human let out an audible gasp when Lucifer dug one of his fingernails into his forearm and sliced open his own flesh. He dabbed his fingers in the blood that welled to the surface and painted the necessary symbols to bind his daughter onto the walls and windows, the floors and ceiling.

He painted what was needed onto the door and then took Ambrose by the wrist, pulling him into the room and tracing a single symbol onto his forehead with his thumbnail, breaking the skin so their blood would mingle. The man went grayish-green and grew clammy, but he didn't faint.

"Won't she notice all the blood?" Ambrose croaked.

"Shh!"

The Devil closed his eyes, gathering his power and letting it build until he had what he needed. Quietly, in a tongue not meant for the ears of man, he cast his spell and the blood soaked into the walls and carpets, absorbed into the very fabric of the room so that it could not be undone.

Ambrose fell to his knees, his hands pressed to his forehead, and began to scream. He had witnessed magic not meant for the eyes of any mortal thing, something beyond the arcane magic worked by mages, the low spells and potions crafted by witches, or even the natural talents possessed by the descendants of any of the Fallen.

When the spell was done, Lucifer pulled Ambrose back to his feet and inspected his work. "She will not be able to leave the room without her skin on yours. Others can come and go, but she will be trapped. If you ever let her out, what you just experienced will be pleasant in comparison."

Ambrose nodded, eyes buggy.

Lucifer patted his cheek, escorted him from the room, and closed the door. "She'll be angry. It would be wise to keep others out of her reach for a while."

He nodded again.

"I'll stop by tomorrow."

Ambrose continued to nod and Lucifer wasn't sure if he'd understood anything he'd been told. He brought the man back to the penthouse, helped himself to a drink from the credenza and, once he was sure Ambrose hadn't been driven into gibbering suicidal madness, took his leave of the place.

The blue of the sky above grew dark as he walked to his next destination, an apartment building on the Lower East Side. It was not anywhere as nice as the Weller building, but Junius would need to live somewhere that no one would pay him attention, blue-skinned and horned as he was. Socialites would probably not take kindly to him, but he would be able to find work among the teeming masses of immigrants where women might, behind the backs of their husbands or fathers, slip him a few dollars for the right mix of herbs to keep a pregnancy at bay.

He hadn't gone to visit Junius since he'd put him in place as Watcher of Manhattan a few years past. He might not have visited him now if not to tell him that a dangerous thing indeed was taking up permanent residence in his borough.

He stood before a door he knew to be the right one and made himself take a breath before he knocked.

Junius pulled it open, dressed as a man of the times. He wore a white shirt tucked into dark trousers, with his suspenders hanging down. His sleeves were rolled to his elbows and his tie was half undone. He'd been working at something or maybe had been getting undressed.

He stared, wide-eyed, for a minute, before dropping to his knees and touching his forehead to the ground. A surprising amount of illumination came from within the apartment and Lucifer saw several orbs of light bobbing about.

"Rise, Junius."

The blue-skinned demon stood, his hair messy as ever, one lock caught in his horns. Lucifer reached out to fix it and though Junius allowed it, he didn't seem pleased.

"Did you need something?" the demon asked.

"You don't sound happy to see me."

"You're my king; how could I feel otherwise?"

Something didn't ring true in his voice and it bothered him that Junius was lying to him. He had never lied to him, not to weasel out of something or gain anything. "May I come in?"

Junius stepped back and opened the door wider. "Of course."

Lucifer looked around the apartment. Neat, with potted plants on every surface. On the couch sat a Chinese man, though at second glance, he could not be altogether Chinese, because his fangs and red eyes marked him as one of Lucifer's own descendants.

Junius nodded towards the man, who had a scar across his face and only one arm. "This is Wei."

Wei turned to scrutinize Lucifer, then, in a surprisingly English accent, said, "Oy, that's him, innit?"

"Yes."

Wei appraised the Devil and said, "Ain't he supposed t'be tall?"

"He changes size," Junius said and turned his eyes back to Lucifer. "You came for something, though, didn't you? What is it?"

"Since I've appointed you my Watcher, I thought you should know that Elisa is moving into a suite in the new Weller building."

Junius nodded.

"She won't be able to leave."

Junius's face showed his shock plainly. "Oh. Didn't think things were that bad between you two."

"It's not about us, it's about what she's been up to. It's...distinctly problematic, even from my point of view."

Junius shrugged. "You always pretended to be more brutal than you are."

Lucifer frowned; Junius always made him out to be sweeter, kinder than he was, even though he had watched the Devil rend people limb from limb, watched him shove dissenters down his gullet, and worse.

Junius noticed the Devil's frown. "It's not that I think you're decent, it's just that I think you're full of shit."

The Devil's mouth popped open and he could not think of a single thing to say. Junius had never, not in all their time on Earth, or in Hell or Heaven, said anything unkind to him. He stared, then remembered to close his mouth. "Junius..."

Junius shrugged. "Sorry, I'm just telling it how it is."

Lucifer thought of all the things that could have happened to put him in such a mood. He had not been close with Elisa, so it couldn't be resentment for her imprisonment. He had always liked to live in the country but had lived well enough in cities through the ages, so it couldn't be Manhattan. "Is something wrong?"

"Would you know if it was?"

Wei cleared his throat and walked out of the room, taking his jacket and heading out into the hallway.

Lucifer insisted, "If something's the matter, you've got to tell me."

"When was the last time you saw me?"

"When I made you Watcher."

"And before that?" June pressed.

"Um...I don't know, years ago. But I'm busy and you know Hell is always open to you if you want to come. You came to help...was it Siobhan? No, couldn't have been, she hasn't got any children..." Satan thought for a moment and the memory came back to him. "You helped Malketh with her twins."

Junius crossed his arms. "You don't even know."

"Know what?" He looked over the demon again, searching for something that could be different. His nose had been broken and healed a little crooked since the last time Lucifer had taken a good look at him, but that hardly seemed like something Junius would worry about. "Did someone die?"

"No. Well, I mean, *yes*, people have died, but that's not..." Junius sighed. The defiance had gone out of him with that sigh. He rubbed his eyes. "Never mind. Thank you for telling me about Elisa. I'll go visit, probably. She never hated me."

"What am I supposed to know?"

Junius shook his head. "Nothing."

He took in the circles under Junius's eyes, the way he hunched his shoulders; he'd lost weight, too, since the last time the Devil had laid eyes on him. "You're not sick, are you?"

"No, I'm not sick!"

"Please."

"I..." Junius rubbed his eyes again. "I realized that I don't mean as much to you as I thought I did. I thought..." He let out a harsh laugh. "I thought we were close."

"You mean the *world* to me. You are, of all the Fallen, the most faithful, the truest." Lucifer should have hesitated to answer; he shouldn't have been so open with his favoritism, especially when it would rankle the other Fallen.

"Then why didn't you help me!" Junius demanded. "I prayed for years and years, but you never came."

"I didn't...I never heard a thing." There were many prayers that he ignored, but never one from Junius.

"And you didn't ever wonder where I was for *decades?*"

"I..." He hadn't wondered, even once. "Where were you?"

Junius shook his head. "It doesn't matter."

He knew Junius wouldn't tell him; he might have been angry but he wasn't the sort who liked to detail his own woes. He held out his hand, palm up. "Let me see."

Junius shook his head, then looked at the Devil's hand. With a sigh, he placed his hand in Lucifer's. Unlike most people, Junius never pulled back when he felt the Devil inside his mind. His consciousness nestled against the Devil's the same way that he leaned into Lucifer's arms.

When Lucifer learned of what had happened to Junius, of his imprisonment and the things he'd been forced to. do, he understood why Junius would think the Devil didn't care.

"I should have known."

Junius sniffled and wrapped his arms around Lucifer's waist, pressing his face against his chest. "I'm glad you didn't."

"Why?"

"Because it means you weren't ignoring me."

Lucifer kissed his hair and skated his fingers along one of Junius's horns, pale gray and curved like a ram's. "You do mean the world to me, Junius, I'm sorry I've let you forget that."

"No, I..." He sighed and tightened his arms around the Devil. "I miss you. I know you have so much to do, but...I don't know. I feel like..."

"What?"

Junius pulled back and shook his head. He ran a hand through his hair and a few strands got stuck on his horns. "It sounds so petty but...it feels like you've been staying away on purpose lately."

Lucifer shifted uneasily, his gaze skating around the room, taking in all the potted plants. "I have been."

"Why?"

"Because you remind me of how I was."

"I liked you the way you were!" the demon insisted.

"I know. But I can't be the Devil if you're there making me wish..." He didn't have it in him to name his desire. "I will bring us home someday. It wasn't an empty promise."

Junius looked at his feet.

Lucifer wanted to touch his face, to cradle the back of Junius's head in his hand and touch his forehead to his own. He wanted to tell him that he belonged in Heaven still, that he shouldn't have been stupid enough to fall in with an idiotic bunch of rabble-rousers. Junius had loved him in Heaven and had not needed to be cast out when he'd seen Satan fall. He'd gone willingly after him and had gotten nothing in return.

"It won't be the same after being away so long." Junius pressed a hand to his own chest. "This body...you know, it's so different to have one. Even having feelings is different in a body. You hear the word 'heartache' and you think that humans must be such a dramatic bunch of crybabies..."

"Until you have a heart."

Junius nodded. "Do you have to go soon?"

Bound to Hell as he was, Lucifer had never been able to stay on Earth for more than a few days. The currents that bound all things always pulled him back, whether he wanted to go or not. "I've only been here for a few hours."

Junius glanced toward him and straightened his posture a little. "I'm not asking you to stay. I don't want you to go thinking I'm love-struck or anything."

"What?"

"All that about missing you, liking you the way you were, I don't want you to get the impression I've got all these secret feelings about you," Junius clarified.

"Of course."

"It wouldn't work, the two of us."

"No, of course not," Lucifer agreed.

They stood together quietly for what couldn't have been more than half a minute.

"Are you seeing anyone?" Lucifer asked.

Junius shrugged. "Not really. Not really looking to, either, right now. You?"

"There's, well...hmm. I don't think so."

"You don't *think* so? There's a story there. I'd listen if you'd tell it to me. Do you want a drink?"

He found himself nodding before he'd really thought the offer through. At Junius's urging, he sat at the small, rather wobbly kitchen table and accepted the glass set in front of him.

Junius put in some ice chips and covered them with vodka. "I hope you like vodka, it's all I've got to drink. The Russians almost exclusively pay in vodka."

"It's fine."

"Wei makes a great sloe gin fizz...I mean, if we had all the ingredients. But you were saying about not thinking you're seeing anyone?"

Lucifer sipped his drink. "There's...well, there's this woman who tried to kill me but we slept together on a very strange whim."

Junius raised his eyebrows. "Do you mind if I smoke?" he asked and once Lucifer had given a shake of his head, he prompted, "Uh, and you have feelings for her?"

"No, it's just an interesting footnote."

"And...?" Junius plucked a cigarette from its pack and lit a match, taking a drag, but keeping his eyes on Lucifer. "You don't smoke, do you?"

"No."

Junius waved his hand to indicate he should continue his story.

"And there's this couple, a human and one of the Hell-born...no, don't look at me like that, I'm not with them either—"

"You know I don't judge people's relationship dynamics."

"No, I know. But it's not about them, it's about what they have. And what I don't." Although Junius said nothing, only took a sip of his drink and a drag on his cigarette, Lucifer felt compelled to add, "It sounds maudlin, I know."

"No, not to me."

"But you were always so tender-hearted, love. They're young, or, well, Eodus is young for a demon, and not as rough as the usual lot."

"The Hell-born *do* tend to be a little tamer than the ones you made." He tapped his cigarette over a dirty plate that must have been left over from dinner.

With a guilty grin, Lucifer said, "Well, you remember my wild days. And so many years have gone by! The viciousness gets bred out after a while. They're sweet together, the two of them. Is it so bad of me to envy that?"

"You want to be sweet and young?"

Lucifer shrugged. He didn't know what he wanted.

"You haven't been looking for her, have you?" Bringing his glass to his lips, Junius sipped, then made a face at the vodka.

"I'm not nearly stupid enough to go looking for Tabby when she doesn't want to be found."

Without making eye contact, Junius took another sip. He stared into his glass. "Do you want her to come back?"

"I don't know. Sometimes I miss her, sometimes I'm glad she's gone. She wasn't always easy to be around. She was..." He searched for the right word. "I don't know. I loved her, though."

Junius touched his cigarette to his lips, breathing in deep. He seemed to consider his words carefully and spoke them without making eye contact. "She hurt you."

"Only because I liked it."

Junius pressed his lips into a thin line and said nothing. He finished the last of his vodka and filled his glass again. He swirled the glass, the ice chips tinkling, and tapped his claws against the side, the movement abrupt, impatient. "So will you ever tell me about this person you don't think you're seeing?"

"He works in one of the brothels in the Ninth. I don't see him much but..."

"But you like him."

He nodded.

"And you think about him."

"Yes."

"But...?" Junius prompted.

"But I'm just someone who pays for his time."

"You're more than some customer."

With a scoff and a roll of his eyes, Lucifer said, "Sure, Prince of Darkness and all that."

"You're the King of Hell."

Lucifer made a face. "I hate that word, just the sound of it."

"You're *my* king."

"Then for you, I will be a king."

Junius grinned. "And what will you be for your friend in the brothel?"

Lucifer shrugged. "I don't know. A client, nothing more. Probably."

With a sigh, Junius took a final drag on his cigarette, stubbed it out, and lit a new one right away. He sipped his vodka again and Lucifer watched him, taking in the motion of his hands, the dangle of his wrist as he smoked, his tenuous grip on his glass. It hung from his fingers as if it might fall.

"What?" Junius must have felt the Devil's eyes on him.

Smoking looks good on you, he wanted to say, transfixed by the way he brought his fingers to and from his lips, the way his tongue would touch the rim of his glass when he drank. There had always been something about Junius that was not like most men, not something strictly feminine, but markedly different from others. "You're still chewing your nails."

Junius laughed. "Bad habit. I've got plenty of those, I guess."

"How's the fertility business here?"

With an ambiguous movement of his head, Junius said, "Good, if I can convince people I'm not working for the corruption of their immortal souls." He took a drag. "Actually, I guess my business is more infertility these days. Working in the garment factories doesn't pay much so fewer mouths can be better sometimes."

"And what about that other man? Wei, I think?"

"Oh, he lives here. Comes and goes a lot. I think he might be...I don't know, I think he's involved with some gang or another, always has women hanging around. But he seems decent, you know, nice to everyone that comes by to see him."

Lucifer nodded.

"He, uh, actually, a fair amount of the women who come to see me come because he gave them my name. Especially the younger ones."

"Ah."

"But I'm not here to tell people what they should do. I've got no moral high ground, anyway. I'm just lucky Wei doesn't give me a hard time...God, what are they calling us now? Sexual perverts? Sodomites? Homosexuals?" Junius took a drag on his cigarette, a sip of his drink, and ran his hand through his hair. "Whatever it is, they've got laws against it. Nonsense."

Lucifer couldn't believe what he'd heard. "Just lucky?"

Junius shrugged. "Humans are..."

"Small-minded and putrid," Lucifer finished for him.

"Harsher than what I was thinking of."

"Junius, you were handmade by God to be exactly as you are, in every way."

"Did He make me a chain-smoker, too?" the demon asked as he stubbed out his cigarette.

"Don't let these horrible human *things* make you feel bad."

Nails clinking against the glass, Junius explained, "It isn't that I feel bad. It's just...exhausting. To worry all the time, to hide." He knocked back the last of his drink. "To feel bad about hiding." He rubbed his eyes. "But I keep getting arrested and I don't like that at all."

Lucifer reached out and put his hand over Junius's, the one in which he'd been holding his cigarette. "We do what we must to survive."

"Do you want another drink?"

As Lucifer contemplated the choice, the door opened. Wei stepped into the apartment and glanced at the two seated at the table. "Y'tellim?" he asked and Lucifer could not quite make out what the man had been trying to say.

"Very interesting fact, Junius, in England there is a man currently writing a play called *Pygmalion*. I suggest you take in a show when it comes to stage."

"Sure, I'll make a point of it," Junius said, seeming a little put-off by the Devil's change in topic. "Drink?"

"No, thank you. I should get home."

"Are you sure?"

Leaning back from the table, Lucifer nodded. He didn't want to go. "I told Ambrose I would stop by tomorrow."

"Stay the night."

"No, I don't want to intrude."

"You are my king. All that I have is yours," Junius insisted.

Wei let out an odd snorting giggle, but shook his hand and walked away, muttering that he was sorry. He went into one of the bedrooms.

Quietly, June told him, "And I know you hate going through the in-between place."

The thought of the crawling feeling the threads left in his head and on his skin was enough to make him want to stay the night on Earth.

The offer to stay with Junius for the night tempted him as well.

"Maybe one more drink." He pushed his glass towards Junius. When it was filled, he took a sip and made a note to send Junius something nice to drink. He mulled over what he had seen in Junius's memories of his imprisonment. "He was a mage, right? The one that had you."

"Reinhart? Yes. A powerful one too. Had these books all about, well, us. Magic for creatures like us."

Lucifer nodded. He'd imagined as much, recalled the books and what the Reinharts had done to get them. "He must have warded you. Hid you from me. Reinharts are a slippery bunch, I don't recommend them."

"How did you think they'd turn out with you doing all that meddling?"

Lucifer took a drink instead of answering. He had always found himself drawn to members of that family, no matter how often he said he was done with them. Generations of deals and assorted romantic entanglements with the Devil had left its mark on the family, no doubt spurred by the mental infirmity that lurked within their genes. But the family was exactly his sort of crazy. Morose, brooding, self-loathing, prone to paranoia and dark thoughts, never quite in touch with reality.

"Oh, most of them are generally harmless to anyone but themselves. It's just that the really bad ones get remembered."

The set of Junius's mouth said that he did not agree with his king. Instead of arguing, he lit another cigarette.

"How has Manhattan been?" Lucifer asked.

"Quiet. There's a fairy, three vampires and a handful of ghosts that don't do anything more than wander through walls. A few mages and witches."

"Things will change."

"They always do," Junius agreed.

Lucifer yawned into his elbow. Neither of them said much after that. They finished their drinks and Junius didn't light another of his cigarettes. He tapped on the table then chewed his lip for a moment. "So. Do you want to stay?"

"Yes."

"Bedroom's over here." Junius stood and gestured for Lucifer to follow him.

They settled easily into bed together, their path to sleep aided by what they had imbibed earlier.

"You aren't upset with me, are you?" Lucifer asked once Junius had nestled against his chest.

"No."

"I would have come for you if I'd known."

Junius confessed, "I used to imagine you coming and ripping them all to pieces for me."

"I would have done so much worse than that," Lucifer promised. He pressed a kiss to the top of Junius's head. "I'll do better."

Junius slipped an arm around the Devil's waist and with that gesture, Lucifer felt his chest tighten. "I forgive you," Junius murmured into his chest.

In the morning, shortly after Lucifer had woken up, Junius turned on his side, facing toward him. He put one arm under his pillow, nestled cozily beneath his blankets. "What's his name?"

"Who?"

"The one from the brothel," Junius clarified.

"Oh. Ira."

"And the woman?"

"Mercy."

"Do you mind if I do something?"

"No." Lucifer would not have minded anything Junius could have done to him.

Junius took his arm from beneath the blankets and placed the back of his hand on Lucifer's forehead as if he was checking for a fever. Lucifer felt little tendrils of Junius's magic trailing over him, warm and calm.

He removed his hand and asked, sounding rather surprised, "She's human?"

"Why?"

"I can send you home with the right herbs to take care of things if you want."

"Take care of what things?" Lucifer asked, feeling dense.

"When was the last time you slept with a human woman?"

"I don't know, a few hundred years ago. As I rule, I try not to..." Lucifer struggled to remember why it was he avoided human women. There had been a reason ingrained enough that it had become a habit, though it had nothing to do with their gender or race.

"Because..." Junius prompted.

He sat up to think. "Because they..."

"Because *you*..."

The reason came back to him with a sudden and unwelcome clarity. "Because I always get them pregnant."

"Remember when you came to visit me and Kavi?" Junius asked. "And you got half the village women with child while you stayed with us?"

Lucifer flopped back down onto the bed and into the pillow, groaned, "Fuck."

"Herbs, then?"

"No. I don't know. She's a Moralist, I don't know what she'll want to do." He let out a heavy sigh. "Shit."

"There's always the chance it didn't take. What compelled you to fuck a Moralist? They're worse than Puritans."

She reminded me of Tabby, he almost confessed, but instead asked, "What chance?"

"One in ten."

"That can't be right. That it *didn't* take?"

Junius shrugged. "Angels and humans are uncommonly fertile together. I don't know what to say except that most of us are smart enough take precautions."

"Oh, what do you have to worry about? You only sleep with men."

"It's a lifestyle I recommend," Junius said with a grin.

"Will you do me a favor?"

Junius promised, "Anything."

"Will you go to Ambrose later today and check in on things?"

"Yes, but why?"

"Because I thought I had it in me to see Elisa but now..." Lucifer trailed off.

"Dramatic, as always. Yes, I'll go."

Lucifer stood and glanced around. He had brought nothing with him but had the sense that he'd forgotten something. "I, uh, I've got to go."

Still nestled beneath the covers, Junius said, "Don't be such a stranger."

It made Lucifer never want to leave.

He nodded in response, not sure he would find any acceptable words for the situation, then took a breath. His shoulders tightened and he had to make an effort to relax. He reached into the nothing-and-everything between worlds and brought himself back to Hell.

He found himself, foggy-minded and ears ringing, in his bedroom. Marlow leaped off the bed and tried to claw her way up his leg. He scooped her up, let her rub her face on his for a moment, then returned her to the floor.

He made his way to Imogen's office. "Where's Mercy?"

"You smell like tobacco."

"If I had a mother, you would sound like her. Where's Mercy?"

"I don't know. Probably in your study with those atlases, like she has been since you had Shiraz bring them over."

"How long has she been here?" he asked.

"Since Halloween."

He sighed. "No, I mean, months, days, what?"

Imogen examined one of the several calendars on her desk.

"Um. On Earth above, it's January fifteenth. So...two and a half months for her timeline, about three in ours. Whatever that means for her, I'm not sure."

He nodded and walked away. The passage of time had never sat quite right with him; in Heaven, there was no time, it was all the time and never there. Hell had its own timekeepers; they were demons carefully crafted to do their job, with an understanding far beyond his own.

At the table in his study, Mercy sat with one of the atlases open in front of her. The illustration showed a pleasant meadow near the Swiss Alps.

"Didn't Shiraz show you how to work the pictures?"

Mercy turned and looked at him. With her tight bun and one of her usual boring dresses, Lucifer wasn't sure how she had ever reminded him of his wife. "Magic isn't something I meddle with."

He leaned in and touched the picture, running his finger over the string of runes below, murmuring their names. The illustration floated off the page and he cast it into the room so that it spread out behind them.

The enchantment would bring them into an approximation of the view that had been captured in the illustration. It wouldn't be possible to walk more than a few yards, but the smells and sounds, the warmth of the sun and caress of the wind, would feel real enough.

"Come on." He held out his hand to her.

She didn't take it.

"Mercy, really." He put a hand on her arm and coaxed her out of the chair. She didn't resist, nor did she really give in; he led her into the illustration. "A little magic never really hurt anyone." He released her arm.

They stood together in the meadow, a breeze bringing the smell of flowers and the sound of happy, fat bees.

"Do you smell that?" he asked. "It's rained. Probably just a shower."

She regarded him briefly.

"Do you know how long you've been here?"

"Less than a month, I think," she replied.

"Two and a half, as time goes on Earth, and more than three as time flows here. More than enough time for a human to spend here."

She gazed out over the meadow, took a few steps forward.

"Kicking me out?"

He looked down at the grass and found himself wanting to sit down. "Mercy, you and your husband, do you have children?"

"Not for lack of trying." She played with her skirt. "Webster...his first wife left him because of it."

"But you wanted them?"

She nodded.

"What about him?"

"It tore him up not being able to."

"Is he clever?" he asked.

"Why?"

"Go back to your husband, Mercy, tell him something miraculous happened. Tell him you're with child, tell him that it's his."

She crossed her arms and turned to face him. "What good would that do? He'd just think it's Reg's."

"And let him think that."

"A demon isn't a child. Besides, I'm *not* with child, he'd know that soon enough."

He knelt and picked a cluster of pale blue flowers. He brought it to his nose and found that it smelled as real as anything that grew on Earth. "We did have a rather interesting time together in the dungeon."

She scoffed. "You've got a high opinion of yourself."

For a moment, he thought she meant that their time had not been interesting. "There's always a chance." He handed her the flower.

She took it, rolled the stem between her fingers, then dropped it. "Webster wouldn't raise a child with unnatural blood, even one more dilute than Reg."

"Would you?" he asked, then backpedaled. "Not that I care! I mean, it's not my business if you would or wouldn't."

She nudged the flower with the toe of her boot. "I wouldn't."

"Did Reg know that?" he asked before he could help himself.

She walked away from him, out of the illustration. He remained a little longer, but followed her out and returned the enchantment to the atlas.

She had taken a seat at the table again.

"Reg wasn't like you," she said.

"You can say that with confidence? You've known me for hardly any time at all. And for how long, really, did you know him?

Less than a year, I'd bet."

Mercy closed the atlas. "I won't."

"I've got a man for that, then, if you want. Better to get it done before your belly starts to swell. It's worse the longer you wait."

She played with the ribbon that marked her page in the book, running her fingertip along the frayed edge. "You've done everything to me I ever feared you would."

"And I didn't even have to try that hard to do it. Imagine what I could accomplish if I applied myself." He reached over and with a small bit of heat, melted the end of the ribbon to stop it from unraveling more. "I'll have my man come down."

She shook her head. "No, I won't do that either."

Baffled, he sat beside her at the table. "You're sort of between a rock and a hard place on that one, then, Mercy."

She wrapped her arms around herself; her whole body shuddered and a wracking cry escaped her throat. It wasn't weeping or crying, but the type of deep belly sobbing that hurt all over. Lucifer watched for a moment, unsure what to do.

Between her sobs, she managed to ask, "What have you done to me?"

"Mercy, come now, it's not that bad."

He put his hand over hers and patted her back. The gesture angered her, which he had worried it might, though he hadn't expected her to lash out at him, her palm connecting with his face. He recoiled with his hand to his cheek.

She continued her wracking sobs and he watched, not sure that he should leave her alone. Her face became bright red and he grew increasingly worried.

"Mercy, dear, come on..."

He could think of nothing to say. Well versed in torment and manipulation, he had little practice with comforting the distraught. He scooted his chair closer and hesitated to touch her again. She was not his friend or relative, they were by no means close. Without friends or family to go back to, she stood alone in his world and in hers.

His hand hovered near her back. Not knowing what else to do, he went to his knees before her chair and put his hands over hers. She had her fists wound into her skirt and he could only think how much he hated her dresses.

"Tell me what to do, Mercy, and I'll do it."

"Get away from me."

He moved away, standing, and taking a few steps back. He didn't know where to go or if he should leave her alone. He reached into the underneath and pulled Junius through.

The demon arrived, cigarette in hand, and looked around. He laid eyes on Lucifer, then saw the woman. He shook his head, then tucked his cigarette safely between his lips so that he could kneel, touching his head to the carpet.

"Rise."

Junius rose and walked right over to the woman. He crouched in front of her. "You must be Mercy. What's this terrible monster done to you?"

She heaved a sob.

"Oh, love, can you look at me?" Junius implored gently.

She tightened her arms around herself but looked up at Junius. That was all he needed. Despite the horns and claws, the blue skin and the fangs, people, particularly parents and parents-to-be, trusted him.

"I'm here to help."

She shook her head. "You can't help me."

"I can help you calm down. Come on, we'll find the kitchen, I'll make you something to drink." He offered his hand to her and she took it.

"I don't traffic with your sort."

Junius smiled and led her out of the room.

Not for the first time, Lucifer wondered if he had ruined someone's life, but the thought came without the usual detachment or mild satisfaction. He sat at the table, pulled the atlas over closer.

Imogen found him like that, he didn't know how much later. "She's stopped crying."

He didn't take his eyes from the atlas. "I can hear that."

The vampire sat beside him, in the chair where Mercy had sat. "How could you *forget* that you can get people pregnant?"

He glanced over.

"Every other monster in this place has contraceptive charms or prophylactic tattoos and I mean, Christ, even on Earth we know enough to pull out."

He thought back to his time with Mercy and imagined, odd and lustful as their encounter had been, how much odder it would have been to pull out. He giggled.

"What?"

"I would have probably dropped her."

Imogen shook her head.

"Besides, pulling out doesn't work."

"Works better than nothing. Why'd you fuck her in the first place?"

He shrugged. "Don't you ever do something just because?"

She answered, "No," and he didn't doubt it. She glanced at the page of the atlas at which he had been looking. "I came to give you this."

He took the folded piece of paper she offered him; he flipped it over to see Siobhan's seal. The letter, once he'd broken the seal, told him that she'd taken his advice to hire Jack. She'd invited him to come take in a show.

It wouldn't be right, he thought, to go see a show with Mercy so distraught and all because of him.

"Do you think she hates me?" he asked Imogen.

"She tried to kill you," the vampire answered helpfully.

"Do you think she'll ever hate me less?"

"She fucked you," she said and he began to suspect that she knew how unhelpful that answer was.

He closed the atlas. "You're miserable at this."

"At what? You don't trust me, what counsel can I give?"

"Pretend I trust you, then, what would you say?" he asked.

"I'd ask what you even intend with this woman. I mean, she's been your assailant, your prisoner, your houseguest. You wanted to know how she got here, now you know. You wanted her gone, but she's still here. Who is she to you, what do you want her to be to you?"

His fingers, without his permission, played with the ribbon bookmark. He could not stop them from touching the melted end over and over. The ribbon was not original to the book. When the atlas had been made, this type of fabric hadn't existed yet. He'd brought it back from some trip or other, not on purpose. It had ended up in his pocket somehow; Mercy must have found it in his study.

How could he remember that this synthetic fiber would melt with applied heat but not know his own intentions for Mercy?

"I lied, take it back, I don't want to pretend I trust you."

"As you wish, Your Highness."

"They're in the kitchen, right?" he asked, but left without getting an answer. They would be in the kitchen. Junius always gravitated toward kitchens.

Instead of going in, he lurked outside the door, not eavesdropping, but feeling that his presence would be unwelcome.

"If you think I don't know you're there," Junius called.

He stepped into the kitchen. Mercy had a mug gripped in both hands and her face was less red than it had been, but she had tear streaks down her cheeks. "Can I sit?"

With a wave of his clawed hand, Junius invited him to sit. Mercy didn't look at him. Lucifer glanced at Junius and asked, "Any, um, progress?"

"No. But we've calmed down," Junius shared.

"*I've* calmed down, you mean," Mercy said, eyes fixed on the tea in her mug. "I don't want to talk to you."

Lucifer didn't really want to talk to her either. He wanted this whole thing to go away. He wanted, more than anything, to send her back to Earth where she belonged. "You don't have to."

Junius advised, "You two should come to some kind of decision."

"It is an impossible choice," Mercy pronounced.

The Devil, unable to help himself, snorted at her distress.

She glared at him. "How dare you mock—"

"How dare I? What about how dare you? I understand the hesitation to end a life, especially one that grows inside you. I understand if you don't have any desire to bear a child and it is your choice either way. What I cannot understand is how you can condemn a thing before it is born because of its blood."

Her grip tightened on her mug.

"I mean, she is pregnant, isn't she?" he asked, looking at Junius. "This isn't all some overwrought hypothetical?"

Junius nodded. "She is."

"So Mercy, end it or don't, take what time you need to make your choice, but for Christ's sake, get over yourself."

She threw the mug at him but missed by a broad margin. He felt her aim should have been better, considering her ability to fight, but it wasn't a fair judgment.

They sat silently, with her glaring and his guts starting to twist.

Junius searched himself and swore when he didn't find his pack of cigarettes.

Lucifer handed him a cigarette and Junius took it with a flirty smile. "Did you conjure that just for me?"

"The world for you, Junius."

Junius lit his cigarette. "I guess, Mercy, I mean...I'm not a therapist or a philosopher but we have to examine the source of this impasse. Not between the two of you, but in yourself."

Again, Mercy said, "It's impossible."

"I could kill you, how would that be for a solution?" Lucifer offered.

Junius shushed him. "Ignore him. Now, with your unfortunate cult association, you believe that we unholy things are evil by nature, yes?"

She nodded.

"But not with such conviction that she won't bed us," the Devil pointed out.

Junius gave Lucifer a look. Mercy tried his patience as much as she tried Lucifer's and it showed in the set of his shoulders, the tightness with which he gripped his cigarette. "You pulled me here. If you don't want help, send me back."

"I'm sorry, but I haven't got the patience for this." Lucifer stood and as he turned to leave, he stepped on a shard of the mug she had thrown. It cracked beneath his shoe. This couldn't continue. *He* couldn't continue.

Every so often, something would come to interrupt the ennui of his days. It would remind him of the place his father had carved for him in the world.

His throat closed somewhat, the way it did right before he was going to throw up and his body was trying to fight it. The world seemed a little less firm than it had before. This was his place and he could not leave. He would never leave, no matter how much he schemed to get out, to bring his Fallen back to Heaven. Even when his heir sat the serpent's throne and ruled Hell, Lucifer would have no place in Heaven or on Earth.

He had the impression that Junius was talking to him, that he might have touched him. "I just needed help."

"You're alright."

"No," the Devil whispered.

"You are. You're alright. Come sit."

He shook his head, then squeezed his eyes shut. With a few deep breaths, he pulled himself back to reality for a while longer. He pulled his hand back from Junius's grip. "No, I'm fine."

"You sure?"

"Yes."

Not appearing reassured, Junius stepped back.

Lucifer bent and picked up the pieces of the mug, gathering

them all down to the smallest sliver, then mopped up the spilled tea. He abandoned the rag and the shards in the sink, not sure what else to do. He took a few steps toward the exit, then paused in front of the table. He leaned in, resting his hands on the wood, a table so old the ghostwood had darkened from gray to black.

"Mercy, I'm sorry, I haven't been fair."

She retreated somewhat, leaning back in her chair and letting her hands slide from the table to her lap. "What?"

"It's a hard choice. I'm sorry I contributed to your predicament. Old as I am, I should know better."

Mercy looked at Junius, pine green eyes meeting his sea glass ones. Two pairs of green eyes, least common of all the colors in the world, and Lucifer had two pairs here with him.

"If you want my opinion, I think you should go to your husband, pretend to have a life with him. If you pretend long enough, it starts to feel real," Lucifer shared.

"Webster knows a demon when he sees one," she said.

"He knows them even in the cradle?"

She gave a shake of her head, little wisps of pale blond hair swaying, having escaped from her bun. "Demons don't act right, they're *different*. You can tell."

With a glance at Junius, who had gone quiet, he asked, "Junius, is that true? Even newborn?"

The Fallen gave a shrug. "Babies are babies. They cry, eat, sleep, mess their diapers. And demons don't really start to be...odd for a while. Their baby teeth aren't even sharp."

Leaning in began to feel overbearing and Mercy still sat as far back in her chair as she could; he sat and placed his hands close to himself.

She relaxed marginally. "Put a thing with red eyes among my family and it will meet one end."

Her answer gave him hope. She had stopped flat out refusing to consider either side of the issue. "Head bashed so hard you can see brains? Burned on the pyre?"

"I haven't seen it go any other way," Mercy confirmed.

About a dozen questions bubbled in his mind. "Would Webster leave to be with you?"

"No."

The flatness of her answer made him reconsider that she should go back to her husband. "I could get you a new husband. I have a handful of favors to call in with decent but foolhardy men.

Or a nanny, it doesn't have to be a husband. But babies are a lot of work, it's easier with two."

"I never said—"

He cut her off to say, "I'm only trying to let you know that you won't have to do this on your own. I will take whatever amount of responsibility you want me to take, within my ability to do so."

"What if I wanted you to bear the thing instead and leave me free to cavort around, doing as I pleased?" she asked.

Lucifer turned at Junius, who shook his head emphatically. "No, don't ask me to try that. It's beyond my ken, dangerous for everyone involved. I won't do it."

Rarely had Junius refused him anything, so for him to draw a line here told Lucifer that he shouldn't push the issue any further. Not knowing what else to say, Lucifer looked at his hands. Words pressed at his lips, dying to be heard, and heard by Mercy most of all.

"They're bad because of me, you know. Not because they've inherited any sort of ill nature from me, but because of what the world does to them on account of them being mine." He pressed the tips of his fingers together to keep them quiet. He pressed so hard he could feel it through his arms, up to his chest. "Your whole life people expect the worst of you. How long before you give it to them? Does it take you till you're thirty, twenty, ten?"

"What's your point?" she asked.

"What if someone loved you, expected good things? It's happened, there are more than a few of mine who grew to be...normal enough."

"And what hand do you have in any of that?" Mercy asked.

"I'll bring you to meet the daughter I raised someday and you can tell me why I keep my distance," he told her.

Out of the corner of his eye, he saw Junius catch Mercy's eye and shake his head, mouthing the word 'dramatic.'

She started to smile but suppressed it.

"Think, Mercy. Sleep on it. I didn't mean to pressure you all at once. I'm sorry." He stood. "I've got to go. I mean, I don't *have to* but I need to. Want to. Junius, should I send you home?"

The demon shook his head and said, "Just give me the strings, I'll go when I'm ready."

Lucifer nodded and gathered what Junius would need, tethering them to the Fallen's wrist. "Be careful."

He left the two of them in the kitchen and heard Junius

offering to make Mercy another cup of tea if she promised not to throw it this time.

The Trade House rang with more laughter than it should have, bustling though the morning had not yet ended. A glance showed that Ira was not on the floor. He approached Nial's desk and asked, "Ira's still working days, right?"

"That one is booked for most of the day."

Lucifer couldn't check his expression quick enough. He hadn't imagined having to compete for Ira's time.

Nial noted his expression. "Of course, if Your Highness is displeased, things could be rearranged."

"When's he free next?"

"His lunch is coming up. I'm sure he would be amenable to seeing our Prince."

The offer wasn't what he'd expected, but he took it. "Please."

Nial nodded. "Would you like to see anyone else while you wait?"

"No. I can just...sit, right?"

"You may do as you please," they informed him.

After paying, Lucifer selected an armchair in the corner and settled in, wondering how many fluids had soaked into the fabric. The smell of herbs comforted him more than it should have. He watched the people come and go, braiding his hair with little interest in his surroundings. When he saw Ira emerge from behind the curtain back into the main room, he nearly leaped out of his chair.

He made himself move more slowly and watched as Nial approached the demon and said something to him. Ira's shoulders sagged and he turned to look where Nial gestured.

Lucifer approached and Nial returned to his desk.

"It's my lunch," Ira said, his voice small and flat.

"So we'll eat."

Seeming on the verge of tears, Ira nodded, putting his hand on the curtain, ready to bring Lucifer to one of the rooms.

"Where's the kitchen?" Lucifer asked.

"Uh." Ira took his hand back and turned his body away from the hall, taking half a step.

"Go on, I'll follow," Lucifer prompted.

Ira led him past Nial's desk to a door with acknowledgment but no protest from the bookkeeper. Past the door, he found a hallway lined with doors, as the one behind the curtain was. Halfway down the hall they turned left to enter a small kitchen with an austere ghostwood table and half a dozen chairs around it. An apron-clad demon by the stove gave Ira and Lucifer a hard look.

"I just want my lunch, Koal," Ira said.

"Does Nial know—"

"Nial knows everything."

Koal, brow still furrowed, handed Ira a hunk of dark bread and a tin cup of water. Ira headed out of the kitchen but paused to glance at Lucifer. "Do you mind? I was going to eat in my room."

"Whatever you want."

Back in the hall, they walked down a little farther. Ira pushed open a door to reveal a room the same size as the ones in which customers were seen, but instead of a bed, there were three cots and a hammock.

Ira sat on one of the cots, tucking one leg beneath himself, letting the other hang off the side. "You can sit wherever you want."

Lucifer chose to sit on the floor beside the cot. Ira ate, ripping the bread into little pieces, chewing and washing down each bite with a sip of water. He did this without vigor; every so often he would rub his eyes or yawn. He said nothing.

"Up late last night?" Lucifer asked.

"We've just been busy lately."

"Nial mentioned you were booked."

"You'd be surprised how bad people want to fuck something just because *you* fucked it. You've made us fashionable, at least for a little while."

"And your mistress wants to capitalize on that."

He nodded.

"I...Ira, I didn't come here to impose."

"I'm a whore, you can't impose," Ira told him.

"I'm taking up your lunch, that's got to count as an imposition. It's...I'll go, of course, if you want, I just..." Lucifer didn't know what to say.

Ira waited, stifling a yawn in his elbow.

"I wanted to see you, that's all. I didn't want you to think I wasn't coming back. I promised, after all."

Ira nodded, his mouth going tight. He drew in a shaky breath, emptied his tin cup, and set it on the table. "Sure."

"Would you mind if I came to sit next to you?"

Ira shook his head. "Whatever you like."

Lucifer came to sit beside him, but as soon as he did, Ira's whole body seemed to go slack, as if he'd let out a deep breath or gotten unwelcome news. On instinct, Lucifer wound his arms around the smaller man. "I didn't come to sleep with you."

"I'm sorry. You can."

"No, I don't want to, I just...I wanted to see you, that's all."

Ira leaned in, resting his head against Lucifer's chest, tucking his arms close to his own body.

"You have appointments for the rest of the day?" the Devil asked.

"Yes."

"And all day tomorrow?"

"Yes."

"You shouldn't stay here, Ira."

"Where would I go?" the demon asked. "So many places are worse and I'm not good enough to work somewhere nice."

"You're the one I come to see. Take that to any other brothel in the Ninth and it will be enough."

He shook his head. "No, I can't leave."

Lucifer tightened his arms. "Do you mind if I stay?"

"No."

Ira yawned again and Lucifer scooted back, leaning against the wall and stretching out his legs across the cot. As soon as he'd settled, Ira nestled against him. He smelled of the usual herbs, but also of someone else's perfume.

"I'm just going to close my eyes for a second," the demon told him.

"Of course."

Sleep took the demon in mere minutes, giving Lucifer the chance to become acquainted with the things tacked to the wall beside Ira's cot. One of them was a poem by Phaedrus Queen, hand-copied onto the blank backside of a leaflet. A silly drawing done on a bit of newspaper, a dried flower, and a blue jay feather. A butterscotch wrapper and a glossy picture of a two-headed snake that must have been ripped out of a book because it had a bit of text beneath it.

Ira snuffled, rubbed his nose, and turned to one side.

If Ira had been sold to this place during the Wasting Plague, whatever his mistress had lost in the transaction must have been paid off by now. She might have levied some fines against him for the cost of raising him to adulthood, as well as continued fees for room and board, but Lucifer couldn't imagine the cost for an unlucky twin had been too high.

Maybe, before he left, he would have a word with Ira's mistress.

Ira sat up suddenly, peering around like he'd forgotten where he was or why Lucifer was in his bed.

"Bad dream?" Lucifer asked.

"Did I oversleep?"

"I don't know. Ira, listen, can I ask you something?"

"What?"

"Do you *want* to work here? I mean, do you like it?"

Ira moved away from him somewhat, turning to look at him and running a hand through his curls. "Why?"

"Because there are other places to work."

There was a hint of defensiveness in his tone when Ira said, "Whoring is as good a job as any."

"No, I'm not talking about working in *a* brothel, I mean *this* one."

Ira rubbed his arm.

"Be a whore, Ira, if you like, but why do it like this?" Lucifer gestured around the room. "You could do it somewhere nice. Somewhere to earn coin instead of just a hunk of bread and a bit of water."

"I've got debts to pay off."

The corner of Lucifer's mouth tugged down. "Debts that all the jewels I've traded for your time can't pay off?"

Ira pressed his hand to his mouth, the side of his forefinger touching the tip of his nose, his thumb against his lips. "I don't know. Mistress will tell me when I've paid my debt."

"Imagine you have no debts. What would you want then?"

"I don't know."

"Ira, you're not stupid or boring. I know that you must want something more."

"I don't know," Ira said again, but his voice had gone quiet. He took his hand from his mouth and rubbed his chin. He ran his hand over his cheek and gripped his hair.

"Tell me when you do and I'll give it to you," the Devil promised.

Ira put his arms around Lucifer's neck and squeezed him tight. "I'm sorry. I'm so tired, I can't think right."

"It's fine."

"This can't be what you wanted, I'm sorry," he breathed.

"I wanted to see you, that's all."

Ira drew in a breath, his thin body shaking as he did so.

"You should get some sleep."

"I've got someone booked soon."

"Lie down, dear. Someone will wake you when it's time," Lucifer assured.

"Are you going?" Ira asked.

"Yes. I've got some things to do."

"You'll come back, though, you have a promise to keep."

"I know." Lucifer untangled his limbs from Ira's and knelt beside his cot. He took Ira's hand and kissed his knuckles.

"How come your teeth are black?"

The question and the sleepy way Ira had asked it made Lucifer smile. "I don't know, it happened after I fell."

Ira nodded and nestled his face into his pillow, his eyes fluttering shut. Once he was sure Ira had fallen asleep, Lucifer whispered a small spell of protection over him. Others would feel the need to leave him alone, let him rest, until he woke.

When he walked past Nial's desk, Lucifer paused and said, "Ira isn't going to be seeing anyone else today."

The creature looked up. "He has appointments—"

"No, he's in no shape to see anyone else, I've seen to that."

Nial blinked a few times and turned his eyes down toward his book.

Lucifer told them, "Anyone displeased in missing their time with him can contact me directly. I'll make recompense for the inconvenience."

"Your Highness, I..." the creature began.

"And as for your mistress, I'd like to speak with her. Tell her she's invited to my palace whenever she pleases tomorrow. If she can't make it, I'll come back to see her. You'll relay that message, won't you? Or should I leave a note?"

"I will tell her, Your Highness."

"Thank you, Nial."

Lucifer left the brothel and headed for the library. He greeted Shiraz but didn't stop at the desk to talk. He knew where to find what he needed. Beneath the library, in a vast underground office, two score accountants kept track of all the financial transactions that took place in Hell and managed the Devil's holdings on Earth. Unlike the demons that he had made and let run wild, these accountants had been made to be orderly and honest.

As soon as he stepped into the office, one of the accountants peeled away from their desk and knelt briefly before him. "What can I do for you, my Prince?"

"I need the records for a building in the Ninth. Called the Trade House. Dating back to just before the Wasting Plague and ending now."

The accountant nodded and gestured to an empty desk. "I will bring you the records, Your Highness, if you'd like to have a seat."

"Thank you." He went over to the desk, rummaged through the drawers to find a piece of paper and a pencil.

By the time the accountant returned with an armful of books, Lucifer had doodled on the front side of the paper. "Anything else?"

"No, thank you."

The demon placed the books on the desk and walked away without another word.

Lucifer opened the first ledger, skimming through all the lines, but found nothing. In the second, he found the information he sought.

"Ira" Hell-born male, age four – unlucky twin. Traded 20 lb. flour, 30 lb. asstd. vegetables, 1 lb. honey...

Ira had been traded for a few months' worth of food and nothing more. Lucifer jotted down the sundry items his family had gained in the trade and read through all the ledgers that came after. He tallied up all the expenses that Ira had incurred—room, board, clothing, treatment for a broken arm—during his childhood. Ira's name didn't occur as an earner for about a decade after his sale.

He listed all the things that Ira had earned the brothel starting on a fresh sheet of paper. Even without precise values, it became clear that Ira was in the black.

When he thought he had enough information, he gathered all his papers, bid the accountants farewell, and headed home.

He stopped by Imogen's office and rapped on the doorframe.

"Yes?"

He handed her the papers. "Will you have another set copied for me?"

She studied them. "What are they?"

He ran fingers over the doorframe, hesitating. "Brothel records."

"From the brothel at which you made that scene?" She asked it with an arched eyebrow.

"Yes."

"Your Highness, it isn't my business either way, but don't you think you've got enough on your plate?"

"The copy, please, before tomorrow," he said.

"Of course."

"Thank you."

He passed Mercy on the stairs. They made eye contact and he paused to speak with her. "Your friend went home," she told him.

He nodded. "Feeling better?"

"He's a good listener."

"It's why he's my favorite."

She almost smiled but shook her head and banished the expression. They both watched a cat come tearing down the hall and gallop down the stairs. "He's different."

"No, he's not, not like you mean it. He's a person, like the rest of us. Maybe that's easier to see with Junius, sweet as he is."

"I don't know."

"No one knows anything today," he said.

She rolled her eyes. "You smell like lady's perfume."

He sniffed himself. "Oh."

"Maybe you'll get her pregnant, too."

He grinned. "Unlikely. Do you like dancing, acrobatics? I mean to watch, not to do."

She walked away, shaking her head and muttering to herself. He caught the word *idiot* and didn't blame her for thinking him one.

Going to see Jack perform in his pretty stockings and leather slippers wouldn't repair any part of the rift between humanity and unnatural creatures, he knew that. Still, there was the small and ridiculous hope that maybe she would be able to shed some of her prejudice.

He thought about following her but continued upstairs. Once in his room, Marlow greeted him happily. Her mother had long since left, as had the other kittens, but Marlow stayed. She insisted on being near to him and even now, she went up on her hind legs, stretching and putting her front paws on his leg.

He picked her up and cradled her like a baby; she began to purr immediately. Marlow worried him and he really believed that he should not have brought her back from the dead, but she was only a cat. There couldn't be that much harm in bringing a cat back to life.

With Marlow still held in one arm, he went to find Mercy, changing his mind about asking her to go out for the night.

He found her in the kitchen, stirring a bowl of soup with her spoon. She leaned in to blow on it and frowned when she saw him.

"What do you want?" she asked.

He set Marlow on the table. "Come out with me."

"No."

"Stay in with me?"

"Why?"

He came to sit with her. "You don't want this baby because you think it will be like me, but you don't know me."

"You're the Devil," she said as if that explained everything about him.

"But I wasn't always, Mercy, the Devil is…it's more than a job, of course, but it's not *who I am*. It's not who my children are."

She let go of her spoon and it clacked against the edge of the bowl. She leaned back and crossed her arms.

"I'm not telling you what to do, I'm not saying that you have any obligation to keep it or end it. I'm…I'm asking you to be better informed because I think it will make your choice easier."

"You're the Prince of Lies; how can I trust anything you say?"

Seriously, he asked, "How can you trust anything anyone says? I didn't invent lying."

She ignored him for a while, taking her spoon back up and eating. She glanced at the loaf of bread on the counter and he handed it to her before she could stand to get it. She ripped a piece off, dipped it in her soup, but before she had it halfway to her mouth, she brought it back to the soup. She tossed it in as if the bread had offended her.

"Don't you care?" she demanded.

"Care about what?"

"The baby! You keep trying to get me to think that you're not so bad, but you don't even care," she accused.

He tilted his head. "It isn't up to me. I don't want you to think I'm trying to coerce you into anything."

She sighed. "That's a weak answer."

Marlow stretched out and reached her paws towards the Devil. He gave her belly a rub. "I don't know what to tell you."

"Do you care what I do?"

"Of course I care, Mercy. I care for all the things I create, for all my children, born or made."

"If you cared—"

"It's not my choice, I can't tell you what to do."

"I'm not asking you to tell me what to do!" She pushed her bowl away from her; soup slopped over the edge.

He reached for a towel and started to wipe up the soup.

"Is that what matters to you now?" she demanded.

He stared at her. "I...I don't like messes. I mean...clutter is one thing, but I don't...it's better when things are as they should be."

"Do you feel anything?" she asked.

"Everything," he breathed.

She snatched the rag out of his hand. "Then tell me what you feel about *this*."

The words came unbidden but once he started, he couldn't stop. "I don't think you'll end your pregnancy. You're alone now and you don't want to be. You've never even taken the life of a grown demon, let alone a child, and you already, in your heart, consider that scrap of life to be a child." He took the rag back and finished cleaning. "You even loved one of mine already, but Reg was grown and he was strong enough to survive what your family does. But a baby? A baby isn't strong, a baby can't...a baby can't *try* to be good for you, a baby can't try to make you love it. Babies just need to be loved no matter what. And I don't know if you can do that, Mercy."

She wrapped her arms around herself.

"So if you can love the thing, if you can love another monster, if you can *stand* the idea of putting a demon to nurse at your breast, then I want the babe to live. Loving someone is never the wrong choice. But if you can't, then it is better to end things."

He hadn't meant to talk so much. He put the rag on the counter, not sure what to do. He sat back down and put one hand on Marlow's side, feeling the rise and fall of her ribs. She twisted herself, licked his finger, then wrapped her front legs around his wrist.

He didn't want to raise his eyes to Mercy and find her staring at him, but he raised his eyes anyway. He found her with her face buried in her hands. "If you really wanted to know what I thought."

When she looked up, her eyes were red-rimmed, but she hadn't started to cry yet. She reached out to touch Marlow, her fingers brushing the cat's fur. "But you won't be a father to the child," she said.

He shook his head. "I can't. I can't stay on Earth and you can't stay in Hell. Well, you could, but it would make you miserable. And it's really no place for a baby, not one that's got human blood."

Mercy shook her head again. She rubbed her eyes.

He put some heat back into her soup and pushed the bowl

toward her. "You should finish eating."

"You're right."

"It's good soup."

She clucked her tongue. "Do you play stupid on purpose?"

"Well, I was going to invite you to play cards, or maybe checkers, since you didn't want to go out, but then you started asking all these questions. I had sort of planned to be subtle, but you're not one for subtlety, are you?" he asked.

"I don't like being played with."

"Then you shouldn't have come to Hell." He stood, tired, though it was nowhere near nighttime. "I meant what I said, Mercy, whether you believe me or not."

He walked away with Marlow on his heels.

Ira's mistress did not come to visit the palace, so Lucifer went to her. He walked past Nial, though the creature protested, and went to the woman's office. She looked up, surprised but not as concerned as he wanted her to be.

"We have something to discuss."

"Do we?" she asked.

He took the sheaf of papers that Imogen had copied from his pocket and placed them on her desk. He took in all the fine things she had collected in her office and saw a trove of finer things beyond the doorway that led to her bedroom.

She eyed the papers, getting halfway through before she set them down.

"It is the judgment of your Prince that he has paid back all that he owes." He pointed to the seal and signature on the last page he'd given her.

"I—"

"You will give him a share of what he earns or you will release him from service here."

She sighed and looked him over, her mouth pressed into a thin line. "I suppose you meant to make him your personal whore. He could easily have been reserved for your use only if you'd wished."

Lucifer thought about arguing, about telling her that it was not about having exclusive access to Ira or his body. "Have him brought to me."

"He is with someone currently."

"I'll wait."

The woman sat a little straighter and picked up the papers again, shuffling through them. The quick motion of her hand, the sound of the paper, didn't sit right with the Devil, so he turned and left the office.

He stopped at Nial's desk and said, "Bring him to me."

"He is with—"

"I don't care, bring him to me now." He had meant to wait, to settle into one of the chairs and bide his time, maybe ask for a book, but that felt impossible now. He wanted to take Ira from this place as soon as possible, to get him away from the people who preyed on him.

Nial bobbed their head and went, disappearing behind the curtain.

Lucifer waited beside the creature's desk, touching things that didn't belong to him until he heard a pained yowl come from behind the curtain. He moved without making a conscious choice, pushing the curtain aside and rushing down the hall.

In the doorway of one of the rooms, he found Nial hopelessly explaining things to a large man who held Ira by the hair.

"I paid for my time—"

"Yes but—" the bookkeeper tried.

"You can stay and watch if you like but I'll finish what I started," the man growled, pulling Ira back toward the bed.

"Release the lad, Wil," Lucifer said. He recognized the demon and, brutish as he knew him to be, did not like at all that he had come to bed Ira.

Ira, his hands holding on to Wil's wrist in an attempt to alleviate the hair pulling, said, "Please, just, it's fine, I'll let you finish, just—"

"You'll let me!" Wil threw him to the floor.

"For fuck's sake!" Lucifer shoved the man to the floor and away from Ira. "Did you forget who *made you*, Wil? Is your dick so hard you can't think!"

Wil stood, twice the breadth of an average man, though he didn't stand as tall as the Devil. Lucifer recalled watching the man hunt down souls with an unequaled fervor.

"Go, before I unmake you," Lucifer warned.

Wil stepped forward, his hands clenched, and Lucifer smiled his widest smile, growing taller and reaching for the unruly demon. He caught him by the arm and picked him up off the floor. It would have been embarrassingly fruitless to grapple with Wil at his usual size.

Wil thrashed in his grip, which grew tighter with each buck and twist; Lucifer deposited him outside the room, where he stayed, red-faced but defeated.

"Whatever he wants, bill me for it," Lucifer told Nial.

The creature nodded and hurried Wil into another room before the bigger demon could take issue with the offer.

Lucifer returned to his normal size and knelt beside Ira, who lay curled on the floor. He had tears on his face, not just new ones, but dried streaks that left a white crust on his skin. His back held evidence of a recent lashing.

The thing that worried Lucifer most was fresh blood on his ass and thighs.

"Christ, Ira..."

Ira pushed himself up and wiped his eyes. "I would have let

him finish, everything was fine..."

"I find you like this and things are fine?" Lucifer couldn't keep the disbelief from his voice.

Glowering, Ira moved away from the Devil. Not much, but enough to show that he wished Lucifer hadn't come. "It's a little rough, nothing I'm not used to."

"More than rough, Ira. You're bleeding!"

"So what?"

Lucifer rubbed his face.

"Wil always gets rough, but he trades fair for it. It was all under control, I don't need *you* to come save me," Ira spat.

"If you know he's going to hurt you—"

"Because whores don't say no."

"Yes, they do! And more than that, Ira, whores get paid," Lucifer insisted.

Ira pulled his knees close to his chest and hid his face, wrapping his arms around himself. He began to sniffle and Lucifer put a hand on his shoulder. He shrugged it off. "Don't! Why couldn't you just wait? You're going to get me in trouble again."

"When did I get you in trouble?"

Ira accused, "You let me sleep through all those customers the other day."

"I..."

"I don't belong to you, you know, just because you've had me a couple of times."

"You don't belong to her, either."

"Yes, I do!"

"No, you don't, you've earned enough to pay her back, I know you did. Your debt is squared, official and everything. That's what I wanted to tell you."

At that, Ira came undone. He started to weep, pressing his forehead to his knees and twisting his hands in his hair.

Lucifer sat back heavily and watched Ira cry, wanting to pull him close, but sure that would be unwelcome. "Ira."

"She won't let me stay, where am I supposed to go?"

"Ira, shh..."

"Why did you do this!" Ira screamed at him, giving him a push.

"You can go anywhere you want."

"Fucking easy for you to say!"

Lucifer had thought this whole thing would be easy, especially compared to his business with Mercy. It should have been straightforward: release Ira from his debt, find him somewhere nice and safe and paying to work, and continue to visit him without feeling like he was leaving him behind whenever he left.

"Please, can you let me explain?"

Ira shook his head, but he wrapped his arms around himself, his fingers digging into his own ribs, and stared at Lucifer. "What?"

"We can find you somewhere good to work. There are a dozen brothels in the Ninth alone. I promise I didn't come here to make you destitute. I thought...shit, I don't know, I thought you'd be better off. I..." He took a breath. "Come back with me, for a little bit, you can get yourself back on your feet, and we'll go to find you another place to work."

Ira sniffled, an ugly sound, sucking snot back into his nose. Lucifer handed him a handkerchief and he took it, blowing his nose. He stared at Lucifer. "You don't..."

"I don't what?"

"You don't want me just for you?" It was a cautious question, as though he didn't know if it would be good or bad.

"I want whatever you want. If you want to be mine, you can be. I'll keep you well, somewhere clean and nice. You can have whatever you want."

"And if I don't?"

"That's fine, too, I just...I want to know you're safe when I go home."

Ira scooted closer to Lucifer, but didn't touch him; when Lucifer put a hand on his shoulder, Ira leaned against him. "I'm sorry I yelled at you."

"You're allowed to."

Ira shook his head.

"You should see a healer, you know."

"I'm fine."

"Alright, but you aren't. You're not supposed to bleed, really, from any of your orifices post-coitus. Or at any point, now that I think about it."

Ira only shrugged. "I don't like healers."

"I can try if you want. I've always been kind of rubbish at healing, fair warning."

"You saved Phaedrus's husband."

"It's different on Earth."

Ira wrinkled his nose.

"Like I said, I can try," Lucifer offered again.

"My stomach does sort of hurt," the demon admitted.

Lucifer stood and helped Ira to his feet. He walked him to the bed and gestured for him to lie down. "On Earth, I can...I can sort of do whatever people think I can, and they think I can do anything, so I can. It's part of being the Devil. You said your stomach hurt?"

Ira gave a small nod.

Lucifer rubbed his hands together, not liking that Wil had done so much damage. Of course, Wil probably wasn't the only one who'd contributed, considering Ira's busy schedule of late. Durable as demons could be, repeated use would cause wear and tear, especially in more sensitive areas.

He placed his hands on Ira's belly and called up his power, sending it out to find whatever wounds he might have. "It's not to say that on Earth I can run unchecked, the magics there still have rules that ought to be followed, but...things are easier, let's say that."

"Is this supposed to hurt?"

"Does it?" Lucifer asked, panicking somewhat.

"Uncomfortable, I guess. Or like...when you lose a tooth and can't stop playing with the hole."

"Oh, that, that's normal. I am poking around." Lucifer didn't like what he found and couldn't quite believe that Ira had only described his stomach as 'sort of' hurting.

Having a better idea of what ailed Ira, Lucifer felt comfortable using his power to mend the flesh. There was no infection to contend with, which made things easier. The wounds on his back, though already scabbed, could stand to be fixed, and the tearing within definitely had to go. Before he started, he warned, "This might hurt. Kind of a pinch on the inside."

Ira nodded. When Lucifer cast the spell, Ira inhaled sharply and gripped the sheets. He held his breath, his eyes squeezed shut. A small grunt escaped and he let out a shuddering breath after that.

"You're alright, it's almost done."

Ira, eyes still closed and lips pressed together, nodded. A small squeaking sound escaped his throat.

After a few minutes, Lucifer took his hands back. "Should be all set. Might get a little tenderness yet, but that's all. Do you mind if I come sit next to you?"

"No." Ira pushed himself up to sit.

"Do you feel better?"

"Yes."

"You don't have to come back to mine. We can just as easily put you up in a boarding house."

Ira picked at a loose thread in one of the sheets.

"Was I so wrong to think that you'd prefer to be somewhere other than here?"

"I don't remember anything else. I mean, reading is just reading, it doesn't tell you what things are really like." Ira took his fingers away from the thread, clenching his hand, then looking around the room. His eyes landed on his clothing. "If I do go home with you, will you make me a promise?"

"What?"

"That you won't make me stay."

"I won't."

Ira nodded, stood, and went to gather his clothes. As he pulled them on, he examined a torn seam on his sleeve. "Maybe…"

"What?"

"Maybe I shouldn't," Ira said.

"I won't make you. I'm sure your mistress will let you stay and continue to take no recompense for your work if that's what you want," Lucifer assured.

"It sounds stupid when you say it like that."

"Change is hard, love, but I'll help in whatever way you'd like."

Ira nodded and adjusted his clothes.

Lucifer offered tentatively, "Even if it means not coming to see you."

Ira stopped tucking in his shirt, his eyes snapping to the Devil's face. "No, you're the only, uh…I'll lose all my other customers after this, I bet, I can't lose you, too. I'll be in the Eighth working in the alleys at that point."

"I doubt it would come to that. Have you got shoes?"

"Somewhere, I think, I'll go check."

Lucifer followed Ira out of the hallway. They were greeted with sudden silence when they entered the main room.

"I'll go check, you can wait here," Ira told him and headed past Nial's desk.

A few people followed Ira and several more started to whisper, their eyes occasionally darting over to Lucifer.

"I told you!" one girl hissed to her friend.

When Ira returned wearing shoes and stockings, as well as a jacket, Lucifer had to stifle a laugh, but Ira must have noticed the twist of his mouth, because he asked, "What?"

"You sort of look like an English schoolboy but...you know, if he was trying to get with the other schoolboys."

Ira crossed his arms and sulked, "It's all I've got. Are we leaving or not?"

"After you." Lucifer hadn't meant to hit a sore spot. "You look fine, I wasn't trying to make fun."

The demon didn't say anything back.

"Uh, you never said if you wanted to come to the palace or not?"

"It doesn't matter."

Lucifer had the feeling that it did. He wasn't sure in what way, but the clipped tone Ira used told him the demon wanted something he hadn't gotten yet. "I'd like it if you did."

"Then I'll go."

Although he found himself wishing for a more enthusiastic answer, Lucifer didn't press the matter. He'd accidentally-on-purpose turned the poor thing's whole world upside down less than an hour ago.

"I saw your room, after all. It's only fair I invite you to see mine."

Ira nodded. "Mmm."

Lucifer left him alone after that. They walked in silence to the palace and when they entered together, Ira glanced around, taking in the half-dozen cats lounging throughout the great foyer. He took a few steps in, then stopped.

"Do you want to come upstairs?" Lucifer asked.

"Sure."

Lucifer offered Ira his hand; the demon took it, though not without some hesitation. He didn't twine his fingers with the Devil's or walk close to him. Lucifer got the impression that he was leading a lost and dazed child to find his parents.

"That's the washroom and to the left is Mercy's room."

"Mercy? That woman?" Ira asked.

"Yes."

"I thought she was your prisoner."

As casually as he could, Lucifer told him, "Things change. Imogen is downstairs, second door off to the left of the stairs, if you ever need anything." He thought about adding that the first door was a closet, but the information seemed useless.

"Who's Imogen?"

"My butler. This is my room." Lucifer pushed open the door

and was immediately accosted by Marlow.

Lingering in the doorway, Ira looked around the large bedroom, taking in the wardrobes, the desk cluttered with letters and books, pens and bottles of ink; his eyes slid over the settee and remained on the red and gray ceiling for a while. He stepped in further, his head tilted back a little as he gazed at the pattern until he turned his attention to the bed.

His hand slipped out of Lucifer's grasp as he took another step in. "Bigger than five of our rooms put together, at least."

"Makes it easier to lose things."

"Not a problem if you haven't got any things to lose."

Marlow sat back on her hind legs and trilled at Lucifer, distraught that he hadn't picked her up yet. He scooped her up and she settled into his arms.

Ira regarded the cat warily. "Is it true what they say about the cats?"

"Which thing? That they're my children or that they're my enemies?"

"Either, I suppose."

"Both untrue, I'm afraid. They're just cats." He brought Marlow over to the bed and set her down, running his hand from her head to her tail. She began to purr, walking around in circles so that she was harder to pet. He beckoned Ira over to the bed and the demon came, his pace slow and his shoulders hunched.

Ira allowed Lucifer to take him into his arms.

"I'm sorry this has distressed you so much," Lucifer told him.

"No, it's...I never thought I would leave. I don't know what to do anymore."

"Take time. Here or away from me."

Ira stepped back. "Why do you keep doing that?"

"What?"

"Saying that I should be away from you. Don't you want me here? Or did you really want me to stay in a boarding house?"

"I want you here, but I don't want you to do it out of obligation or anything like that."

Ira opened his mouth, then shook his head.

"What?"

Ira replied, "You're so, well, I always thought that you'd be more forceful about things."

"I can be when the occasion calls for it. But you're here as a guest, not a hostage. I didn't think force was needed."

Ira admitted, "It doesn't really seem like you care one way or another."

"If I didn't care, you'd still be with your mistress."

Letting out a long sigh, Ira rubbed his eyes with the back of his wrist. He ruffled his hair, looked around the room again, and held out his hand for Marlow to sniff. "I'm tired."

"Should I have Imogen prepare you a room?"

"Only if you don't want me in yours."

Lucifer picked up Marlow and set her on the bedside table so that he could turn back the covers. If he'd thought that morning that Ira would be coming home with him, he would have had someone change the sheets.

Ira slipped off his shoes and peeled off his stockings and breeches. He pulled his shirt over his head and slid into the Devil's bed wearing nothing at all. Getting dressed and undressed so often probably made undergarments a nuisance.

Lucifer began to pull up the covers for him, but he took the Devil's hand and said, "You'll stay, won't you?"

"Yes."

A tug indicated that Ira wanted him to lie down too, so he did so, stopping only to shed his shoes. Ira put an arm around Lucifer's waist and, his forehead against the Devil's chest, said, "I must be the worst whore you've ever had."

"No, I've had much worse."

Ira snorted. "I didn't even sleep with you half the times you paid for me."

"That's not what this is about." The words came out unbidden and Lucifer regretted them.

He regretted them more when Ira asked, "What is it about?"

"That I like to see you."

Lucifer felt the prickle of small claws on his skin as Marlow climbed over him to aggressively worm her way between the two of them.

Ira pulled his arm back from Lucifer's waist and pulled the covers tighter. Lucifer could not, from the droop of his eyelids or the languor in his movements, tell if he was sad or tired. He could easily be both. In a day or two, when he'd had time to adjust and to sleep, to eat a real meal, things would be more telling.

He fell asleep quickly, but Lucifer couldn't keep his eyes closed. He filled with nervous, uncomfortable energy that sat in his chest and throat, demanding to be released. Ira had wanted him to stay, but Lucifer didn't feel settled. He didn't feel right.

When he slipped out of bed, Ira barely stirred. Lucifer left his bedroom, closing the door and then standing in the hallway, not knowing where to go or what to do. He sat, leaning against the door.

A cat walked past, glanced over him haughtily, then continued walking.

In moments like this, he was weak. He thought about how badly he wanted to go home. He had watched the humans and envied them; he had walked among them and become bloated with arrogance when they had loved him too, when they had praised his beauty and stood in awe of his powers. A hollow ache had grown within him the longer he spent among the humans and that had grown into anger, rebellion, spite.

His father, in the end, had given him what he'd wanted in the most backhanded way. Lucifer had wanted humanity to bow to him, too, so now they cowered. He had wanted to feel as they had and now he could not be within arm's reach of a human without experiencing the unrelenting tide of their emotions.

He'd been stupid; he wondered sometimes if God had made him stupid on purpose, if He had put that seed of envy within him out of nothing more than curiosity.

Some days it was easy to feel righteous in his rebellion, to scorn his maker and the banal paradise he'd left behind. But when he was alone, when he still didn't know what to do or how to fix things after thousands of years, he wanted that easy peace back. Heaven had been boring, but it had been simple.

He heard feet on the stairs and thought that he should stand, make himself appear less pathetic, but Imogen reached the top before he'd gathered the will to do so.

She paused at the top of the stairs, then approached to stand before him. She held out the envelope she carried.

He took it and tore it open. It was a flier, folded to fit in the envelope, for Jack's performance. The note jotted on the back said, *Don't worry, I'm still working with Pythea. You might like the show, though!* It had his name scrawled beneath.

"Do you need anything, Sire?" Imogen asked.

"Perspective."

"You've got that more than I do."

"It doesn't feel that way."

She suggested, "Well, why don't you come eat something?"

"I ate before, I'm not hungry."

"Have a bath, that always makes me feel better."

He tried to imagine Imogen soaking in a hot bath to unwind and couldn't imagine her needing to unwind. Even when frustrated, she maintained a level of calm that few could equal.

She crouched beside him. "Should I draw you a bath?"

"I brought him back with me."

"Who?"

"Ira."

Her face contorted for a moment as she thought. "The whore?"

He nodded.

"Well, you're the king around here, I suppose you can do as you see fit," she said.

"Probably."

"I did sort of warn you, though, about having a lot on your plate."

"You did. But I never listen when people warn me. Even if they're as clever and beguiling as you are."

Imogen's eyes narrowed briefly. She straightened up and walked away. A moment passed before he heard the crashing of water into the bath. She returned with wisps of steam following her out of the bathroom.

She offered her hand to help him, but he stood without assistance. He lingered by the door to his room. "He's asleep."

"I'll be sure to direct him your way if he comes searching for you." He must not have looked soothed, because she added, "I promise, nothing bad will happen if you go unwind for a bit."

He stepped away from the door, not sure that a bath was what he needed, but with no other ideas.

The bath helped, no doubt because Imogen had spiked the water with a few drops of herbal oils meant to calm him. She'd lit only a few candles, leaving the room dim but cozy. He didn't mind that she'd taken the liberty to do so since he hadn't been collected enough to do it himself.

The door opened and he opened one eye, expecting to see Imogen. Instead, he found Ira there, clad in a robe Imogen must have found for him. Lucifer sat up a little, both eyes open now.

"Your butler said I'd find you in here."

Sheepish, Lucifer admitted, "I thought you'd be asleep for longer."

Ira rubbed his arm and shrugged.

"Do you want to come in?" Lucifer asked.

Without saying anything, Ira let his robe fall to the floor and climbed into the tub, making a face, then settling in. He faced toward Lucifer but didn't make eye contact.

"Ever been to Dreams of Eulalia?"

Ira shook his head. "Heard of it, though."

"Do you want to go? They've got a new act starting."

"If you'd like to go," Ira agreed flatly.

"Ira, love, what's got you so glum?"

His eyebrows rose. "Me? What about you?"

Lucifer admitted, "I've got some ghosts that need dealing with."

"Ghosts? I thought those were only on Earth."

"Oh, no, metaphorical ghosts. Or, maybe figurative ones. Either way," the Devil rambled.

"Do you want to tell me?"

Lucifer played with the surface of the water, making ripples and waves with his hand. "I imprisoned my daughter and I haven't got the guts to go see her. And now there's this business with Mercy."

"Elisa?" That Ira knew his daughter's name surprised him since she'd spent most of her time on Earth lately. It must have shown because Ira added, "They still tell stories about the things she did."

"Ah."

"And, um...they say she was the one doing those things in the Eighth a few months ago. Those murders? But it's got to be just rumors."

"It wasn't."

"She really ripped apart those people?" Ira asked, leaning

forward.

Murder wasn't unheard of in the city, but those with the urge for truly graphic crimes tended to get their jollies with the souls instead of other demons. They could pick a favorite victim and have their way over and over again without any repercussions.

"She did. She comes down here every so often to remind me that I can't do anything to stop her."

Ira leaned back, settling against the side of the tub. He sunk down further in the water, not appearing as morose as he had before, but cozy and ready to gossip.

"Do you remember all those heads impaled in front of the university? With the guts strung between like party streamers?" Lucifer asked.

"That was her?"

"Yes."

"Good a reason as any to lock her away." Ira glanced around the tub but didn't find whatever he'd been looking for. "She's not much like you, is she?"

"She's...she's the way she is because of me."

Ira didn't seem convinced. "I can't imagine you hanging up people's guts like decorations."

"Only because you don't know me very well."

Ira swallowed and licked his lips. Lucifer's tone had been darker than he'd meant it to be, and here, with the lights so dim and steam still rolling off the water, it must have seemed menacing.

Lucifer felt the urge to move closer to Ira, to climb on top of him and press him against the side of the tub. He wanted to smile his worst smile and whisper the most monstrous things he had done into Ira's ear. He wanted to set him trembling, make his breath come quick and his heart flutter. Maybe he could scare him so bad that he would run away, fleeing the palace and the Ninth altogether to take his chances in the alleys of the Eighth rather than let the Devil have him again.

"Maybe if you knew me better you'd be smarter about things." A smart person wouldn't consort with Satan, no matter how self-indulgently lazy and gloomy the Devil had grown; a smart person knew there was only one way for things to go when the Devil got involved.

Digging his teeth into his lip, Ira shrank back further. He pulled in on himself, his shoulders tight and close to his body, his hands gripping his upper arms. "I'm sorry."

All his desire to frighten Ira dissolved at that. "You haven't done anything to be sorry for."

"I'll do what you tell me, you just have to tell me what you want," Ira pleaded in a small whisper.

"I didn't mean it like that."

Ira nodded, his eyes fixed on the surface of the water, his arms still pressed close to his chest. "You just have to tell me what to do."

Tight as his throat had gotten, he still managed to say, "Come here."

Ira moved toward him, the sound of the water's movement seeming too loud. Lucifer embraced the smaller man, trying his best to be gentle. Ira lay stiffly against him for a moment, took a few deep breaths and slowly relaxed against Lucifer. It must have taken a lot effort, but Ira had to be used to making himself do things.

"I'm sorry, love, I haven't got my head on right these days." His voice came out as a whisper; he'd meant to speak normally, even dismissively, but he'd barely been able to force out the words. He pressed his lips to Ira's hair, taking in the always-there smell of herbs, and tightened his arms around him.

Ira rested against him, his breathing less forced than it had been previously.

"Did you ever think about me while I wasn't with you?" Lucifer asked.

"Yes."

"I thought about you, too."

"You didn't visit much for someone who was thinking about me."

Lucifer let out an amused breath, not quite up to an actual chuckle. "The only one who gets my attention every day is Marlow."

"Who?"

"The cat."

Ira laughed at that, the sound echoing against the tiled walls. "Well, she demands it, doesn't she? Maybe I should be more demanding."

"What would you demand of me?" Lucifer asked and knew that he would hand over his guts if Ira requested them.

"Something better than a few pieces of candy and those lousy poems."

"You didn't like the poems?" Lucifer asked, managing to keep most of the hurt out of his voice.

Ira pulled back a little, smiling. "No, I did. I liked the candies, too. You can buy me lots more nice things and I can charge you a whole barrel of coins for the privilege to fuck me."

"I'm amenable to that arrangement."

Ira sat up straighter, his expression more serious. "You don't care at all if I go to work in another brothel?"

"As long as you don't let anyone do things you don't want to you."

Ira sighed. "You're caught up on that, aren't you?"

"I can't emphasize how important it is."

Ira shook his head, as though Lucifer's worry was naïve. "Fighting makes it worse. At least if you let them, they're paying for it."

Lucifer contemplated not letting him leave the palace until he understood that no one had a right to him, no matter how much they'd paid. He also considered devouring his former mistress for the damage she'd done to his understanding of consent. "Maybe you should go on holiday first."

"Holiday? To where? The Empty Plains? To the shore of River Elde? I could go take the air at one of the rutabaga farms, I suppose, or spend some time in the Ghostwood Forest."

"The Elde actually feeds into this lovely little lake, the beach is nice if you don't go during the fen crow migration. But you'd never get any sleep among the ghostwoods with the way they groan in the wind."

"I guess a holiday is out, then."

"I could send you to Earth," Lucifer pointed out.

"Earth!" Ira scoffed. "I'd know what to do there less than I'd know what to do on a rutabaga farm."

"I do know a few people up there, you know, I wouldn't just toss you somewhere and let you flounder."

Ira shook his head and lay back against Lucifer. "Earth," he huffed, but he did so in an amused way.

Lucifer would have to go to see Jack's show some other time. He'd send a note or maybe stop by the barracks tomorrow to tell him in person.

Ira asked, "You really think Queen's poetry is sappy?"

"Not all of them, just the last book."

"You know what I meant."

Lucifer put an arm around him and pulled him up so that he could kiss him. "I like Bécquer when it comes to love poems if that's what you wanted to know."

"I don't know them."

"Another book, then, you'll have a proper library by the time I'm done..." Lucifer cut himself off, not quite able to believe what he had almost said. *By the time I'm done courting you.* The idea of him courting anyone was ridiculous and Ira did not deserve to be subjected to that.

Ira didn't notice the odd way he'd strangled his sentence, or if he did notice, decided not to say anything. He kissed the Devil, quick and almost chaste. "Are you done in the bath? I'm sort of hungry and I don't know where anything is."

Lucifer nodded and gestured for him to stand.

Both of them, once dried and wrapped in robes, went to the kitchen. Lucifer's heart gave a joyous flutter when he opened the pot on the stove and he realized that Oris had prepared a cream of mushroom soup.

He ladled quite a lot into Ira's bowl and then reflected that maybe the demon did not share his love for mushrooms. "That's not too much, is it?"

"It's fine," Ira said, his eyes as big as saucers as he stared at the bowl.

He tucked in as soon as he was seated and Lucifer felt compelled to warn, "You'll give yourself a stomachache."

"Sorry."

Lucifer woke before Ira, as he had the morning before. The demon had spent two nights in his bed and already Lucifer could imagine him as a permanent fixture. He gave Ira a gentle shake.

"Hm?"

"I'm going to Earth today," he informed the demon.

"Oh."

"I'll take you up."

Ira stretched, burying his face in his pillow, then rolling onto his back. The covers slid down as he moved, exposing his chest, a bit of stomach. He looked delicious, absolutely cozy, and Lucifer knew how warm his skin would be. "Why do you want to get rid of me?"

"I don't." He could not stop thinking of the taste of Ira's lips, no matter that it was first thing in the morning.

"You act like it."

Lucifer shook his head.

"You'll send me away and forget all about me. By the time I come back you'll have found someone else and I'll be giving head on Prate Street for two bits."

Lucifer moved in closer, pressing his mouth to Ira's throat. "I won't. But you should go out and live a bit."

"I've lived a lot."

"You've been whoring since you were fourteen, that's not living any more than bricklaying is." He fought the urge to bite him, just a little, not even enough to leave a mark; he lost.

Ira arched his back and moaned, "Fifteen." He put his arms around Lucifer's neck.

"Go, spend a week where you don't have to work, where you don't have to worry about that woman breathing down your neck or if someone will hurt you. Feel the sun, see the clouds, taste the ocean. Forget about earning your keep or pleasing people. Fuck someone because they caught your eye, not because they traded a basket of raspberries for it."

"Half a basket." Ira kissed Lucifer and the Devil hoped that he did it for the want of it, not in response to Lucifer's advances or as a distraction. "If it had been up to me, I'd have done it anyway."

His tongue flicked out to touch Lucifer's mouth, and then he kissed his jaw, his throat, and Lucifer forgot why he wanted Ira to go to Earth. He nibbled the Devil's ear and Lucifer moved on top of him, only thinking that he needed Ira to stay, to be in his bed each morning so that he'd never worry about him again.

Ira drew him closer, opening his mouth against Lucifer's, and the kiss was as sweet as Lucifer had hoped. He wanted to wind himself around Ira and spend an eternity like this, he'd wanted it since he'd seen him lounging on those cushions. He could keep him here forever, keep him dressed in silks, with jewels at his throat and on his fingers, and with warm food in his belly. What a gilded cage the palace could be for him, so pleasant that maybe Ira would never notice that he was a hostage, that the Devil was his newest owner.

"Make me a promise, Ira."

"What?"

"That you won't come back unless you really want to."

Ira rolled his eyes and gave the Devil another kiss. "You want so badly to save someone, don't you?"

"Is that wrong?"

"No, but it's sort of silly" Ira said. "But I'll promise if it will make you feel better."

"It does."

Ira put one hand on Lucifer's bottom and gave a squeeze. "Good. Have you got any oil? Or that...you can do that spell, can't you?"

Lucifer nodded.

"Go ahead, then." He took Lucifer's hand and placed it on his own cock, his eyes on Lucifer's face as though he were waiting for a protest.

Lucifer had none to give. He applied what he'd conjured to Ira, glad to hear the demon's breath catch with pleasure at his touch.

Ira put his hand on the back of Lucifer's neck, bringing him in for another kiss and to ask, breathily, "Ready?"

"Yes."

Ira slid inside of him, slow and careful, and Lucifer let out the breath he'd been holding. He touched his forehead to Ira's shoulder, his skin hot; he kissed his neck and Ira trailed his fingers along Lucifer shaft, his thumb rubbing the head.

Together they moved, together they let out gasps and breathy moans and together they came, with Ira giving a final, deep thrust and Lucifer pushing back, wanting more of him. They stayed like that, catching their breath, and trading small kisses until Ira turned his head to the side and sneezed.

Lucifer winced, as Ira was still inside of him, and moved away to sit beside him.

"Sorry, snuck up on me." Ira sneezed again, then once more. "Alright, I'm good now."

"You sure?"

He nodded, then looked down at his stomach. "Have you got a washcloth?"

"I've got a whole bathtub." He scooped up Ira and lifted him out of bed.

The smaller man threw his arms around Lucifer, clinging in surprise at first, but after a moment, he relaxed in Lucifer's grasp.

Not bothering with clothes or robes, Lucifer brought him to the hall and stopped dead when he saw Mercy heading toward the bathroom.

She stopped too, her eyes grazing over them with an odd expression on her face, somewhere between surprise and irritation. "Did you need to get in here?"

"Mercy, love, it's a palace. There's more than one bathroom. Go ahead."

"You're sure?"

"Yes." He turned away and stopped before the room between his bedroom and the study. He had to set Ira down so that he could undo the lock with the requisite spell and drop of blood. He hadn't ever meant to come back in here, but somehow that seemed pointless now.

Ira stepped into the room, at first following Lucifer as he went around to light the glass lamps; he peeled off to look around on his own soon enough. The room, as large as Lucifer's bedroom, must have seemed extravagant, with a circular pool set into the floor, large enough for three or four, as well as a closed-off sauna in the corner and a shower area enclosed in blurred glass. Ira wandered to the vanity and touched the phials of oils and perfume, the silver combs, and the small jewelry box.

Lucifer intentionally stayed away, going to the pool and turning on the taps.

"Why keep it locked?" Ira asked, his hand still on the vanity.

"It wasn't my room."

Ira let out a breath of disbelief. "It's your palace."

"This was Tabby's room. It was up to her if I could come in or not."

Ira quickly replaced all the things he'd disrupted on the vanity, closed the jewelry box, and stepped away.

"No, it's fine." Lucifer went over and opened the jewelry box, picking through the contents. He could recall seeing her wear almost every piece. "If she left it all behind, it can't have meant much to her."

"Still, I don't know…" Ira peered around. "Knowing it was hers."

"It was the last place I saw her."

Ira met his eyes, one hand holding his opposite elbow.

"She was taking a bath, told me to go to bed without her. And that was it." He thought Ira might take a step forward, or that he would say something comforting, so he broke eye contact before it could happen.

Water had filled the bath halfway now. Lucifer examined the oils, picked one, and asked Ira, "Do you like primrose?"

"Wouldn't know."

He offered the phial for him to sniff and Ira nodded, so Lucifer dribbled some onto the surface of the water. He didn't expect Ira to put a hand on his arm, so when Ira did, he looked over, eyes wide.

"She was wrong."

"What?" the Devil asked.

"She said that love can't be had between unequal people, didn't she? That smart people can't love stupid ones, or that the strong can't really love the weak, that the brave won't love the cowardly."

"Yes."

"She was wrong. There's not a better way to be a person."

Lucifer teased, "And a philosopher, too. I knew you had hidden depths."

Ira shook his head. "And she was wrong when she thought you had to be more to deserve her."

Lucifer's throat ached.

"And you were stupid to believe her."

He laughed at that, pulling Ira close and crushing him against his chest for a moment. "If she ever comes back you can be the one to tell her," he joked, but worried by the set of Ira's jaw and the disappointed look in his eyes that he might try.

Lucifer brought him into the water and they soaked until the bath had filled. Soap, undisturbed for years, still sat beside the tub. Lucifer wondered if soap could go bad, but it still smelled of lilies and lathered into a froth of bubbles, so he supposed it would be fine.

He had the thought that if Ira returned then he would give him the room. It would be his as it had been Tabitha's, but he pushed it aside. He washed Ira, dried him, and oiled him so that his dark ash-gray skin took on a beautiful gleam. He did all this with tenderness and care, but with the unsettling feeling that he was preparing a corpse for burial.

Don't come back, he prayed.

Ira took the silver comb from the vanity and brushed Lucifer's hair, carefully working out knots. "Do you ever cut it?"

"It just grows back."

Ira laughed. "Hair tends to do that." He set aside the comb and began to braid the Devil's hair. "My mother always braided her hair. Or, I guess, that's how I remember her. Always braided and pinned up. I think she worked in the Fifth and I know the souls get feisty there."

"Do you ever—"

"No." After a few heartbeats of silence, he continued, "But she never braided it like you do. Your braids always look so fancy. Lots of them, all woven together."

"If I can leave them alone." In the mornings, when he could manage it, he braided his hair intricately, but his hands almost always ended up undoing his work so they could braid it over and over again. Some people chewed their nails, he braided his hair.

When they had dressed and eaten, Lucifer wrapped an arm around Ira, pulled him closer, and stepped into the underneath, his hand wrapped around the strings he needed.

Lucifer stepped out onto the sidewalk in front of Junius's apartment. Ira had his face buried in Lucifer's shirt and when he stepped away, he shaded his eyes and squinted at the sky.

His response to his first sight of the sun and the cloudless blue sky was "Eugh."

"Oh, give it more of a chance than that, Ira."

The people on the street gave them concerned stares, some hurrying away, others crossing themselves.

"I look ridiculous," Ira pronounced when he'd surveyed the people around him.

"Junius can take you shopping."

The demon raised his eyebrows in a way that suggested the ludicrous proposal intrigued him. Of course, he'd never been shopping.

Lucifer took him by the hand and brought him inside the building, climbing the stairs and knocking on the door to Junius's apartment.

Wei answered, looked over Ira, and called, "June! Granddad's brought you somefink."

Lucifer grimaced.

Junius came over, went to his knees, and touched his head to the floor.

"Rise." Once Junius had gotten back to his feet, Lucifer said, "I'd like a favor."

"Whatever you need."

"Put Ira up for a week? Show him around?"

"Of course."

"Hope he don't mind sharin' beds," Wei said.

Junius gestured for Ira to come in. Ira's eyes flitted to Lucifer, uncertain.

"If I didn't trust him, you wouldn't be here," Lucifer assured.

Ira shrugged. "Easy for you to trust him, you're the Devil. He fell for you."

"Well, either way, I'll be back in a week." He took an envelope from his pocket and handed it to Junius. "This should cover any expenses. New clothes, I think, would be good."

"I don't know, is he even old enough for long pants?" Junius asked, an unexpected smirk on his face.

Ira straightened his back and tilted his chin up to add to his height. "I was born before the Wasting Plague."

"Am I that out of touch? I don't have any clue how old that makes you. Anyway, come in." Junius gestured for him to come in again.

This time Ira stepped inside the apartment.

"Have fun." *Don't come back.*

Ira nodded, but when Lucifer stepped back, he grabbed him by the hand and pulled him close. He pressed a kiss to the Devil's mouth, long and deep, wrapping his arms around Lucifer's neck.

When he moved away, Lucifer's world seemed to move a little and he had to stop himself from taking a step forward. *Please don't come back.*

Junius had his hands pressed to his mouth, not as, Lucifer first thought, in shock, but to hide the fact that he had started to giggle like a madman. He tugged on Ira's sleeve and closed the door, saying, "We will have to get you something else to wear. Nothing of mine will fit you..."

Lucifer floated hazily out of the building and had to take a few minutes to orient himself in the city. People stared at him, edging around him uneasily as he stood in the middle of the sidewalk and tried to remember which way to go. When he finally remembered, he set out with a sense of purpose that soon flagged.

On his walk from the Lower East Side to the Weller building, he steeled himself for his time with his daughter. It seemed wrong to imprison her without visiting afterward.

As he walked up the stairs to her suite, his feet grew heavy and his legs could barely lift them.

He knocked on the door and she opened it.

They stared at each other for a moment that seemed to last an hour.

It had been so long since the first time she'd said she hated him; she'd given up on that route. She'd stopped threatening to hurt herself, instead hurting others when she felt it necessary or the whim struck her, and she'd found more effective methods of hurting his feelings.

"Elisa."

"Father."

"I thought we should talk."

She smiled. "Then you should come in."

He stepped inside, not sure what he'd expected. The sitting room had been furnished with all the things for which she'd asked, as well as items he recognized from her last residence.

Elisa walked away from him, gesturing to a sofa. "Anything to drink?"

"No. Thank you."

She made herself whiskey on the rocks and sat opposite him, in an overstuffed armchair where once she'd sat on his lap as he'd read to her. He remembered the feel of her small body, the smell of her hair, the way she'd held on to his wrist while he'd read.

In the peace between her tantrums, she'd been sweet and gracious, she'd been his constant companion; he had brought her everywhere and maybe that had been her undoing. Hell had not been made for a child's eyes, but Lucifer had never been a child, he hadn't known. In between the times when she'd threatened to bash her own head against the wall or jump off balconies, she'd been comically erudite for a child and always asking questions.

Even when she'd hated him, he'd loved her.

"How've you been?" he asked.

"Better if I could go outside."

"I warned you."

She sipped her whiskey. "And I overestimated how spineless you were." She paused to think. "Although I shouldn't have. I've seen you devour enough people, punish enough souls. Maybe I overestimated your love for me."

"If I didn't love you, you'd be tortured in Hell, not subject to a pleasant house arrest on Earth."

She chuckled. "Did you come to warn me to be good or else?"

"No."

"I will get out someday."

He agreed, "Of course you will."

They both went silent again, the only sound the clinking of the ice in her glass.

"Have you seen your mother?"

Elisa laughed, harsh and short. "Have you?"

He looked at his hands. He wished she could have behaved a little better. Mischief and wildness could be managed and certainly even had their place. But she sowed dissent just for laughs, she hurt people to get her way, killed people so she could play with their guts, and that had no place.

"You might have driven her away, but she certainly wouldn't have stayed for me," Elisa reminded him.

"Your mother loves you."

"Ah, love is one thing. And it always meant more to you than it did to us. But we were Hell-born and you were an angel."

"Now you're being pretentious," he scoffed.

"No, but think about it, Father. Angels were made to crave God's love, weren't they? To need it as...as a mind needs books or song. And what were we created to do? Punish."

"But you don't punish the guilty!" he protested.

Elisa gave him a bit of a smile. "I suppose we disagree on what it means to be guilty."

"Looking at you the wrong way isn't a crime," he reminded her.

She shrugged and gestured around the room. "That much has become evident."

"I'll come visit if you want."

Her lip curled in a sneer. "When will you stop pretending?"

"About what?"

"That either of you wanted me."

"We made you on purpose," he said.

It had been Tabby's suggestion; she had always been the one

who'd been careful *not* to make a life, but he had complied wholeheartedly when she'd watched him create one of his demons and commented, "I'd like to make something living, too."

"You made a baby on purpose, sure, but once you got it..." She shrugged again and took another sip.

He pressed the tips of his fingers together so hard he felt it in his arms. He could argue, profess his love, plead for her to understand, but it wouldn't change anything.

"Are you seeing anyone?" he asked.

"No."

"Pets?" he asked.

"No."

"Friends?"

"Here and there."

"For fuck's sake, Elisa, aren't you lonely?" he demanded.

"I don't get lonely," she said, but right away he knew it was a lie. "Maybe *bored.*"

"You should make some friends."

"How? I can't go anywhere," she reminded him.

He shrugged. "I'm sure you could find a pen pal."

She really laughed at that. She finished her drink and set down the glass. "Did you need something else?"

"I was in the city."

"Well, if you don't mind." She glanced toward the door. "I have someone coming over."

He felt his body tense. "I will put a warning sign outside your door, I swear."

She waved a hand dismissively. "He's an artist."

"Oh, playing muse is worse than when you kill them," he teased.

"Goodbye, Father."

"I will visit if you'd like," he said and it felt insistent. It felt like begging.

"I'll think about it."

He stood and saw himself out, doubting that she'd ever ask him to come or that he would stop by uninvited. If she did something horrible, of course, he'd come back, but until then, he'd stay away, as he always did.

He'd stay away from her, he'd stay away from Junius. He'd never search for Tabby or plead for Ira to stay in his palace, and he'd never ask Mercy to continue her pregnancy.

He thought about Jack and Eodus, the same uncomfortable feeling of wistfulness and envy bubbling over his skin.

Walter and Shanley Circus had moved from outside Amherst to a horrible, boggy part of West Virginia.

Lucifer approached from a distance; he hadn't been sure what he wanted to do, so he'd given the circus a lengthy observation first.

As he walked in, people stopped their juggling and unicycling, they'd paused their fire breathing and sword swallowing to watch him.

A sweaty young woman in a worn leotard came up to him. "Hey, mister, we're not open. Show starts after dark."

"I'm here to see Mylas."

She ogled him. "Mr. Shanley?"

He nodded.

"Is...is he expecting you?"

"No."

He saw a tent with exclusively boys and young men practicing in front of it. It took no leap of deduction to tell where Mylas would be. He walked past the young woman and past the acrobats into the tent.

One boy of maybe twelve sat on a chair with his leg in a cast and a book in his hand. He ogled up at Satan, his eyes going wide. Off to his left sat Mylas, who at first didn't notice Lucifer's entrance.

The boy reached over and grabbed Mylas's hand, tugging urgently. "Mr. Shanley!"

When Mylas glanced up, he stood immediately. He looked at the boy with concern. "Get out, Pete."

"I—" the boy protested.

"Out!" Mylas barked.

"Let him stay and watch, Mylas, it'll be a day to remember," Lucifer suggested, smiling his biggest and worst smile.

The boy grabbed his crutches and hobbled out the tent doors, his face gray and drawn.

"What do you want?"

"I have one of your boys."

Mylas's hands balled into fists and he took a step forward. "Jack."

"Sweet boy, lovely curls. Sighs like a tired puppy when he's been worn out."

Mylas bared his teeth.

"I told him if he brought me your head that he could stay in Hell." He looked over Mylas, six feet of wiry, hard muscle and realized that he'd condemned Jack to death more surely than he'd ever thought.

"Jack?" Mylas snorted. "He's soft, he could never."

"He's terrified of you, Mylas, he knows how possessive you are. He knows what you would do if you caught up with him."

"And you came to rub it in my face. Typical," Mylas sneered.

"No, darling, I came to do what I should have then."

Mylas shook his head. "And you couldn't then—"

"I loved you dearly, then, Mylas. I love you not at all now." He stepped forward.

Mylas stepped back, his eyes darting around, searching for something to help him. He found nothing. His tent was filled with cushions and mats for tumbling. Things meant to break falls, not bones.

Lucifer pounced, tackling Mylas, though he held the Fallen in his grasp for only a few seconds.

Mylas slipped away, backing up, but Lucifer gave him no chance to recoup. He leaped after him and grabbed him so hard he felt his nails cut into Mylas's skin; this time Mylas struck him, one quick jab to the ribs followed by a kick to the knee.

The blow to the knee made him stumble and he pulled Mylas down with him; soon they were grappling on the ground, Mylas no longer trying to worm away. He pulled Lucifer's hair and Lucifer sunk his teeth into Mylas's neck.

The Fallen howled and kicked at him, but the Devil crawled on top of him, putting his knees on Mylas's chest.

It took strength and perseverance to pull Mylas's head from his shoulders; Lucifer had done it before, but he had liked it more in the heat of a pitched battle than on the floor of a circus tent.

A knife would have been better, but he didn't often travel armed.

The screams must have echoed through the circus, but no one came in.

Lucifer stood, grasping Mylas's head by the hair, then stepped through the underneath.

He arrived right outside Eodus's door and rapped sharply, still winded from the skirmish. The feeling of the in-between place slithered over his skin and filled his brain so he could barely think.

Eodus opened the door and got halfway through his kneel before he saw the head, the blood that covered Lucifer, the odd way the Devil held himself. He straightened up right away, his concern plain. "My Prince?"

"Is Jack home?"

"N-no, he's at the barracks."

Lucifer handed over the head. "This is for him."

Eodus held the head gingerly by one ear. "Why?"

"Remind him he owes me Shanley's head."

"I will." The white cat came from inside the house and started to lap up the blood that had dripped onto the floor. "Pumpkin!" Eodus tried to move that cat away with his foot but had little success.

When Lucifer walked inside the palace, he stopped by Imogen's office. "Will you have Gila clear out the master bathroom? Get all of Tabby's things out."

"You are getting blood on my carpet," she said, her words clipped.

A vampire should not have been so upset over blood. "My apologies."

"Who'd you kill?"

"Mylas."

"I thought that was what Jack's supposed to do."

"It was a death sentence, I always knew it was."

Imogen shook her head. "Christ, you're all over the place. What did Mylas do to you in the first place?"

He debated momentarily. "Mylas and I were lovers...but there was also Jiro. Mylas took offense to the idea of sharing."

"Never heard of Jiro."

"He was human."

Imogen's gaze stayed on the blood drips on her carpet; he wondered if she wanted blood more than she wanted her office to be clean.

"I loved him. Loved them both."

"You like conflict, don't you?" she asked.

"No."

"Two lovers at once, what did you think would happen?"

"I thought we could be adults about it. Jiro and Mylas would have gotten along if Mylas had given things half a chance."

Not sounding like she wanted to know, Imogen asked, "What did Mylas do to Jiro?"

"Ate him."

She finally lifted her eyes from the stained carpet. "Christ!"

"I ate him too. It wasn't on purpose, though, it was...it was supposed to be dinner, after a fight."

"God in Heaven, man, and you let him live after that!" she cried.

Lucifer couldn't help but laugh, surprised by Imogen's exclamation. "I still loved him. Or, at least, I had an attachment to him that I couldn't shake."

She examined him, her eyes lingering on his, and he got the impression she understood what he'd done better than he did. "That's really a lot of blood."

Of course, it is. "Gila has a spell for bloodstains."

"Not for that much blood, I bet. The clothes have to be ruined." He shrugged and stepped out of her office, but she cried, "Don't! You'll just track it everywhere."

He stripped off his bloodied clothes, not much caring about the blood, but compelled by Imogen's tone. He wanted to sleep. Needed it. The day had taken it out of him already and it couldn't be much past midday.

A quick wash rid him of the rest of the blood, except for what would have to be scraped from beneath his nails. He crawled into bed and Marlow ignored him.

He'd locked her out of the room the other night and apparently, she needed time to forgive him, but she'd hissed and swatted at Ira.

He gave her head a pat anyway. "Should have left you dead."

She glowered and walked six paces away. She turned her back on him.

"Be that way." He pulled up his covers and put a pillow over his head, asleep after a few hazy moments.

Sometime later he became aware of a weight on his arm. He reached up to give Marlow a pat. "Knew you wouldn't stay away..."

The thing he touched was a hand, not a cat.

"Uh. Your Highness?"

He released Imogen's hand and rolled over to look at her. "What?"

"You have a visitor."

"Oh, thanks, dear, show them in."

"To your bedroom?" she asked.

"I'm not getting up."

She left and he burrowed further into the covers, training half-closed eyes on the door. She returned with Jack.

The acrobat carried a sheet-wrapped bundle stiffly, trying to keep it away from his body. He stepped towards the bed uncertainly. "Um."

Lucifer held out a hand. "Give it."

Jack passed him the bundle.

He unwrapped it a little to confirm what it was, compelled to do so by the deal they'd struck, unable to not confirm things, then dropped it on the floor. "Come here."

He pushed himself up and put his hands on Jack's face when he approached.

The acrobat flinched a little.

"Won't but sting, love, don't worry." He cut the runes for citizenship into Jack's other cheek with his thumbnail. He should have rescinded the ones that marked him as a refugee but losing that might have put his life at risk. The youth trembled in his grip the entire time, his eyes squeezed shut.

When Lucifer finished, he kissed his forehead. "One of us now. Or as good as it gets. Welcome home."

"Why'd you do it?"

"Because you would have died."

Blood ran down his face, his neck and soaked into the collar of his sweat-stained shirt. "I didn't think that mattered to you," Jack said, his voice hushed.

"I wasn't sure if it did. I guess we'll never find out how sad it wouldn't or would have made me."

Jack rubbed the back of his neck.

"Tomorrow night I'll come to see your show."

He nodded. "You'll like it."

"Of course I will. Goodbye." He lay back down and pulled up the covers.

Jack left, closing the door behind him.

It was easier to kill Mylas than it was to find out how much he wanted Jack and Eodus to live their simple, happy life together.

And, the more he thought about it, Mylas's death at the hands of another would have been empty, though Jack had the right to hate him just as much as Lucifer did.

He tried to get back to sleep, but couldn't, disturbed by the sound of Marlow smacking her lips as she cleaned herself. He sat up to shoo her off the bed, but found her on the floor, chewing at the scraps of flesh that dangled from Mylas's neck.

He grimaced, took the head, and set it outside his door.

"Imogen!" He peered over the railing of the hallway, from

which he could see the foyer.

She emerged from her office. "Yes?"

"Could you have the head taken care of?"

"Leave it, I'll send Gila," she called up.

"The cats."

He saw her shoulders slump.

She headed towards the stairs. She came and collected the head, then asked, "What do you want me to do with it?"

He shrugged.

"Should I keep it or...?"

He shook his head. "No, sorry, get rid of it."

After that, he slept easy.

Lucifer encountered Mercy coming up the stairs as he descended them; she paused and looked him over.

His eyebrows knitted. "What?"

"You're not wearing black."

"Do I have to?" he asked.

"I didn't think you owned anything else. Same color he is."

He frowned but couldn't stop his hand from plucking at the buttons on his charcoal gray shirt. "Isn't."

She smiled.

His eyes skimmed over her. She looked pregnant now, her stomach swollen somewhat. From time to time, she would rest her hands on her stomach or give her belly a gentle rub. The sight of that always made him feel like he would vomit. "Do you know where you want to go?"

"Yes."

"Were you going to tell me?"

"Yes, but then I saw you carry a severed head out of your room, so I thought you might be up to something," she said.

He had to concede the point. "Fair enough. Come out with me, we can talk."

"Where are you going?"

He'd expected a flat-out refusal. "Jack's got a show."

She appeared to think things over. "Whose head was it?"

"You don't know him."

"Of course I don't know him! Who was he to you?"

"Oh. Um." He didn't particularly want to rehash the messy way he and Mylas had split, but he didn't think he should lie to her. "He killed someone I loved."

She nodded. "Let me get my boots."

He hadn't expected her to accept his offer.

On the walk to Siobhan's, he asked, "So where do you want to go?"

"I want a house of my own, somewhere quiet. There's a town in Vermont that's...I don't want to say it's a haven, but the people there are friendly to things like you. Enough that they helped creatures evade us when we went hunting."

"And they'll let you in?"

She shrugged. "I can hope."

He wanted to ask but knew he shouldn't. "So have you decided, then?"

"I told you already you were right," she said, "I didn't know you expected a proclamation. Did you plan to send your birth announcements to all our friends and family, too?"

He almost agreed to her proposition before he realized she was making fun of him. "I'll visit if you'll let me."

"Do you visit your other children?"

He hesitated, then admitted, "To be honest, I usually don't find out about my children for years after they were born. I wasn't usually around for more than a night or two. I go to collect on a deal or visit a friend and there I see a wee thing with red eyes. It actually took me a while to put two and two together."

She gave him a scowl of disgust and he couldn't be sure if it was because he'd slept around or because he'd been an absentee father.

"But that was centuries ago. And I don't think those women would have wanted me around much either, a lot of them had husbands. Not to mention that old-fashioned love for burning witches and the like."

She prickled.

"No perks to having the Devil hang around you during the Inquisition," he said.

"They must have known that when they took you to bed."

He stopped walking for a moment. "Why would they have known?"

"You didn't tell them?"

"Oh, hello, I'm the Devil himself, mind if I sit here? No, don't be silly, I'm not here to torture you or steal your soul, just hoping to have a bit of a chat," he mocked. "I don't think that would have gone over well."

"You really are a beast."

He resumed walking, not sure if she was right and not sure how he felt. He had liked sometimes to go to Earth and be someone other than the Devil for the night.

Of course, maybe he wasn't giving his trysts on Earth enough credit. He didn't change his form often, other than waffling between genders and heights, and he knew without a doubt that he didn't look human. Maybe they had suspected that he was some sort of unholy thing. Maybe they hadn't cared. Maybe they had even liked it.

Mercy had to be wrong, he decided.

He pointed to the building coming up on their right. "This is it." He opened the door for her.

Siobhan appeared as soon as he entered. He bent and they kissed each other's cheeks. When he straightened up, he gestured and said, "This is Mercy...uh. What's your last name, dear?"

"Mercy Specter."

"Siobhan."

The women shook hands.

To Lucifer, Siobhan said, "Two humans? They'll be calling it an infestation soon."

"She's not staying for much longer."

"No good for your reputation," Siobhan warned.

"Let them try what they'll try, I haven't feasted in a while."

"Maybe in too long," she suggested.

"I'll be sure to devour the next person who irritates me."

Siobhan walked away toward the stage, waving for them to follow. "I hear you finally dealt with Mylas."

"I did," he confirmed.

"Ripped his head clean off, that's what his circus boys are saying."

The statement disoriented him. "How could you know that?"

"You don't think people went to see!" She laughed. "You get the guts to go after Nimble Mylas and you don't think Pythea and a dozen others are up there asking questions? Luci, you are *dense*."

He considered all the demons he'd given permanent privileges to go to Earth and wondered if he should rein that in. It was easier, though, to pick a handful of people he trusted to make the trips than to always have to send them himself.

No. Gossip aside, they hadn't breached his trust enough to do anything about it.

"Here, have a seat, the show's going to start soon."

They settled into their seats and a serving girl brought them drinks, though Mercy didn't sip hers. He wasn't surprised, considering that she thought rich food had made her indulge in casual sex.

When he'd finished his drink and the servant came to replace it, he put a hand on her arm and leaned in to request something non-alcoholic for Mercy.

"And for you, my Prince?" the server asked.

"Get me as drunk as you like."

She smiled, showing slightly crooked teeth.

The first act featured a ballet, the second a handful of girls who performed daring balancing acts. The third was trapeze. The same girls from before, but this time with the addition of Jack.

Several people catcalled when he appeared.

Mercy glanced at Lucifer, then turned her eyes away when she noticed that he'd seen. She'd been checking to see if he'd noticed the flush in her cheeks, he knew; he heard her worrying about it with such intensity that he hadn't been able to ignore it.

"He's pretty," Lucifer conceded.

"Shut up."

"If he didn't love Eodus I'd fancy tasting him."

She wrinkled her nose. "Tasting him? What, are you going to eat him?"

He clucked his tongue. "Mercy, tell me you don't like the taste of another's skin on your lips."

She didn't say anything.

"Of their seed on your tongue."

She fully grimaced at that.

"You need to relax about these things, love, especially if you're going to think about them all the time."

She glowered.

"But he is very pretty..." He put his glass to his lips and took a drink. He hadn't taken his eyes from the stage the whole time, though he had made his way through four drinks.

Jack moved with control, grace, smiling the whole time. He loved this and it showed on his face. It lent a degree of vitality to his performance that drew the eye.

Afterward, Lucifer and Mercy met Jack backstage. Lucifer wobbled, or at least, he felt like he wobbled, on the walk back.

Eodus had beaten them there; he had Jack's face in his hands, kissing him. "You're beautiful, you know."

Jack laughed, gave him a squeeze, and pulled away, grinning at the Devil. "You came."

"Couldn't be gladder that I did. He's right, you're beautiful." He took Jack by the hand and kissed his cheek. "We should celebrate."

"Celebrate what?" the acrobat asked.

"You, Jack, darling."

Eodus wrung his hands so Lucifer pulled him close, wrapping an arm around him. "Celebrate the two of you, sickeningly sweet as you are. What do you think, Mercy?"

"That you're an idiot. Why does he look like the other one?" She nodded towards Eodus.

"Twins, I think."

Eodus frowned and then pulled out of Satan's grasp. "What other one?"

"The other one that looks like you," Lucifer clarified when he released Jack, not sure why Eodus appeared so unsettled.

Mercy sighed, giving the Devil a dirty look. "Some other demon he's bedding. A whore, if I'm not mistaken."

"You don't mean Ira," Eodus whispered. "The Wasting Plague took him."

Lucifer spoke before he considered his words. "Your parents sold him, Eodus, he didn't die."

The ash-gray demon went pale. "Where is he?"

"Just brought him up to Earth, he's on holiday for a while."

Eodus began to tremble and Jack put an arm around his partner.

Seeing the demon so upset didn't sit well with Lucifer and he felt that he needed to set it right. "I...I don't think he wanted...he...well, he got sold, I don't think he was hoping for any kind of reunion!"

Eodus shook his head.

"I'm sorry, Eodus."

"No, just...no, my Prince, it's a shock is all!" Eodus's voice had gone high and thin.

Lucifer rubbed his eyes, his vision somewhat muddled. "Fuck."

With a sad dog, pleading look on his face, with his hands twisting viciously, the demon asked, "Will you tell him...I mean, does he know that I'm, that he has a brother?"

"He knows you're alive." That felt cold, so he added, "But I'll tell him you asked about him."

"We should go," Jack said.

"I'm sorry."

"No." Jack smiled, but it was fake. "It's fine. Maybe you could come back, though."

Lucifer promised, "I will, Jack, you were lovely."

The human's smile looked real this time.

Jack and Eodus left through the back, but Mercy and Lucifer headed to the front. Patrons and performers milled together.

The crowd parted for Siobhan as she approached the two of them. "Stay for another drink."

He almost said yes, but Mercy didn't seem thrilled with the idea, so he said, "No, thanks, maybe a different night."

"Oh, Lila will be disappointed, she thought you fancied her."

He grinned. "I've got enough on my plate. Maybe some other time." He kissed her cheek and took his leave.

The walk home progressed precariously, as he kept trying to put his arm around Mercy, half to steady himself, half because he wanted to touch someone, but she shrugged him off each time.

"What do you think for names? I like Maliyah for a girl and Tharnak if it's an incorporeal monster."

"No."

"Well, it probably won't be incorporeal," he conceded.

"I'm still not sure how I ever let you touch me."

"Because you miss him. Because even though you don't want a demon in your life, you're going to a town that harbors them in the hopes that maybe someone else like him will be there. Someone else who will make you laugh."

"You talk like you're so complex," she said, scowling at him.

"No, I'm simple, Mercy. I know what makes me tick at the core."

"What?"

"Fear, pride, insatiable bloodlust."

She snorted.

"In that order."

They walked for a while longer, quiet and slow.

"I'm going to raise the babe to be Christian," she told him.

"It never hurts to have faith in something."

He right away felt that he had spoken too soon because a light appeared in the sky and an angel descended. It was not the one he had locked in with Elisha, but one of the identical soldiers, with golden curls and orange eyes.

Mercy paled and drew back, especially when the angel turned his gaze to her.

Lucifer shielded his eyes from the light reflecting off his glittering armor. Before the angel could ask what a human was doing in Hell, Lucifer scoffed, "Have you been just waiting around for me to say something like that? Always so theatrical."

"I came for the boy," the angel announced.

"Which one?" Lucifer asked.

"The trapped soul."

"Oh." His stomach grew cold. "What changed His mind?"

"Bring me to him."

Lucifer glanced at Mercy, worried the turn this interaction

could take. "Love, would you like me to send you home?"

She nodded and he wrapped her in his arms to whisper the right spell, not liking the idea of her walking home alone. She disappeared from his arms, leaving him embracing the air. He hoped the spell wouldn't have any repercussions; transportation magic had notorious side effects, but even those would be better than the angel finding out she bore his child.

"Where is he?" the angel demanded.

"About the boy, he's...not here anymore."

The angel must have known the boy hadn't made it to Purgatory or Heaven, because his immediate response was, "What did you do to him?"

"You can't go leaving things behind and expecting them to be as they were."

"He is not a thing! What did you do to him?"

He couldn't avoid the truth, the angel would know soon enough, but he hadn't meant for Heaven to find out about Elisha. The Almighty had been hard to provoke of late, but this could be a tipping point.

Lucifer clasped his hands behind his back so they wouldn't reach for his hair; he stood up straighter, taller than the angel, though far less powerfully built. "I made him mine."

The angel knocked Lucifer to the ground with a single swing of his weapon and had his spear point to the Devil's throat before Lucifer, drink muddled as he was, could react. "You'll undo it."

"Can't be undone." He tried to knock the spear away but only cut his hand in the process.

The angel pressed the spear point closer, pricking his throat. "Bring me to him."

"Let me up."

The angel stepped back and Lucifer stood, his hand dripping blood onto the street. It smarted for now, but he knew the cut would do more than that soon enough. It would burn, maybe even fester, unless he treated it. Not that he knew how exactly to treat it.

Angels worth their salt came to Hell with poisoned blades when they had to come. Strong and fast as they were, they didn't share his inability to die. The poison wouldn't kill him, at least, it hadn't yet, but it would slow him, weaken him, cloud his mind.

If he couldn't get rid of this angel soon, he'd be at his mercy.

"He can't go with you. The thing is done." Lucifer reached within himself, trying to summon his monstrous form, but it slipped from his grasp each time he touched it. He pressed his fingers to the nick on his throat. That, too, had started to sting. "Angels can fall but a demon cannot rise. He saw to that and He doesn't break the rules."

The angel's hands tightened around his spear.

"He must have known..." Lucifer mused.

If God had sent this angel, then he had sent him on a fool's errand. If God had been paying attention to the boy, He would have known the moment he'd touched the book. He would have known that the soul had been corrupted.

"He didn't send you."

The angel stepped back when the Devil grinned, but Lucifer followed after him. He grasped the angel by the face, pulling him close. "He didn't send you, friend, and if He didn't send you, you'd better go home before He doesn't let you back in."

The angel writhed away, breaking Lucifer's weakened grip. He had the Devil's blood smeared on his face.

Lucifer grabbed him again, putting an arm around his waist, pressing their bodies together. He could feel the angel's heart pounding in his chest and it made his own heart quicken. Fear rolled off him and Lucifer wanted to sink his teeth into his flesh, to taste his blood, and make him scream his throat raw.

He put his mouth close to the angel's ear. "If He finds out, He'll do to you what He did to me. He'll send you here and you'll be mine, too, and it has been *so long* since I've been bad."

The angel broke away again, knocking Lucifer to the street, dropping his spear and reaching for Heaven.

Lucifer let him go, watching on his knees as the angel disappeared.

The poor idiot had better hope the Almighty didn't care enough to punish this transgression. He'd better pray that no one else had noticed his absence.

He knelt for a while in the street, the world moving in an unpleasant, woozy sway. He had to get out of the street, he knew, before the denizens of the Ninth encountered him like this. Some would help, he knew, but more would take advantage. Someone always thought they'd be better at being Satan.

He'd had to dig his way out of enough graves and didn't fancy the idea. Not when it still gave him nightmares, made him dizzy in tight spaces.

A cat watched him from a yard away, its bright green-yellow

eyes blinking slowly. He blinked back.

Of course, if he was stupid enough to grab a poisoned blade, maybe he didn't deserve to be Satan anyway.

He made himself stand. He swiveled around, trying to recall which way would bring him home.

He walked, the world tilting, his feet heavy. He leaned against buildings and stumbled in the gaps between them.

Several times he looked about and realized he didn't know where he was. His hand continued to drip blood, his throat continued to bleed. The sky grew lighter.

"You alright, mister?" a small voice from behind him asked.

He had been wandering down an alley without much of an idea where he was headed. He knew he hadn't left the Ninth, at least.

He turned to see a child, maybe ten or eleven, with pinkish orange skin, standing at the mouth of the alley. "Fine."

She had her eyes fixed on the bloodstain on his shirt. "You sure?"

"Do you..." He tried to swallow, his mouth and throat dry. "You know where the palace is?"

She nodded. "Sure."

"Take me there."

She hesitated, then shook her head. "Momma says the Devil will eat us if we go too close."

"Only naughty ones and never children. Please. You don't even have to...to walk all the way." He closed his eyes. "Just close."

"I...I'll show you."

"Thank you." He shuffled toward her and she took a few steps away from him.

A few other children had stopped to watch.

"This way," she said.

Another little girl came over to her. "Praeta, what are you doing?"

"I've just got to show him to the palace."

"You'll be late for school, Yatha will yell at you."

Praeta kept walking and Lucifer followed after her. Children rarely had aspirations for the throne.

Half of the other children walked behind him, whispering together, some of them screeching with laughter or terror every so often as they grew closer to the palace. He began to recognize things around him.

Praeta stopped and turned. She pointed. "That's it."

He nodded. "I owe you a boon."

He walked on after that, once she and her friends had hurried away. He made it inside. Almost.

He ended up slumped against the front steps when he couldn't make himself walk any further.

He woke with a gasp when someone jabbed something into his chest, not just hard enough to wake him but to break the skin and cleave flesh.

Above him stood a gardener and buried three inches deep in his chest was a garden trowel.

When Lucifer opened his eyes, the gardener screamed and fell over himself trying to get away, bumping into the woman behind him.

"Told you he wasn't dead," the woman said.

"Fuck off, Kaless!"

Lucifer pulled the trowel out of himself. A gout of blood dribbled down his shirt. "Get. Imogen."

The gardener hesitated.

Teeth gritted, Lucifer warned, "I cannot die and I will come for you."

Kaless gave the gardener a push. "Go on, you idiot, get the butler."

The gardener ran inside.

Kaless stood over the Devil, her arms crossed. "If you eat him for this, our mother might thank you."

"Not hungry."

She laughed and sat beside him on the steps. "They've been searching for you, you know, and what does he try to do?" She glanced over. "You sure you can't die? You look awful."

"I'm sure." He tried to push himself up only to be reminded of the cut on his hand as it sent a shot of pain through his arm.

Kaless took him by the upper arm and righted him somewhat. "Delusions of grandeur, he's always had them. Makes him a gambler. Makes the rest of us always have to get him out of trouble."

Imogen came down the stairs, her hair flying behind her. He'd never seen her look so lovely. She, without hesitation, swooped down, putting one of his arms around her shoulders and her arm about his waist to lift him up.

She carried him like that all the way to his bedroom, where she placed him into bed, surprisingly gentle.

"There was—" he began.

"An angel, I know, Mercy told me. Why didn't you stay put! I had people looking all over for you."

He'd forgotten that he'd sent Mercy ahead.

She examined his hand, tilted his head back to inspect his throat. "Someone could have done you in."

"Couldn't have."

She undid his shirt and poked around the gash the trowel had left. "Done you in enough to bury you again. You'd have been coughing up dirt for weeks."

Gila entered the room, with the cat keepers and Oris on her heels. "Thhould Irunn for a healer?"

"No, I can manage it."

"You can?" Lucifer asked.

"Descended from seven generations of herb wives."

"Weren't."

She amended, "Well, I mean, I was adopted but I don't think that should matter too much since I paid attention during my lessons. Don't move."

She left the room and returned with a pitcher of hot water, as well as a mortar and pestle that reeked of astringent herbs. She cleaned his wounds, stitched them shut, applied the herbs she'd brought, then bandaged him.

He asked, "What do herb wives know of angel's poison?"

"Nothing, but what does anyone in Hell?"

He had to concede the point.

"You can't die, anyway, and what I've done should...*should* stop things from getting any worse."

"Wonderful bedside manner."

She shrugged. "There's a reason why I became a vampire instead."

He put his good hand on her arm and had the sense that he should say something but had no clue what to say. He gave her arm a pat.

She stood. "I'll get you something to eat."

"Don't bother, I'm going to pass out."

Lucifer sent word to Junius that he'd be a few days late in picking up Ira because he thought that if he made himself go into the in-between place he would pass out again. He'd been doing that on and off for a while, though it had only happened once yesterday and hadn't yet today.

When he'd managed to go an entire day without fainting, he took Mercy with him into the underneath and brought her to the town in Vermont she'd requested. They appeared together in front of a colonial-style house with fresh paint.

He handed her an envelope stuffed with cash, as well as a key. "Deed's in the envelope, too. I had Imogen put everything together. Would have done it myself, but you know, I've been barely conscious. Let me know if you need anything else."

"How?"

He shrugged. "Someone around here can get in touch with me, I'm sure. The place is buzzing with we unholy things. Can't you smell it?"

She toyed with the key.

"I'll come visit." He thought that their goodbye should be longer but didn't know what else to say. "If you want."

"I suppose I wouldn't mind."

He smiled. "Can I give you a hug?"

"If you feel that you must."

The consent she'd granted, begrudging and marginal as it was, satisfied him and he swept her up in his arms, embracing her as though he cared about her. He could feel her rounded belly press against him and he realized he still hadn't come to terms with the existence of the little thing inside of her yet. "I'll come visit even if you don't want me to, you know, so you should just get used to the idea."

She snorted and stepped out of his arms. "I did assume as much. Especially after how distressed you were about whether I'd keep the child."

"I wouldn't say I was distressed."

"Oh, you only think they're bad because of me, don't judge the poor babes so harshly. I'm so tragic and misunderstood." She put a hand to her brow for dramatic effect. "If the thing turns out to be like you, you're taking it back to Hell with you."

"Well, if it turns out like you and tries to kill me, I'll be incredibly disappointed."

She shook her head. "That's all behind me now."

He raised an eyebrow. A lifetime of cult indoctrination did not dissolve in a few weeks. He wondered if he gave himself too much credit; she had loved a demon before she'd ever set foot in Hell. "Have you got any names picked out?"

She shook her head.

"Do you know when you're due?"

"No. I don't even know the date here."

He thought for a moment. "I think...I think less time went by here than it did in Hell. It's...early spring, right, or maybe late winter...March is my guess. *Feels* like March." He searched around and spied someone walking by, a man with a small girl's hand clasped in his. "Oy, you, what day is it?" he shouted.

The man looked over, eyes wide, then pulled the child closer and hurried away.

Mercy gave him a push. "Don't. I have to live here, I don't want people thinking I've got some kind of maniac hanging around me."

"Goodbye, Mercy."

"Get thee behind me, Satan."

He laughed at that. Sour-faced and frumpily clad, he didn't think anyone would ever appreciate how funny she could be. Maybe her face was less sour when she wasn't trapped in Hell. Maybe he would return to find her bright-eyed and laughing.

A warm nervousness, one that bordered on excitement, bloomed in his chest when he imagined her like that, happy with a baby in her arms. He imagined her glad to see him and thought of what it would be like to hold a child in his arms again.

He steeled himself for the trip to New York, leaving Mercy behind before he could grow sentimental.

He stepped out of the in-between right in front of Junius's apartment.

An old man in a cap dropped his newspaper and crossed himself as he fled back into his apartment, crying out what he'd seen in Russian.

Lucifer leaned against the wall, resting, taking long slow breaths for a moment, waiting for the black edges around his vision to clear before he knocked.

When he could stand up straight, he rapped on the door.

Junius pulled it open and touched his head to the floor.

"Rise," the Devil said.

Junius popped to his feet and threw his arms around Lucifer. "I was worried, you know! We heard what happened."

"Angels these days aren't hardly worth their salt."

Junius stepped back and opened the door wider. Lucifer stepped inside and spied Ira hovering by the couch. He had dressed in trousers and suspenders, a crisp white button-down shirt, a vest, and a tie. Lucifer badly wanted to loosen his tie, undo his buttons, if to do nothing more than touch his skin.

"How was your holiday?" Lucifer asked.

Ira shrugged. "Good. Fun." His eyes slid towards Junius and he twisted his hands together. "June showed me around the city."

"And?" he asked. Ira didn't seem pleased to see him, which should have made him glad. He hadn't wanted the demon to come back to Hell anyway.

He straightened up and lifted his chin, but his eyes gave him away. He looked at Junius again.

Junius didn't seem nearly as concerned. He lit a cigarette and shook out the match. "He thinks it'll put you out of sorts if he tells you we kissed."

The words came to his lips before he realized he was saying them. "Oh, no, good for you!" He turned his eyes to Ira. "Are you going to stay here, then?"

"No!" the two said together.

"It wasn't anything like that." Junius took a drag on his cigarette and let it out.

Lucifer nodded. He'd quietly hoped that the two of them would like each other, hit it off, maybe even fall in love. Of course, a handful of days might not have been enough time for that, but one had to hope.

He held out his hand to Ira. "Home, then, let's go. Thank you,

Junius, love."

Junius nodded. "Take care."

Ira took his hand and Lucifer brought them back to Hell. He brought them to his bedroom because he wanted to lie down, wanted to be somewhere safe.

When they stepped out of the underneath, Lucifer had tears streaming down his cheeks. He tried to wipe them away, but Ira appeared to notice anyway.

"You've gone gray," he said.

"So have you," Lucifer tried to joke.

Ira pulled him towards the bed and he went without resistance; he needed to lie down or he would pass out. He curled up on his side and Ira sat beside him. "I thought you were going to leave me there. That you'd keep coming up with excuses."

The confession had come unprompted and Lucifer didn't know what to do with the information. "I wouldn't have."

Ira took the Devil's hand and studied the bandages. The skin around the cut had gone greenish-black and he had continued to apply herbs to it. The discoloration hadn't gotten worse, which satisfied him.

"Other than tussling with angels, what did you do?" Ira asked.

"Brought Mercy to Vermont."

With a bored huff, Ira said, "Wherever that is."

"Saw Jack's show."

"Whoever Jack is."

More quietly, Lucifer admitted, "Accidently let slip to your brother that you aren't dead."

Ira sat up straighter and released Lucifer's hand. "My brother!"

"He wanted, I don't know, I think he wants to meet you."

"Well, I don't want to meet him," Ira grumbled.

"It wasn't him that sold you."

"No, but it was him that got kept!"

Lucifer yawned, burying his face in the crook of his arm. "I've got an apartment set up for you at the Inverness. Or, well, Imogen picked it out. Says it's nice. You can stay there as long as you want."

"Oh."

"She'll bring you over."

In a soft voice, Ira said, "I thought it was my choice."

"Hm?"

"About if I stayed with you or not," Ira clarified.

Lucifer pushed himself up. "You can't stay."

Ira's eyes glimmered. "Why not?"

"Because you'll never leave."

Tears slid down his cheeks. "Already bored of me. Knew you would be."

It was a misunderstanding, plain and simple, and an easy one to make considering how Ira had worried about such a thing before. Lucifer's voice had been cool and flat and he had meant it to be. He wanted Ira to go, but something in him couldn't let Ira go thinking that he was the problem.

"No, not that. You'll never leave because you'll be mine and I won't let you go. Every gift will be a shackle, every kind word will be blackmail."

"That doesn't sound so bad," Ira said.

Lucifer grabbed him by the arm, squeezing hard. "Because you don't understand! I won't be a lover or a client or a friend, I'll be your jailer. I *promised* I wouldn't make you stay."

He let go of Ira, realizing how hard he'd been holding on. He rubbed his own face and wanted to rip out his hair. A thousand things buzzed in his head and the feel of Earth, of the underneath, of his own guilt, crawled over his skin. His tenuous grasp on reality threatened to take its leave.

"Then why pretend you were ever going to let me stay? Why make me think the choice was mine if you were always going to do this?" Ira asked.

Lucifer swallowed.

"Why not just leave me on Earth if you didn't want me?"

"I *do* want you. Just not here, not with me. I can come to you, you can see other people, find whatever work you want. Keep me as a client, Ira, but don't let me be anything more."

"Does it matter at all what I want?"

Lucifer shook his head and couldn't lift his eyes. "You think you know me—"

"Don't tell me what I think! Here you are trying to save me again, save me from Mistress, from rough clients, now you're trying to save me from *you*, which is the stupidest thing yet. Let me decide."

"If you stay, I'll fall in love, I know I will," the Devil whispered.

"And maybe I want someone to fall in love with me! Maybe I want someone to remember my name for once!" Ira gave him a push, barely even a tap to the shoulder. "I've never loved anyone, never even had the chance. Maybe I want that chance."

He shook his head again. "It's a bad idea."

"Then it's on me."

Lucifer pulled his knees to his chest and hung his head.

"Unless you're kicking me out."

"No." He wasn't kicking Ira out, but he should have been.

"Because I haven't seen you in fifteen days and that feels like longer than it should." Ira moved closer, put a hand on his arm.

Lucifer wrapped his arms around Ira, drew him closer and buried his face in his neck. "I missed you."

"He says immediately after trying to make me leave."

He nuzzled against Ira's neck. "You'll see someday."

"Stop it. You really are dramatic." Ira kissed Lucifer's temple. "I don't like the ocean."

Lucifer wondered, for no more than a moment, if maybe this could work. "Why not?"

"Too many things live in it," Ira said. "People talk about Hell like it's bad but at least it's not full up with things that want to eat me."

"Well, no, not in the city, silly. Go out into the wilds and see what you find there."

"The city suits me fine."

"What else didn't you like?" Lucifer asked.

Ira pulled out of his arms and flopped onto his back. He stared up at the ceiling. "Humans are...well, they've got a lot going on. They're hard to figure. Always *worried* about something. You see someone, give them that look, you know, the 'let's go somewhere private' one, and suddenly they've gone bright red, choking on their drink."

Lucifer lay on his side, glad for the sight of him.

"Some of them are good enough, though. I like the clothes, too, the suspenders. You should have seen June..." Ira trailed off.

"Seen him what?" the Devil prompted.

"Nothing."

"Junius is a good man," Lucifer told him.

"Oh, no question."

"Did you do more than kiss?"

"No. Not really. But I'd had a lot to drink and he didn't want to do anything because of it. Good enough call on his part, I threw up all over someone's shoes ten minutes later." Ira turned on his side to face Lucifer. "I know he's special to you."

"*He's* special?"

"Everyone knows it. Junius, the one who leaped after you. Your most trusted and faithful, all the way up on that pedestal where you keep him."

He ran his fingers through Ira's curls. "What else did you do?"

Ira told Lucifer of the trip to Coney Island, of the clandestine rooftop party where he had kissed Junius, of riding the IRT. He told of hours exploring the New York Public Library and the Museum of Natural History. He shared the horror of gasoline-powered taxi cabs and the chugging rumble of trains. The bad taste of cigarettes and strange carbonation of Coca-Cola.

They had gone upstate and to the shore. Ira had tasted every fruit he could get his hands on, every cake and pie, every type of meat and fish.

"I would have stayed for the food."

"It isn't too late," the Devil offered.

"Why bother slumming it up there when I can have you bring me whatever I want down here?"

Voices hissed and things slithered over his skin, tiny invisible things that might not have been real but definitely should have stayed in the in-between place where they belonged. He moved closer to Ira, took in the smell of his skin. "Tell me what you want and it's yours."

"I'll come up with a list of demands soon enough."

"I'm going to close my eyes for a minute, but I'm listening. Tell me more about the subway." New as it was, he hadn't ridden it yet; the Temporal Parliament would have had a field day if he'd moved around in time just to ride on fancy trains.

Ira talked and Lucifer, eyes closed and his face nestled into the covers, fell asleep, though not before Marlow came and lay across his ribs, fixing Ira with a distasteful glower. She had purred, though, when Lucifer had scratched her behind his ears and he assumed he was forgiven for bringing an interloper into the room.

In the morning, Ira woke him and asked to be taken to the Inverness to see his apartment.

Lucifer found himself almost protesting. "I thought you wanted to stay."

"I do. But not right now. Not all the time."

That morning, Lucifer let him go, all the while knowing that someday he wouldn't be able to. He brought him over to the Inverness and watched as he inspected the rooms. A bedroom, a parlor, a bath, and a kitchen. More space than he'd ever had for himself, Lucifer was sure.

He took Lucifer's hand in his and leaned his head against the Devil's arm. "You really think one of the other brothels will hire me? I don't like the idea of customers being here. Or of trying to find them on my own."

"Someone will hire you," the Devil promised.

"And you don't mind? It must cost a lot to rent this for me, I'd understand if you didn't want to share." Ira's voice didn't hold notes of accusation or worry; instead, he sounded calm, curious. Rational. Their relationship still represented a series of transactions to him, things he had relied on for food and shelter.

"I don't mind anything you do." He wondered if he should tell Ira the room was not rented but owned, but it seemed a discussion for another time.

Ira gave him a look, one raised eyebrow and a slight downturn at the corners of his mouth.

"Did you want me to mind?" Lucifer asked.

"No." He stepped away from the Devil and ran his fingers over the sofa, then examined the drapes hung in the window. "Not yet."

"Not yet?" The idea being unfamiliar to him, Lucifer asked, "When would it be appropriate for me to mind who you're sleeping with?"

"Someday I might not want to be with anyone else. I might not want you to be with anyone else either. If it was only the two of us would that be, um, an issue for you?"

"I don't know. I've never done it before," he admitted.

"Not even with your wife." It wasn't a question.

"No, but it wasn't something we ever talked about. I don't think Tabby would have wanted to give anything up to keep me."

Ira nodded.

Lucifer had not felt a strong desire to take anyone else to bed in a while, not anything more than a passing thought brushed away like a cobweb. It couldn't be that hard and Ira was much more reasonable than Mylas had ever been if exclusivity proved to be more of a trial than he anticipated. "But I'd give it a try. If you wanted me to."

"Maybe someday." He glanced at Lucifer and grinned. "Maybe someday I'll let you save me, too, keep me safe and sound and wonderfully pampered in that palace of yours."

Lucifer smiled, just a little. He was tired. More tired than usual.

Ira lay down on the sofa, his feet hanging over the arm. "Come here."

Lucifer approached, kneeling next to him.

Tucking a lock of Lucifer's hair behind his ear, Ira said, "When you come to visit me, it won't be at work. If you do visit me at work, it better only be to ask me to lunch."

"Fair."

"I don't want you trying to keep me safe from people."

"I don't want you to let people hurt you," Lucifer countered.

"I'll set my boundaries now that I can afford to have them."

"Good." He leaned in to kiss Ira. "You shouldn't come back to the palace."

"But I will. And you'll let me walk out when I want to go."

"I can't promise that," he warned.

With a shake of his head, Ira exhaled, irritated perhaps, or somewhat amused. "I think you will."

He rested his head on Ira's chest, listening to the steady sound of his heart. "I won't want to."

Ira put his arms around his shoulders. "Don't you owe me a book?"

"I don't, it's on the shelf."

Ira laughed. "I can't believe you have the nerve to call Phaedrus Queen sentimental."

"The things we don't like in others always ends up being what we don't like about ourselves."

"Is that a quote?" Ira asked.

"I can't remember. Probably, though, it doesn't sound like something I'd say."

Ira laughed again and pulled Lucifer closer. He pressed a kiss to his lips. "I still don't believe that you're the Devil."

"Wait until you see me eat someone."

"You say that like you're the only thing in Hell with a taste for flesh."

Ira sounded brave, but he'd wept at the sight of his Prince's more monstrous form. He would weep again, too, Lucifer knew, when he saw it again. When he saw bodies disappear down that gullet, when he saw entrails on the claws.

"Then who am I?" Lucifer asked.

"Fuck if I know. I don't even know who I am yet."

An acceptable answer, really, Lucifer decided, for such a stupid question. "I don't want to go."

"I haven't asked you to yet."

"My knees are starting to hurt, can I come on the sofa?"

"Yes," Ira told him, a smile in his voice.

Lucifer slid onto the couch with Ira, nestled beside him, prepared to stay for as long as he was allowed.

ABOUT THE AUTHOR

Dan is a writer and educator who has lived in or around Wolcott, Connecticut for their entire life. They received their BSED from CCSU in 2013 and has written their Master's thesis on representation of women in same-sex relationships in contemporary Spanish literature and cinema.

WHAT EVERYONE DESERVES

2017 Rainbow Awards HONORABLE MENTION
"Although the story deal with some real 1950's issues – discrimination, homophobia, interracial couples and hate crimes – it did it in a way that perfectly suited the characters and the story." - Divine Magazine

In this 1950s period drama, Junius is a New York City fertility demon with a crush. Ever since falling from heaven he's been alone. Except for the mothers and children he watches over.

James Kelly Rosenburg, a black soldier with snowflakes in his hair, walks right into his life with a big problem. James Kelly, turned vampire during the war, is new to New York and its prohibition against vampire killing in city limits.

Junius offers to teach him to overcome his bloodthirsty instincts and live a proper Manhattan life. Their growing friendship leaves them both conflicted as they explore a city both welcoming and alienated by their kind.